Valerie's father had reached up and taken down one of the stuffed animals, holding it, stroking it while his eyes gazed into a bleak emptiness. Sister Joan left him there, went back to the landing, drank her too sweet, cooling tea with a slight grimace, and went down the stairs again as Father Malone arrived.

"Thank God, but Mrs. O'Hare is tons better today," he informed her. "You've spoken to the family?"

"Briefly. There isn't much one can say."

"And the poor things will still be in shock, of course. It was good of you to come, Sister."

"You must have known Valerie," she murmured.

"She was a regular communicant." His face was heavy with distress. "Girls these days are not like they used to be, Sister. All late nights and heavy make-up, but Valerie wasn't like that. She was young for her age, Sister. Young and innocent. She was a nice girl."

A nice Catholic girl who went regularly to Holy Communion, who collected stuffed animals and bought religious statuettes during a family visit to Lourdes. A good girl who took no interest in boys. A girl who had risen from her bunk bed in the middle of the night and sneaked out to meet her killer...

By Veronica Black:

ECHO OF MARGARET
PILGRIM OF DESIRE
FLAME IN THE SNOW
HOODMAN BLIND
MY PILGRIM LOVE
A VOW OF SILENCE*
LAST SEEN WEARING
A VOW OF CHASTITY*
MY NAME IS POLLY WINTER
A VOW OF SANCTITY*
A VOW OF OBEDIENCE*

*Published by Ivy Books

A VOW OF OBEDIENCE

Veronica Black

IVY BOOKS • NEW YORK

Ivy Books
Published by Ballantine Books
Copyright © 1993 by Veronica Black

Library of Congress Catalog Card Number: 93-44061

ISBN 0-8041-1245-2

This edition published by arrangement with St. Martin's Press, Inc.

Manufactured in the United States of America

First Ballantine Books Edition: August 1995

10 9 8 7 6 5 4 3 2 1

ONE

✠ ✠ ✠

Sister Joan of the Order of the Daughters of Compassion had never seriously contemplated murder but by the time her train drew in at the station she was beginning to change her mind. The two women who had boarded the compartment in London had glanced incuriously at the grey-habited figure in the corner seat, then proceeded to spread themselves over the remaining seats, depositing bags and baskets with reckless abandon before they settled down to a long, loud gossip in which the most intimate details of their neighbours' marital problems, operations and financial affairs were dissected with relish. It was impossible to read or even to keep one's mind on the passing scenery as the two shrill voices rose and fell in unison, neither of the speakers paying close attention to what her companion was saying because each was anxious to contribute her share.

"A disciplined religious should be able to meditate anywhere, even on the platform at Euston Station," Mother Agnes, her first prioress, had said.

I would like, Sister Joan thought meanly, to see how Mother Agnes would cope with these two.

Had she been wearing the old-fashioned wimple with its heavy veil that stifled unwanted sound it wouldn't

1

have been so bad, but the founder of the Order fifty years before had been in advance of her time in advocating garments more suited to the modern age. Sister Joan's grey habit ended above her black-hosed ankles, and her white veil was a short one, showing at the front two inches of shining blue-black hair. An impossible costume in which to shut out unwanted conversation.

". . . not safe in your beds these days." The fatter of the two women pronounced the cliché gloomily. "Mind you, if I hadn't known her second cousin's first wife I'd have jumped to the conclusion that she'd run off with a young man—you know what girls are! But it seems she went off to bed and in the morning—pouf! Nothing missing except her slippers and dressing-gown. And nobody heard a thing."

"Transported," the other said. "Makes you wonder if those tales about flying saucers aren't true."

"More likely to be kidnapping," said the fat woman. "Not that I've heard anything about a ransom note, but then the police wouldn't say, would they?"

"The police," the other opined, "never say anything worth hearing. They want the public to co-operate and then they put a blanket over every mortal thing."

"Like doctors," said her friend and embarked on a ghoulish recital of a doctor her aunt had consulted who had mistaken a tumour for a boil.

The train slowed and glided into Bodmin. Sister Joan took down her case and the larger bag that contained her painting materials and thankfully alighted. Behind her one of the women said in a piercing whisper, "They say most of them are lesbians, you know."

"How perceptive of you!"

Sister Joan threw the remark smilingly over her shoulder, made a mental note to confess it in general confession, picked up her bags from the platform and headed for the exit. She hadn't notified the convent about the time of her arrival but she half expected to find someone there to meet her with the old boneshaker of a car that Sister Perpetua usually drove when it was necessary to come into town.

The forecourt was innocent of grey habit and veil, however, and she looked round, wondering if she could beg a lift and save what Mother Dorothy would certainly regard as the completely unjustified expense of a taxi fare.

There was no taxi in view and the local bus which would have dropped her off in the vicinity of the convent had long since departed. Nothing for it but to start walking then. She walked on into the main street, her eyes caught by a large poster in the window of the newsagents' opposite.

HAVE YOU SEEN THIS GIRL? demanded the huge scarlet letters. Underneath was a blown-up snapshot of a girl with fair hair and a face in which vacuous prettiness seemed to be the dominating factor. Beneath the photograph smaller letters gave brief information.

Missing from home. Valerie Pendon, aged sixteen. Fair hair, blue eyes. Last seen in nightgown in her bedroom on the evening of . . .

Three days before, Sister Joan calculated. The girl had worn a nightgown which suggested either she, or whoever had given the description, was somewhat out of date. Didn't girls wear shortie pyjamas or something called teddies these days? The face and name were unknown to her, however, and she walked on.

She was approaching the police station which had a similar poster on a board outside. The temptation to linger in the hope someone might be driving out her way was only a fleeting one. She moved on briskly and heard her name called.

"Sister Joan? Hang on a minute."

"Detective Sergeant Mill, how nice to see you." She turned, holding out her hand with unaffected pleasure.

The tall dark man with the greying hair gripped her hand and shook it.

"Back from exile, Sister?" His glance was faintly teasing.

"Back from our retreat in Scotland," she reminded him.

"And how was it? All mist and lochs and wanting to come home? Or did you renew your spiritual strength?"

"A bit of all those things, but I'm glad to be back."

"You weren't thinking of hiking out to the convent surely?" He gave her a sharp look. "Or is this an extra penance?"

"No transport—and don't knock penance until you've tried it."

"But you wouldn't say no to a lift?"

"I'd accept gratefully, but I'd not want to interrupt your work. Unless you're coming my way anyway?"

"Unfortunately I'm not, but Mrs. Barratt is. She's the wife of our new sergeant—they've moved into the new housing estate past Farrer's Field, and her way takes her past the convent gates. She dropped in to make sure we were treating her husband gently." He gave the attractive grin that lit his rather saturnine features into youthfulness.

"But she doesn't know me from Adam," Sister Joan protested.

"She's one of your lot and she knows hardly anybody at all," he assured her. "I'll catch her. Wait there."

He walked swiftly away into the parking space next

to the station where a neat little Mini was being backed out.

Detective Sergeant Alan Mill had never made any secret of his liking for herself or his astonishment that she should have chosen the religious life in preference to marriage and children. They had worked together on a particularly brutal case*—or to be more accurate she had found herself entangled in the affair without realizing it, and his own undisguised admiration had kindled a small spark in herself. Not sufficient to build a fire though, she reflected, but just enough to give a slight *frisson* to what could never become more than an amiable acquaintanceship. It was good to see him again and to reassure herself that his inability to give her a lift hadn't roused in her anything stronger than a mild disappointment.

The Mini backed out and crawled to where she stood, Detective Sergeant Mill in attendance.

"Sister Joan, meet Sergeant Barratt's wife. She's going in your direction," he said.

"I'll be happy to take you, Sister. I pass the convent gates," Mrs. Barratt said, turning her head to smile, somewhat shyly.

"That's very kind of you, Mrs. Barratt. Detective Sergeant Mill, I hope your family is well?"

She asked the question formally, shutting out of her mind the bleak admission of a relationship that was going wrong he had once made to her.

"The boys are fine." He held open the passenger door for her.

"I'll give your regards to Mother Dorothy," Sister Joan said, allowing herself a touch of mischief. Her su-

*See *Vow of Chastity*.

perior's views on policemen tramping through the enclosure had been trenchant.

"You do that, Sister." He saluted as he closed the door.

"Such a nice man," Mrs. Barratt said in a slightly flustered tone, being clearly not immune to charm herself whatever her feelings for her own spouse. "He has been most kind since we arrived here. Mark, my husband, thinks he's splendid."

"How are you settling in?"

"Oh, we came down from Birmingham," the other said, "and rural living is all very new to us both. It's easier for Mark because he has his job and so he can make friends that way, but the people roundabouts are a little bit clannish, don't you think? Of course we've only been here a fortnight so perhaps it's a bit early to tell."

"About twenty years too early," Sister Joan said, and seeing the expression of dismay on the other's face, amended it hastily to, "I was only joking. People here are apt to regard everybody who lives north of the Tamar as foreigners, but when you get to know them you'll find them very friendly and helpful. And being a Catholic will help. Father Malone arranges all kinds of activities down at the church."

"Yes. He came to bless the house," Mrs. Barratt said. "He was very welcoming."

"He's a nice man." Sister Joan glanced at the hands gripping the wheel tightly. Mrs. Barratt was in her late twenties, she guessed, with brown hair which she had brightened, not altogether happily, with an auburn rinse and neat, small features. Her brown coat and skirt did nothing for her at all. It needed a vivid scarf at the neck to give colour to the pale cheeks.

"If you take it slowly," she continued kindly, "you'll soon feel as if you'd lived here for years. I've only been here myself for a year but already I feel like a home-body."

"But a nun would," the other said. "I mean that you aren't attached to any particular spot, are you? The convent, wherever it is, is your home."

"That's the ideal we aim for, certainly. This is where the road forks. You can drop me if you like. It's only a mile further on."

"I'll take you to the gates," Mrs. Barratt said. "The moors are lovely, aren't they? Even at this time of year. But lonely too."

"Solitude isn't only loneliness," Sister Joan argued. "I know what you mean though. One could imagine one was entirely alone out here. Honestly, this is far enough. The gates are just ahead."

"If you're sure." Mrs. Barratt drew to a halt and released her cramped fingers from their grip on the wheel. "I don't actually like driving very much," she confessed suddenly, "but one needs a car out here with the public transport so scarce. Mark has his own car but he bought me this one for my birthday."

"He sounds like a good husband," Sister Joan said, alighting and reaching in for her luggage.

"He's a wonderful husband." The small, tight face beamed widely. "I just can't tell you."

"Well, I'd better get on. Thanks for the lift, Mrs. Barratt."

"You're welcome, Sister. And please do call me Daisy," the other begged. "Only Mark uses my Christian name round here. It makes me feel terribly ancient."

"Daisy then. Thank you again."

The Mini started up again and chuntered off, Daisy Barratt clinging desperately to the wheel. Sister Joan waved, picked up her bags, and went through the open gates.

The Order of the Daughters of Compassion was not a completely enclosed order, its members often taking outside work to augment the convent finances, but always mindful of the rule that contemplation and prayers were their main reason for existence. Sister Joan herself taught at a tiny school high on the moors, taking as pupils those smaller children who couldn't get easily into school at Bodmin and enlivened by the more or less regular attendance of some of the children from the local Romany camp. The teacher's salary, which went straight to the convent, was provided for out of an old endowment established by the Tarquin family who had owned the great house before it had become a convent. There were no Tarquins in the area now. The last of them had left the district the previous year.*

Beyond the gates the drive curved between lawns that were not as well manicured as they had once been despite all of Sister Martha's valiant efforts. The house itself loomed ahead, the original L-shape disfigured by a large Victorian conservatory stuck on one end. The latter was crammed with the various pot herbs and indoor bulbs that Sister Martha and Sister Perpetua raised together, the main façade thickly ivied with the windows discreetly shielded by white net.

Sister Joan stood still for a moment, savouring the return. After only six weeks in Scotland she felt as if she had been away for months; though it was less than two

---

*See *Vow of Silence*.

years since she had first seen the Cornwall House she had the distinct impression that she was coming home.

The main doors stood wide as they always did save in the worst weather and after dusk. The last rays of sunlight arched across the polished floor of the wide entrance hall with its archways to left and right and the staircase rising to the upper storey. The beautifully moulded cornices were evidence of the previous wealth of the owners but the chandelier held only the minimum number of light bulbs.

"You steal upon us like an angel unaware," Sister Hilaria said, appearing suddenly, as was her wont, around the corner of the building and stopping short, her large hands clasped before her, her somewhat prominent mystic's eyes lighting with pleasure.

Sister Joan, surprised that the unworldly novice mistress had even marked her absence, said modestly as they exchanged the ritual touching of cheeks, "Rather a disobedient angel, I fear. I ought to have given my time of arrival."

"But you didn't want to put anyone to the trouble of meeting you," Sister Hilaria said, in the tone of one who always sees stars instead of mud.

"I got a lift home," Sister Joan informed her.

She might as well have saved her breath. Sister Hilaria had concentrated on practical matters for as long as her temperament would allow, and was gazing now at a patch of sunlight with rapt intensity. Sister Hilaria was not, in Sister Joan's opinion, the ideal guide for imaginative young girls but Mother Dorothy disagreed.

"The rest of us can provide the example of common sense, Sister, but in Sister Hilaria they may catch a privileged glimpse of the higher aspects of our vocations."

Mother Dorothy, small, bespectacled and displaying

her usual uncanny ability to appear on the scene the moment one thought about her, trotted briskly into view.

"Are you going to linger on the doorstep all day, Sister Joan?" she enquired with a touch of acid.

"I beg your pardon, Mother." Sister Joan went hastily up the shallow steps to the hall and received the kiss of peace from her purple-habited superior.

The rule that the one elected as prioress for the term of five years, no sister being allowed to serve more than two consecutive terms, wore purple and thereafter wore purple ribbon on her sleeve, one stripe for each five-year term, was strictly kept. Sister Joan who had never aspired to any particular office recognized her own limitations of character as Mother Dorothy said, "I assume you had some notion of begging a lift which is not very wise in this day and age, or did you splash out money on a taxi? Never mind, you will want to visit the Blessed Sacrament immediately. You can take your bags up later."

What she really craved, she thought guiltily, was a good strong cup of tea. That only proved that even after her period of retreat she fell far short of perfection.

"Thank you, Mother."

Turning right, passing the small parlour with its grille dividing it from the equally modest visitors' parlour on the other side, she made her way down the narrow passage to the chapel. It had once been the family chapel and the side door was kept unlocked until dark lest any lay member of the local community might care to visit.

The chapel retained its intimate atmosphere with the candles casting a gentle radiance over the carved altar and the pews where the nuns kept their several places. At the left, at the foot of the spiral stairs giving access to the library and the storerooms above, stood a statue of the Blessed Virgin, its tinted plaster slightly faded, a vase of chrysanthemums at its feet. Sister Joan, who had a sneaking liking for the flower though Sister David complained it was an untidy bloom, blessed herself from the holy water stoup and splashed a little on to the wilting bronze petals.

Sliding into her accustomed seat, folding her hands, she felt the tiny flare of irritation that Mother Dorothy so often roused in her flicker and die. It was, after all, only fitting to greet the Master of the house immediately. She bowed her head and thanked Him for a safe journey and for the benefits of her recent retreat.*

She prayed briefly for the other sisters, living and dead, and added on impulse a request that the missing girl—what was her name? Yes, Valerie Pendon—might turn up safe and sound. According to the posters she'd been missing for three days. Three days was a long time, time for almost anything to have happened. She curbed her straying imagination, murmured a Hail Mary and rose from her knees, the craving for a hot cup of tea returning almost as soon as she was back in the corridor again.

Her next duty was to report to Mother Prioress. She went across to the antechamber and tapped on the parlour door.

"Enter." Mother Dorothy never kept anyone waiting. *"Dominus vobiscum."*

The familiar greeting that never altered when one entered the parlour. Sinking to her knees, Sister Joan responded respectfully, *"Et cum spiritu sancto."*

"Sit down, Sister." Mother Dorothy nodded towards the stools ranged before the severe flat-topped desk on

*See *Vow of Sanctity*.

which she conducted her letter writing and other business.

This had once been the drawing-room. Taking her place on a stool, back straight, feet together, hands lightly clasped, according to rule, Sister Joan kept her eyes firmly on her prioress with no sideways glance at the silk paper on the walls, the long panels of faded and exquisite tapestry. Now no carpet covered the bare polished floor and the furniture was utilitarian but the beauty of the room shone through.

"Did you have a good retreat, Sister?" Mother Dorothy gave her an expectant look.

"In many ways, yes, Mother Prioress. It was cold and lonely at times, but the loneliness was never empty. I found that I actually met several local people, which I did enjoy."

"And your example may have inspired some of them to consider the deeper aspects of life."

Sister Joan rather doubted that but bowed her head meekly.

"And you did some painting?" Mother Dorothy looked at her.

"Yes, Mother. In my case. Unsigned." For the life of her she couldn't repress a faint sigh after the last word.

"We shall find time to look at them later," Mother Dorothy said. "Some of them may be good enough to be sold at the Christmas fair."

How Jacob would mock if he could hear those words. Jacob, with his keen, clever, Semitic face, his scorn of those who wasted or threw away their talents.

"Never sell yourself short even if you're not a Michelangelo," he had instructed her. "And always be proud of what you do. Art is above all the expression of the artist's own personality."

"Personality must be checked and repressed to a certain degree," Mother Agnes had advised. "It cannot be entirely eradicated; nobody would wish that, but we must avoid singularity."

Sister Joan doubted if that counsel of perfection would ever be achieved by her. However, there was no point in worrying about it now. She murmured, "Thank you, Mother."

"Have you any particular observations on our Scottish retreat?" the other wanted to know.

"You do know there's a steep climb up to it? It would be impossible for older members of the community to make the climb regularly."

"That point has been made by several other sisters," Mother Dorothy said. "It may be time for us to consider another site, but that will be a matter for consultation among all our houses. You look well, Sister, despite the rigours you have undergone. Ready to begin your tasks in the community again?"

"And glad to be home," Sister Joan said warmly. "How is Sister David managing at the school or did you decide to defer the opening?"

"The school is closed."

"Then I'd like permission to spend a day cleaning out before we reopen. After such a long break there'll be dust an inch deep."

"Permanently closed," said Mother Dorothy.

"Perm . . . I don't understand." Sister Joan looked at her blankly. "You always said the school fulfilled a real need."

"It wasn't my decision, Sister," Mother Dorothy said. "The new education rules, with the national curriculum and endless series of tests, make schools like the Moor

School superfluous—or so the education authorities inform me. The children are being bussed into Bodmin."

"Which is ridiculous!" Sister Joan's face flushed indignantly. "Don't they understand that the Romany children will start truanting if they're thrust into the Bodmin school? They come to me because we've built up a pleasant relationship. They get as much education in the Moor School as they'd get anywhere else, probably more because they get individual attention. We know the families, the way they think. Officialdom can be so—so . . ."

"Officious?" Mother Dorothy smiled slightly. "I agree with you, Sister, but we have no real grounds on which to make a stand. The number of pupils affected is very small indeed, and you know that when they get older they are already obliged to enter the larger schools."

"But what about the trust? The Tarquins founded it for a school."

"I am in touch with lawyers," Mother Dorothy said. "It may be possible to convert the trust into something else that would benefit the community. The school building is sound and then there are the books and desks and teaching aids. Something can be worked out, I'm sure."

Sister Joan was silent. She hadn't realized until this moment how much she had enjoyed teaching, how close she had become to her pupils. Riding to school on Lilith, the placid pony, every morning she had relished the hours of freedom when she had been in charge of her little world. To have to give it up and submit herself to the cloistered life entirely was a blow for which she was unprepared.

"You did some very good work there," Mother Dorothy was continuing. "You have every right to feel proud of that, Sister. I understand that you feel you have a responsibility to the children, but your first responsibility must be to God and the community. And you need not fear that we will leave you without occupation. After your retreat you will be ready for some practical work, I'm sure."

"Yes, of course, Mother." Sister Joan felt more cheerful.

"My main concern is how to use you in the best possible way," the prioress was considering thoughtfully. "There is one area where you would be most useful but I wonder how you would feel about it yourself. You have been Mary. Perhaps it is time for you to be Martha for a while. I mean that as we have no lay sister at the moment you could fill that gap until we can obtain one."

The lay sisters did most of the cooking and shopping; they kept earlier hours and went to bed later than others in the convent. They slept in the two cells that led off the kitchen. At present there were no lay sisters at the Cornwall House. Women who chose the religious life generally preferred to enter the cloister proper in an order like the Daughters of Compassion.

"It would not," said Mother Dorothy with delicate irony, "be a demotion. Sister Perpetua has been doing most of the work but she has her infirmary duties."

"I would be very happy to take over the duties of lay sister," Sister Joan said, curbing her enthusiasm prudently. "I must warn you that my cooking isn't very good—and that's an understatement."

"We are always in need of extra penances," Mother Dorothy said, her mouth twitching slightly. "Fortunately, Sister Teresa can cook. As novice she must not, of course, take her full place in the activities of the community until she has made her perpetual vows. However, she can be of use in the kitchen."

"Thank you, Mother."

"Your things will be moved to the lay sister's cell," Mother Dorothy said, making the small gesture that signified the end of the interview.

"May I have leave to ride over to the school before chapel?" Sister Joan asked. "I'd like to pick up a few things and . . ."

"Take a somewhat sentimental farewell? Be back in time for chapel, please. Punctuality hasn't been waived during your absence."

"Yes, Mother. Thank you."

She waited until she was outside the parlour door before she allowed herself to grin with delight. Mother Dorothy, for all her prissy ways, knew her nuns. The prospect of being able to go shopping in the car without asking for special leave, of having some precious time to herself in which to let her mind roam while her hands busied themselves with mundane tasks.

"So you're back." Sister Perpetua, reddish eyebrows arched, clumped through from the back premises. "Has Mother Prioress told you?"

"About the school being closed? Yes, it was a shock."

"Trust the government for that," Sister Perpetua said with a sniff. "Always sticking their fingers in the pie."

"But I am to take over the duties of lay sister."

"Leaving me free to get on with my infirmary and leaving you free to do the cooking? I call that a mixed blessing."

"Sister Teresa is to do most of the cooking," Sister Joan assured her.

"Then my pills and potions won't be needed so often," Sister Perpetua said. "So how was Scotland?"

"Beautiful," Sister Joan said simply. "I painted some pictures there."

"Let's hope Mother allows us to hang one of them up somewhere then. Where are you going now?"

"Over to the school to give Lilith some exercise. Then I'll move my things down to the lay cell."

"I can do that for you," the older nun offered. "You have your ride and get your bit of nostalgia over. Don't stay out after chapel or you'll blot your copy-book before you've been back five minutes."

"Sometimes," said Sister Joan, "I have the feeling that those words will be the first addressed to me by Saint Peter when I arrive at the heavenly gates."

Sister Perpetua gave a harsh bark of laughter. "And if you arrive at the other place, which God forbid, I daresay you'll be certain of a welcome!"

Sister Perpetua was evidently developing a sense of humour. Sister Joan smiled as she went on into the narrow passage off which the infirmary and dispensary opened before the large kitchen was reached.

She paused to put her head in at the door of the infirmary but the two old nuns who spent most of their time there were both dozing and Sister Perpetua's loud whisper restrained her.

"Don't go bouncing in on Sister Gabrielle and Sister Mary Concepta now, just when I've got them settled for a nice little nap before chapel."

Sister Joan put her hands on her heart and went on through the kitchen to the yard. Lilith, her head stuck over the half door, greeted her with a whinny.

"Hello, girl. Did you miss your rides?" Sister Joan lifted down the old saddle and led the pony out. It struck her that she was talking to the horse rather in the same way that Sister Perpetua had talked to her, as if she were ten years old instead of thirty-six. However, since only a sixth of her life had been spent in the religious life she suspected that in many ways she could fairly be regarded as a mere child.

She swung herself up into the saddle and trotted round to the front of the building. The sunshine had been deceptive. The light was beginning to fade and the joined shadows of Lilith and herself were long and thin on the grass. When she rode to school she had a special dispensation to wear jeans under her habit, but at this hour it was scarcely likely that she would meet even a casual walker on the moor.

She urged Lilith into a jog, sensing her mount's pleasure at being out again. A gentle walk up and down the lawn on a leading rein was the most she could have expected to get from any of the other sisters.

The moor was brown at this end of the year. Unlike Dartmoor with its high, wild crags Bodmin had a brooding, secretive quality of its own. It yielded its beauties reluctantly, like a veiled woman holding back jewels. Here and there a late clump of heather clung to the turf, and the fronds of bracken were tipped with the pale gold of late autumn.

The schoolhouse lay ahead, its walls and roof softened by shadow. She drew rein and dismounted, thinking with real regret of the months she had spent teaching here. She had grown to love the children, had even managed to weld into one class the dark-eyed Romanies and the more stolid offspring of the farmers. She liked to think they had liked her too, but she was too clear headed to imagine she had had any lasting influence on them. They would move on into other schools and forget her.

"One of the hardest things you will ever have to do is cultivate detachment," her novice mistress had warned. "Detachment from all save the things of the spirit. Detachment does not mean coldness or not caring, but it does mean the ability to set oneself apart from all yearnings for transient things, all possessiveness, even in the end from the very prayers and devotions so dear to our hearts. These are only the finger pointing at the moon. Don't spend all your time looking at your finger."

She had forgotten to bring the key to the school. Sister Joan wondered if that could be attributed to detachment but decided wryly that it was more likely to be absent-mindedness.

Leaving the placid Lilith to graze at her ease, she approached the door and gave it an experimental push. Sister David had evidently been remiss since it swung open with a protesting creak. Within, the cloakroom on the left and the classroom on the right were shadowed and shuttered. There was no electricity in the school. She had brewed tea for herself and hot soup on chilly days for the children on a primus stove. She went into the classroom and opened the shutters, letting the last of the late afternoon sun illumine the desks and blackboard and the shelves where the children had kept their projects.

Sitting at her desk, surveying the room, peopling it with remembered children, she permitted herself her moment of nostalgia.

"So, goodbye and God bless, my dear pupils."

She spoke the words aloud into the sighing silence. No sense in lingering here. Later on, when it had been decided to what use the building could be put, she would ask if she might take a few of the books. There were other books in the cupboard behind her. She glanced round and frowned slightly. The shelves from the cupboard had been lifted out and leaned against the blackboard. Sister David had evidently started clearing out ahead of time.

"And as my deputy she has a perfect right," Sister Joan told herself firmly, rising and pulling open the door.

The girl wedged awkwardly into the shadowy corner wore a white dress and had a garland of fading leaves on her head. She looked as if she were asleep but, of course, she wasn't.

TWO

✠ ✠ ✠

Sister Joan had seen dead bodies before. Death itself held no terrors for her, but the manner of dying did. As she knelt to lift the drooping head she saw the thin, purple line cutting into the neck like the rehearsal for a beheading.

She had seen the face already that day. Valerie Pendon, missing from home in the middle of the night, now bundled into a cupboard, the wreath on her head and the long white dress with its inserts of cheap lace a terrible mockery of a bridal costume. Bitten nails on the fingers added the final touch of unbearable pathos.

It had been an elopement then. A girl of sixteen stealing away in the middle of the night to meet a boy-friend of whom her parents had either been unaware or of whom they would have disapproved. Killed here? Brought here later? It was impossible to tell.

Moving with the calmness of shock, she rose and shut the cupboard door, her hand automatically sketching a blessing. There was no help for it but on her first day back she would have to miss chapel.

Remounting Lilith, she urged her down the track towards the town. Fortunately the pony was in a mood to go fast but it would be dark by the time she reached the

21

police station, even though in Cornwall the day died slowly.

Street lights cast a hard blue light over nun and horse as she rode down the street and dismounted in the parking space at the side of the police station, tying Lilith's rein loosely to the fire hydrant.

When she walked into the station the desk sergeant glanced up, then snapped to attention in the way some people did when a nun appeared.

"Good evening, Sister. Anything I can do for you?" He sounded brisk and businesslike.

"Is . . ." She searched for the one name she knew. "Is Detective Sergeant Mill on the premises?"

"Someone using my name in vain? Oh, hello, Sister Joan." Detective Sergeant Mill had just emerged from the inner office.

"I hoped you'd be working late," she said.

"Catching up on paperwork." His voice sharpened slightly as he took a second look at her. "Is anything wrong?"

"I'm afraid there is, Detective Sergeant Mill. May I use your telephone to let the convent know I'll be late?"

"Certainly. You look as if you need a stiff shot of brandy too. See about it, will you?"

He threw the order over his shoulder at the desk sergeant as he held open the door for Sister Joan.

She accepted a chair gratefully and dialled the convent with fingers that felt suddenly clumsy and chilly.

"Sister Perpetua? Sister Joan here. Please ask Mother Dorothy to excuse me but I'm forced to be absent from chapel and possibly for supper too."

"What's happened?" At the other end of the line Sister Perpetua sounded more resigned than panicky.

"I'll explain what has happened when I get back. I'm

ringing from the police station but I'm perfectly all right, so there's no need for anyone to worry. Goodbye."

She hung up quickly to find Detective Sergeant Mill's eyes fixed on her.

"What has happened, Sister?" he asked quietly.

"I went over to the Moor School—you know it's been closed? I wanted to have a last look at it—not literally, of course, but in a rather sentimental way. I also had some idea of picking up anything that I thought I might need. I'd forgotten the key but the front door was unlocked, so I went in." She paused to moisten her lips, clasping her hands tightly together. "Someone had taken the shelves out of the cupboard behind my desk. I opened the cupboard door and the girl—the one who was reported missing—was there. She was—someone strangled her, I think, and she's wearing a bridal gown with a wreath of leaves on her head."

To her extreme embarrassment her voice choked and tears came into her eyes.

"Drink this." Detective Sergeant Mill handed her the brandy the desk sergeant had just brought in. "You heard that, Stephens?"

"I did." The desk sergeant looked marginally less stolid.

"Lay on a car and get hold of Barratt, will you? He may as well be flung in at the deep end."

"Doctor, sir?"

"And the photographer. A couple of men to rope off the area—you know the drill. Oh, and better get hold of the priest—Father Malone. Don't contact the Pendons yet. Bad news will keep, if it is their daughter. Did you know the girl, Sister?"

Sister Joan, her throat burning from the brandy, her self-possession restored, shook her head.

"I saw the posters earlier," she said. "The photograph was a good likeness."

"I'll have to ask you to accompany me, Sister. I can run you back to the convent afterwards."

"What about Lilith?"

"I'll have someone ride her back. Get things moving, Stephens."

Outside he slid behind the wheel and gave her a keen glance as she strapped herself into the passenger seat.

"Feeling better now?" His tone had the solicitousness of an old friend.

"In myself, yes. About that girl's death, no. It seemed so—blasphemous somehow. The white dress and the fading leaves."

She bit her lip.

"Nobody gets used to it." His voice had changed, becoming rough with what she guessed was suppressed anger.

"The desk sergeant seems fairly unshockable," Sister Joan said, "I don't suppose he's any relation to the curate, is he? Same name."

"Don't think so. Is the curate the stolid, unflappable type?"

She thought fleetingly of Father Stephens with his involved sermons and beautifully polished shoes, and answered discreetly, "Oh, he's a very worthy young man. A great help to Father Malone."

But not the man to break the news of a horrible death to worried parents. His mellifluous phrases would have no comfort set beside Father Malone's simpler vocabulary.

The desk sergeant had been efficient. Two other police cars snaked behind them on the moorland track, their headlamps raking dark peat and bracken that made strange shapes against the wind-swept sky.

The schoolhouse was a darker square against the dark. Detective Sergeant Mill drew to a halt and gave her another glance.

"You don't mind coming in with me, going over what you did when you arrived? Sergeant Barratt, over here. Sister Joan, this is Sergeant David Mark Barratt, our latest acquisition from Birmingham."

There was a faintly ironic edge to his voice as he rolled out the full name. An ambitious police officer who had arrived with the intention of patronizing the rural constabulary, Sister Joan summed up at first glance, shaking hands with the tall, smartly manicured and brushed officer.

"I met your wife, Daisy, this afternoon," she said. "She was kind enough to give me a lift to the convent."

"I'd only just reached home when the call came in so she hadn't had the chance to tell me about it yet," Sergeant Barratt said. "What happened here?"

"Looks as if Valerie Pendon's turned up," Detective Sergeant Mill said. His face and voice were carefully neutral; the process of hiding his feelings under a mask of officialdom had already begun. "Now, Sister, take us through it. You rode here . . . ?"

"I dismounted and left Lilith to graze. She's very good and never wanders. Then I realized that I didn't have the key to the school, but I tried the door and it was unlocked."

"Not forced?"

"Not as far as I can recall noticing, but then the door is occasionally unlocked. I've been guilty of forgetting it myself. It's so remote here and there's nothing of monetary value inside. Anyway I pushed it open and went in."

Repeating her action, poised on the threshold she paused, then said, "There's no electric light here. We have a primus stove to provide heat in the cold weather and brew soup for the children."

"We can rig arc lights," Detective Sergeant Mill began.

"I took the liberty of ordering that done, sir." Sergeant Barratt nodded towards a small group of policemen occupied with trailing cables.

"Did you now?" His superior officer spoke somewhat dryly. "I'm glad to see you aren't afraid of using your own initiative, Barratt. Right, get the lights on and in here. Sister Joan, would you like to lead the way? I have a fairly powerful torch."

She didn't want to lead the way anywhere save straight back to the convent. She didn't want to be the one who opened the cupboard again.

"Of course, Detective Sergeant Mill." She walked into the narrow passage, the beam of the torch lighting the way ahead.

"You turned straight into the classroom?" he said behind her.

"Yes, I did."

"Do exactly what you did before then," he encouraged.

She walked steadily into the classroom and seated herself behind the large desk from which she had been wont to survey her pupils.

"You just sat there?" Sergeant Barratt's tone was puzzled.

"Regretting the fact that the school is now closed," she explained. "Then I noticed the shelves from the cupboard were propped up against the blackboard. I got up and opened the cupboard."

Her hand was on the knob and her stomach was churning.

"What was usually kept in the cupboard?" Sergeant Barratt asked.

"Exercise books, rolls of sketching paper, pencils—general supplies."

"Open the cupboard, if you please, Sister." Detective Sergeant Mill was polite but firm.

She opened it, compressing her brows as she looked down at the huddled figure. In the light of the arc lamps which were abruptly illuminated it had a ghastly, theatrical quality. Juliet in the tomb, the Mistletoe bride.

"Did you touch her?" Detective Sergeant Mill asked.

"I went down on one knee and lifted her head. That was when I saw the red line round it. Must I . . . ?"

"No need to do it again," he said.

"Surely you knew you ought not to have touched a dead body?" Sergeant Barratt said. He made it sound as if she had committed some social gaffe.

"I acted instinctively." She drew herself to her full height which wasn't very tall and gave him the look designed to quell "bold" children. "I didn't know she was dead. Not consciously, that is. If I was thinking anything at all it was that she might have been hiding in the cupboard and been taken ill or something. I didn't touch anything else. I closed the cupboard door and then I remounted Lilith and rode straight into town."

"The convent is nearer," Sergeant Barratt said.

"You mean why didn't I telephone from there? By the time I'd explained things to Mother Prioress and received permission to use the telephone more time would have been lost. You sound," she added acidly, "as if you think I might have killed the poor girl and put her in the cupboard myself!"

"I wasn't implying anything, Sister." He sounded offended.

"And Sister Joan has a perfect alibi," Detective Sergeant Mill said in a voice intended to diffuse hostility. "You had just arrived from six weeks in Scotland when I saw you this afternoon, hadn't you?"

"Sorry, I'm still upset, I'm afraid. Can we go outside?" She kept her eyes turned resolutely from the cupboard.

"Yes, of course, Sister." He took her arm in a soothing fashion. "Ah, here's the doctor—and Father Malone. We shall need your fingerprints but perhaps you can come down to the station tomorrow morning? It'll only be for purposes of elimination. Didn't one of the other sisters assist you sometimes?"

"Sister David would faint with horror at the thought of being summoned to provide her fingerprints," Sister Joan said, with a twinge of humour, "but of course she'll come. Will you want a list of the pupils too?"

"Can I get them from the register?"

"I don't know if it's still in the desk or whether it was taken back to the convent or not."

The purely practical snatch of conversation had steadied her nerves.

"I'll see about it," he said, releasing her arm and giving it a little pat. "I'll be grateful if you'll wait around for a few minutes. Sergeant, can you see that the lights are correctly angled for the photographer?"

His impersonal, courteous tone told her that he wasn't overkeen on his new colleague.

"Sergeant Mill, is it?" Father Malone, an immense muffler around his neck, trotted over to where they stood. "Sister Joan, good evening. Is it true that you found the poor child? This is a terrible thing if it's so."

"We shall need formal identification, Father Malone," Detective Sergeant Mill told him, shaking hands briefly. "That will have to come from one of the parents, but if you can confirm—she was a Catholic."

"And a very sweet girl," the priest said, nodding his grey head vigorously. "The Pendons are regular church-goers which is more than can be said for many these days, more's the pity. She'll be requiring prayers for her soul."

"When the doctor and photographer have finished."

"Will you require me, Father?" Sister Joan asked.

"No absolute need. This must be a sad homecoming for you, Sister."

"Yes," she said simply.

"The poor, poor child."

Valerie Pendon had been sixteen, Sister Joan reflected. At sixteen most modern girls knew more about life than Father Malone himself. On the other hand the girl must have been naïve to steal away in the middle of the night in the belief she was going to be married. Presumably she had stolen away. Nothing had been said about any signs of struggle in that empty bedroom.

"A terrible thing," Father Malone said helplessly, coming out of the schoolhouse again. In the lights from the arcs and the headlamps of the surrounding cars he looked small and impotent. "How could anyone do such a thing to a young girl? I shall have to break the news to the parents as quickly as possible. First we must get you back to the convent as swiftly as possible, Sister."

He made it sound rather as if she'd escaped from the

place, Sister Joan thought. It would have been interesting to drive back with Detective Sergeant Mill who might have something more to tell her, but he was obviously needed here, if only to combat his junior's officious manner.

"That's very kind of you, Father," she responded gratefully. "Mother Dorothy gave me leave to ride Lilith over and take a last look at my old classroom before the building is used for some other purpose. When I found—well, I rode down at once to report it."

"You informed Mother Prioress?"

"I telephoned her from the police station and then Detective Sergeant Mill drove me up here, so Lilith is still in town."

"And yourself just back from a Holy retreat," he said sympathizingly.

"Yes." Settling herself into the priest's woefully elderly car she felt as if the lochs and hills of Scotland, the retreat high in the cliff face where a person had time to be alone with God, growing further away in her mind, like a picture seen through the wrong end of a telescope.

Father Malone drove fast and not altogether skilfully, uttering small cries of self-recrimination as his wheels bounced against clumps of turf. He said nothing and she was grateful for the silence. To have been forced to hear platitudes at this moment would have been unbearable.

"I can walk from here," she offered when they reached the gates.

"Better be safe than sorry, Sister," he returned, turning into the drive with a squeal of brakes.

Surely he didn't fear for her own safety? She cast

him a startled glance, but they were already at the front steps.

"Thank you, Father. Good night." She unbuckled her seat belt and alighted, aware from the look on his face that his mind had already moved ahead, to the ordinary house where two parents waited for the news that would shatter their lives.

"You had better come in, Sister." Mother Dorothy had appeared on the step, her habit fluttering in the wind. "May I say that it was exceedingly peaceful here while you were away?"

"You heard what has happened?" Sister Joan came up the steps.

"That very polite desk sergeant from the police station had the kindness to telephone me and inform me of the circumstances that had delayed you. Sister, have you been drinking?"

Mother Dorothy was sniffing the air, a look of consternation on her face.

"They gave me some brandy and I haven't eaten all day," Sister Joan said, torn between a desire to burst into tears and an almost uncontrollable urge to giggle.

"You need a good hot meal and some strong coffee," Mother Dorothy said, becoming all concerned bustle. "Supper is over but Sister Perpetua will give you something in the kitchen. Go along there now. Blessing is in half an hour."

"Thank you, Mother." Sister Joan knelt briefly and continued on her way across the hall.

"Plaice and chips, Sister," Sister Perpetua said brightly as she entered. "I kept it hot for you. Coffee?"

"Isn't tea better for shock?" Sister Joan ventured.

"Coffee is better for alcohol on the breath. Really, Sister." The infirmarian clucked her tongue and gave

her usual bark of laughter, her face immediately so-
bering as she added, "But very sensible to take a drop.
What a dreadful shock you must have had. I was with
Mother Dorothy when the call came from the police. Of
course we've said nothing to any of the others. If it
turns out to be that poor girl then Mother Dorothy will
make a brief announcement."

"I'm afraid it is true." Sister Joan was tucking into
the meal. "Father Malone recognized the girl as one of
his parishioners."

"And only sixteen." Sister Perpetua poured an extra
cup of coffee for herself and sat down at the other side
of the table. "Poor misguided child. I'm assuming she
was—unlawfully killed."

"Strangled with some kind of cord, I think, and bundled into the school cupboard." There was a definite relief in talking. "She was wearing a white wedding dress
and there was a wreath of leaves on her head."

"Then that is truly wicked." Sister Perpetua's high-
coloured cheeks had paled and every freckle on her
weather-beaten skin stood out. "She had taken up with
some boy or other, I suppose, and he lured her to the
schoolhouse with promises of marriage. Wicked."

"I suppose it might have been like that," Sister Joan
said doubtfully, "but why would she have left home in
the middle of the night wearing a wedding dress? If she
thought she was going to elope she'd surely have
dressed in street clothes first."

"Perhaps she did."

"But her parents said only the nightgown she was
wearing and her slippers and dressing-gown had gone."

"She might have purchased something they didn't
know about."

"I suppose." Sister Joan sipped her coffee, weariness stealing over her.

"Well, thank the Good Lord that the solving of it isn't in our hands," Sister Perpetua said fervently. "The police will deal with it."

"Sister David and I have to go down to the police station tomorrow morning to have our fingerprints taken—for elimination purposes," she added hurriedly. "Both of us at various times worked at the school."

"Such an unpleasant business," Sister Perpetua said, the frown on her face deepening. "And so unfortunate that you should return from your retreat to have to face it. Do let us talk of something more congenial. Oh, I moved your things into the lay cell. Sister Teresa is still in her cell upstairs but since she is to assist you during this period of her training she can be moved into the adjoining cell, if you wish."

"Whatever Mother Prioress deems fit. Thank you for moving my things. I'm afraid we all take advantage of your kindness and hard work."

"Nonsense. If we can't help out wherever and whenever we're needed then it's a poor look-out for our souls," the other said briskly. "Now that you'll be sleeping down here you will keep an ear open if one of our old ladies requires anything? Sister Mary Concepta sleeps like a top but Sister Gabrielle—well, you know Sister Gabrielle."

"An eighty-four-year-old insomniac," Sister Joan said with a grin. "I'm surprised she isn't here right now."

"We held vigil last night to pray for your safe return," Sister Perpetua told her. "Sister Gabrielle insisted on joining in and so she's flat out tonight. Was that the bell?"

The shrill clanging, calling the community to the blessing, rang through the house. Sister Joan put down her half-drunk coffee and crossed herself in unison with her companion.

The community with the exception of the two oldest nuns who were sleeping filed silently into the chapel. This was the part of the daily ritual that Sister Joan most relished. After the day's work all the strands were drawn together as they knelt in their accustomed places, the rosaries at their belts sliding through their fingers as they recited the Litany. Sister Joan knelt with the rest, keeping careful custody of her eyes. She had, in any case, no need to study her companions since their faces were as familiar to her as her own—more familiar since the convent had no mirrors.

Sister Perpetua knelt stiffly, with no more than the faintest intake of breath to betray the rheumatic pain that plagued her knees. Next to her Sister Martha looked as if a breath of wind would blow her away. Sister Joan always felt astonishment when she saw Sister Martha lugging huge bags of compost around the vegetable garden. At the farther side Sister Katharine moved her hands as if she were still spinning the cotton from which she fashioned the exquisite lace that brought in regular profits for the order.

In the row behind Sister David was gabbling softly, always a syllable ahead of everybody else. With her rabbit features and her granny specs she reminded Sister Joan of a Disney creation. A nice, kind, timid, over-zealous little creation, she amended. Empty seats separated her from Sister Teresa, who having completed her two years in the postulancy, was now with the rest of the community to work out her third year of training before the two years of virtual silence that would bring the five-year training to an end. Sister Joan had little knowledge of Sister Teresa who had only just moved from the status of postulant, a change signified by the white veil she wore over her blue habit.

There was a slight rustling as Sister Hilaria glided in, a few minutes late and, as usual, sublimely unconscious of the fact. Behind her the two postulants in their white bonnets settled themselves meekly. Elizabeth and Marie, Sister Joan remembered. She had caught fleeting glimpses of them—both young girls who had turned their backs on discos and boy-friends and secular life in order to immure themselves for the rest of their lives. She herself hadn't entered the religious life until she was thirty—a latish vocation by most standards, but she had brought some experience and a little worldly wisdom with her. Sisters Elizabeth and Marie were scarcely more than schoolgirls, not much older than the girl who huddled in the school cupboard with a red line round her neck and a fading wreath on her head.

"Sisters in Christ, we are very happy to have Sister Joan back in our midst," Mother Dorothy was saying, with what sounded like absolute sincerity. "She has, as we all know, been on retreat in Scotland and we look forward to seeing the pictures she has painted while she was there. She has also agreed to take over the duties of lay sister for the time being until we can find one but Sister Teresa will be doing most of the cooking."

A ripple of laughter ran round the community.

"I have graver news." Mother Dorothy frowned as if she were marshalling her thoughts. "You may have heard of the recent disappearance of a sixteen-year-old girl from the town. She has been found and it seems clear she was the victim of violence. This tragedy does not concern us directly, but Valerie Pendon was a Catholic and I know that all of you will wish to pray for her."

There was a little murmur of assent, hands rising to sketch the sign of the cross. Sister Joan was aware of a few covert glances darted in her direction. Her absence from chapel and supper had been noted and conclusions drawn.

The prioress finished speaking, turned to the altar and genuflected. Then she walked to the door, took the small lamp already burning there and raised it. With one accord, their physical actions perfectly co-ordinated, the sisters genuflected and filed out, each one kneeling before Mother Dorothy in order to receive the final blessing of the day which marked the start of the grand silence.

"If you wish to take a short walk in the enclosure before you retire," Mother Dorothy said unexpectedly, "you may do so for twenty minutes, Sister Joan."

"Thank you, Mother."

Sister Joan hoped she didn't sound as surprised as she felt. Mother Dorothy was not one to bend any rules, but she seemed to have divined the need for fresh air and the healing silence of the outdoors that Sister Joan was feeling. It was good of her to make such a concession.

As she went out into the cool dark, she reminded herself that it was Mother Dorothy who had suggested she wear jeans under her habit when she rode out on the moor. Mother Dorothy, she decided, had more understanding than appeared on the surface.

Turning aside, her eyes growing accustomed to the dark, she unlatched the wicker gate that led into the enclosure garden.

Sister Martha worked wonders here—using the space with imagination, weaving narrow paths between beds of herbs whose fragrance haunted the air even in winter. In one corner white headstones glimmered, each one the last resting place of a sister of the order. If she remained in the Cornwall House her bones too would rest here one day.

The moon, rising, illuminated the flying remnants of roses clinging stubbornly to their thorny stems. Against the wind the high hedge of elderberry afforded more shelter and privacy. She walked through to the further gate and stood, leaning her arms on it, letting the breeze lift her short veil.

A young girl had been killed. She, Sister Joan, had found the body. She had no more personal connection with the tragedy than that. Yet within herself the desire to find out, to know, was becoming stronger. With slight shame she acknowledged to herself that part of her was angry that someone should have used the school where children had spent their days as a hiding place for the body. Not that it mattered to poor Valerie Pendon where she had been put, but the violence that had ended her young life was somehow insulting when it was carried out in a place where the innocence of children had reigned.

Surely the moor had been searched immediately after the news of her disappearance had been given, and the school building included as a matter of course? They would argue that the murder had been committed elsewhere and the body hidden after the searchers had gone away again.

She bit her lip, realizing that she was in danger of getting her thoughts involved in something which wasn't her business.

"This may be the hardest cross you ever have to bear," her novice mistress had once told her. "The Daughters of Compassion are only semi-enclosed which means there is always a fine balance between the life of the spirit and the duties of one's more mundane life. You have lived as an independent woman for several years, have earned your own living, made your own decisions. I am not saying the life of the spirit was not of vital importance to you. I am saying that from the time you enter the religious life the spirit must order and illuminate every pursuit. Your life must become single pointed, with everything subordinated to the one ideal."

How glibly she had responded, brushing aside the idea that she might find some difficulties in her chosen vocation. Even the word "chosen" had meant something different from what she had first imagined.

"We do not choose our vocation," Mother Agnes had said. "Our vocation chooses us and we forget that at our peril."

Then why, Sister Joan asked silently, having chosen me does my vocation hide itself away, constantly thrusting me into situations where I have to face the mundane world again? Someone else could have found poor Valerie Pendon. Why did it have to be me faced with a problem that has to be solved by other people?

She was venturing dangerously close to self-pity, she decided, and with a small grimace at her own foolishness, opened the gate and went down the shallow mossed steps that led to the old tennis courts where the Tarquins had once played. They were unweeded now with the posts rusted and the nets gone. Sister Martha occasionally mourned over the wasted space and there had been some talk of playing the occasional game to provide physical recreation but nothing had come of it, and they stretched before her, echoing to the sound of her feet. At the far end a low wall divided the postulancy from the enclosure proper.

The small house had once been a dower house and served its present purpose admirably. For the first two years of their training the novices were segregated as strictly as if they all carried the bubonic plague, attending the services but not the general confession, taking the lowest place at table, helping with the manual work without exchanging a word with any professed nun except the prioress and their novice mistress, spending an enormous proportion of their time in meditation and lessons. Only those absolutely suited to the life managed to struggle through. She had often thought that if it were as hard to get married as to become a nun there would be fewer divorces.

Her thoughts were threatening to become full circle again. Valerie Pendon had obviously been unable or unwilling to announce her forthcoming wedding to her family. Or had her boy-friend been already married? Perhaps in her own, childish way she had tried to forget that, to go to him robed as a bride in the wistful hope that her sin might then be judged less harshly?

The fresh air had cleared her head and the twenty minutes were ticking away. Nevertheless it had been good of the prioress to grant her this respite. She cast a last look towards the postulancy with its shuttered windows where Sister Hilaria and her two charges slept.

Not everybody had settled for the night. A veiled and habited figure crossed her line of vision as she turned and began to walk back across the tennis court.

Someone else had received permission from Mother

Dorothy to walk for a while. It was a pity the grand silence made it impossible for her to hail the other one, but even if it had been broad day the figure sped into the enclosure and was hidden by the thick hedge before Sister Joan could distinguish its identity.

THREE

✠ ✠ ✠

"Have my fingerprints taken?" Sister David gave an anguished gulp and nodded bravely. "Of course, Mother. When is it to be?"

She sounded like a French aristocrat enquiring when the guillotine would be set up.

"It's really a painless process, Sister," Sister Joan soothed. "Mother Dorothy, may we stay for coffee if it's offered?"

"I have been thinking that as you're going to be in town anyway," Mother Dorothy said, "it might be a gesture of charity to call upon the Pendons with our sympathy, perhaps take some flowers? Do we have anything suitable, Sister Martha?"

"I cut some very pretty dahlias yesterday," Sister Martha said. "I could make a pretty spray of them."

"Go and do it at once, Sister." Mother Dorothy turned to the others. "I know we don't usually supply flowers for every funeral, but this seems such a sad and needless tragedy that I feel we should make an exception. The parents will require every ounce of compassion that we can offer. Oh, and you may take coffee if it is offered."

Breakfast, cooked by Sister Teresa, was over, the nuns dispersing to their various duties. Sister Joan had slept like a log despite the unfamiliar bed in the unfa-

41

miliar cell, though since every cell in the convent was furnished with pure and exactly similar austerity that hadn't been too great a feat. What had been difficult was waking at 4:30 to the muffled vibrations of the alarm clock under her flat pillow and getting up at once, mindful that it was now her duty to rouse the other sisters at five with the cry of, "Christ Is Risen."

She had achieved it but it would take a week or two before she could rely on waking under her own steam. As she had gone past the door of the infirmary a loud whisper had alerted her.

Sister Gabrielle, her nightcap slightly askew, popped her head up as Sister Joan put her own head round the door.

"Christ is risen," she said.

"Praise be to God," Sister Gabrielle said as fervently as if she were hearing the words for the first time. Perhaps at eighty-four each new morning was a joyous surprise stolen from eternity.

"May I get you something, Sister?" She approached the bed, keeping her voice low since only a series of gentle snores came from Sister Mary Concepta's bed.

"Sister Perpetua will be in soon enough to measure out medicines and get us both on our feet for mass, Sister," the other said. "What's all this about a murder? Or did I dream it?"

"Unfortunately you didn't. A girl from the town has been—unlawfully killed and left in the Moor School."

"If you mean murdered," Sister Gabrielle said, giving her nightcap a ferocious tug, "then say so and don't fall into the modern habit of being mealy-mouthed. It makes me laugh to hear people talking about the permissive society. We knew what was what in my day and we weren't afraid to spell it out. Car stealing was theft and not joy riding, and a killer was a killer and not a disadvantaged member of an uncaring society. Who found her?"

"I did."

"Two minutes back from retreat and the peace of the cloister is shattered." The old nun gave her a wry grin. "God bless you, girl, but you remind me of myself at your age, forever kicking against the pricks and not stopping to think that might be God's purpose for us all along. Evil has to be fought in many ways. Come and tell me how things progress. What was her name?"

"Valerie—Valerie Pendon."

"I'll say a special prayer. Now go and wake up the rest."

Talking to Sister Gabrielle was frequently uncomfortable but never dull. Sister Joan hurried out with a lighter step.

Now she went out to the car and checked the petrol level. Sister David came out and climbed meekly and heroically into the passenger seat, clutching a bouquet of tawny-hearted dahlias.

"We had better go to the police station first, Sister." She turned the key in the ignition. "We can find out from them where the girl lived."

"It's an awful thing to think about, isn't it?" Sister David sighed heavily.

"It's a tragedy," Sister Joan said bleakly. "I hope they catch the man who did it."

"Well, I'm only thankful that isn't our task." Sister David glanced nervously at the speedometer which was hovering around forty. "You'll be getting in some driving practice now that you're on lay duties."

"Whizzing around Cornwall," Sister Joan answered cheerfully. There was no sense in sinking oneself in gloom because of what had happened. It wasn't something that directly concerned any of them. Even as she thought that an inner voice contradicted her. All mankind was concerned in every single death, particularly when that death came soon and violently.

"There's Lilith." She forgot her preoccupation as they drew into the parking space and she spotted the pony being led out from the nearby garage. "Is she all right, Officer?"

"Good as gold, Sister." The youthful policeman paused as she wound down the window. "I'm just going to ride her back to the convent for you."

"See Sister Perpetua. She'll give you tea and a bun," she advised. "You're not going to walk back?"

"Sergeant Barratt's picking me up, thanks," he informed her. "He was up nearly all night so he's coming in later today. I'd better get on. Nice seeing you."

"Right, let's get it over with then." Sister Joan gave her companion an encouraging smile as they got out of the car, with Sister David glancing nervously around as if she feared someone might arrest her for loitering.

"You go first, Sister," she whispered as they went in, to be greeted by the desk sergeant with what Sister Joan was glad to see was unaffected friendliness.

Sister David who would have wilted under officialdom or died of embarrassment had he been over-hearty not only perceptibly relaxed but even ventured on a small joke as they were wiping their fingers after their prints had been taken.

"I do hope those are destroyed afterwards. I may embark on a criminal career and your already having my fingerprints might be inconvenient."

"Don't worry, Sister. We'll make it easy for you." Detective Sergeant Mill, coming in, rubbing the cold out of his well-shaped, ungloved hands, smiled at her. "Sister Joan, good morning. You drove here by way of the school?"

"I took the other track past Farrer's Field," she said.

"The area's still cordoned off. I want the building and the moor immediately surrounding it combed inch by inch. I'll be able to get out of your way in a week or so. I assume you'll be using the building for something or other now that the school's closed?"

"Not until we find out the details of the Tarquin Trust. I don't know what Mother Prioress has in mind."

"I got the list of pupils from the register in your desk," he said. "Has anyone offered you a cup of coffee yet?"

"We didn't expect it. You must be awfully busy." Sister David, suddenly aware that she was chatting to a member of the opposite sex, fluttered into silence.

"Not too busy to thank you for coming in so promptly. Sergeant, bring an extra chair in, will you? And three coffees. Sisters."

He held open his office door with a small show of gallantry.

"Have there been any developments?" Sister Joan asked, seating herself. "We're going to call on the parents, just to leave flowers and express our sympathy if you can give us the address. Oh, have you met Sister David?"

"Detective Sergeant Alan Mill, Sister. Do sit down." His manner changed slightly as he spoke to Sister David.

Sister David sat on the edge of the chair and accepted the coffee with a murmur of thanks.

"You asked about progress." He seated himself at his desk and frowned down at the papers on it for a moment. "It's early days yet as they say. The father identified his daughter late last night down at the morgue. Father Malone had already prepared the family. We just had the pathologist's report. She was strangled with a wire; specks of metal embedded in her skin and then the wire was taken off. She wasn't interfered with in any way. According to the doctor the girl was still a virgin. That was some slight comfort to the parents, though little enough. Now we're trying to find out where the dress she was wearing came from."

Sister David looked a question.

"She was wearing a white wedding dress with a wreath of leaves on her head," Sister Joan said.

"She must have obtained the dress from somewhere," Detective Sergeant Mill said. "There was no label in it but it was clearly new. Then there's her dressing-gown, slippers and nightie—she must have taken those in a bag of some sort. The Pendons will have to be asked about that later on. I'm unwilling to intrude on them but it's unfortunately necessary."

"Perhaps Sister David or I could mention it?"

"In the course of conversation? That would be very helpful. Oh, you wanted the address. I have it here." He scribbled it on a piece of paper. "I've a couple of men rounding up your former pupils for fingerprinting. Merely for elimination but the Romany families may kick up a fuss. Funny, ironic, isn't it? As soon as fingerprinting techniques are improved out of all recognition every criminal wears gloves."

"I hope you catch him," Sister Joan said.

"We intend to catch him." He sounded quietly determined, shaking hands as they rose. "Thank you for coming in, Sisters. If you do hear anything of importance you will let me know?"

"Yes, of course." Going out, she glanced back and saw him frowning after them, his mind already returned to the solving of a murder.

"Shall we visit the Pendons now and leave our flowers?" She slid behind the wheel and glanced at her companion.

"Yes, we must." Sister David looked unhappy. "This is the first time I've ever been on such a visit of condolence, Sister. May I leave you to do the talking?"

"Yes, of course. We'll only stay a few minutes."

The street of terraced houses where the scribbled address led them was only five minutes' walk. They reached it by car in a couple of minutes, parked as near to the house as possible and made their way with some difficulty through a crowd of people who had apparently nothing better to do than stand and stare at curtained windows and a closed front door. There were cars parked along the road, and a police constable at the gate by the pocket handkerchief garden.

"Is it all right to take the flowers in?" Sister Joan began.

She was interrupted by Father Malone who opened the front door at that moment and greeted them.

"Good morning, Sisters. Come along in, won't you? The family will be pleased to see you and to have the flowers. I have a sick visit to make so if you can stay until I can get back here it'll be a great help."

Going into the narrow hall, Sister Joan smelt the unmistakable scent of grief. Impossible to analyse it but, if pressed, she might have said it was compounded of over-stewed tea, human perspiration and salt tears.

The front room, curtains drawn against curious sightseers and lamps switched on, was crammed with people drinking tea and conversing in low voices. As they hesitated a youngish woman, her eyes swollen with crying, her expression a strange mixture of grief and importance, confronted them, words spilling over.

"From the convent? Oh, how very kind. Val would have loved these. She was ever so fond of flowers and these are just—people are really being very kind."

"Mrs. Pendon? This is Sister David and I'm Sister Joan. We came to express our very deep sympathy on behalf of our community, and to ask if there is anything at all we can do?"

"Father Malone has been here, arranging for the requiem and all that," Mrs. Pendon said breathlessly. "You will stop for a cup of tea? Someone made cake." She looked around vaguely.

Tragedy, Sister Joan thought, could be covered up with little things—the cup of tea, the kind neighbour, the sense that, for a short while, one was somehow at the centre of a drama. Mrs. Pendon's mourning for her murdered child was undoubtedly deep and painful, but for the moment she laid social ritual round the wound like a bandage.

Someone thrust a cup of tea into her hand and someone else took the dahlias from Sister David. A man with a red face pumped her hand, raising his voice to inform her that he was Valerie's uncle and that he didn't know what the country was coming to. Sister David had been manoeuvred into an armchair and was being assured that she was the poorer for not having known Valerie. Sister Joan left her to cope and headed for the comparative peace of the upstairs landing at the top of the open-plan stairs.

The inside of this late Victorian house had been ripped out to please modern convenience. The wood of the staircase was shiny with varnish and some kind of stick figure made out of steel decorated a small table on the landing where she stood.

She put down the barely tasted cup of tea and prepared to descend again whenever she could see a gap in the milling heads below. A door on the landing opened and a tall, tired-looking man stood on the threshold.

"Mr. Pendon?" She didn't know by what instinct she divined it was him.

"You're from the convent?"

"The one on the moors. Sister Joan of the Daughters of Compassion."

"Compassion?" He repeated the word drearily, not shaking hands. "Not much of that about these days. Ghouls coming to gloat, to thank their stars that their kids are safely tucked up in bed, reporters wanting a quote from the bereaved parents—my wife copes better than I do."

"I came with another Sister, just to leave flowers and condolences," Sister Joan said. "We didn't want to intrude but there is rather a crush down there."

"Ghouls," he said again.

"Surely not," she ventured. "In times of trouble friends do gather round."

"Perhaps." He roused himself with an evident effort. "I've been sitting in her room, trying to work out how it might have happened. Trying to work out why neither of us guessed she meant to leave. You can come in if you like."

He stood aside to allow her to pass into the bedroom. It was a room longer than it was wide but still not large or imposing, with the frieze of an old nursery pattern still round the walls and a blue carpet that looked new. The white curtains were drawn and the overhead light glared from a white shade. The furniture was of var-

nished pine, scratched in places. There were two bunk
beds against one wall, the upper one containing a row
of stuffed animals and a large doll in a frilly dress.

The kidney-shaped dressing-table had a frill round it,
hiding the drawers beneath, and there was a double
wardrobe taking up most of the rest of the space. On the
walls at each side of the door small brackets held
brightly coloured statuettes of the Christ Child and
St. Teresa of Lisieux. There was another small plaster
figure on the bedside table—the Blessed Virgin with
"Souvenir of Lourdes" on its base.

"We went there last year," Mr. Pendon said. "Just before Sandra—that's our elder girl—got married. Very
nice it was too. Commercial, of course, but then people
like to buy souvenirs, don't they? They used to share
this room, but we started doing it up a bit after Sandra
got married."

"Does she live near?"

"She went up north, her and Ronnie—her husband.
We're expecting them tonight. He's in electrics."

"There isn't very much one can say under these circumstances," Sister Joan said awkwardly. "I don't know
if you've been told but I was the one who found
Valerie. I used to teach at the Moor School and I rode
over to see if I needed anything from the classroom last
evening. She looked—she didn't look frightened, Mr.
Pendon. She must have died very quickly."

"In a wedding dress. We can't make it out," he said
helplessly. "Why did she run off in the middle of the
night in a wedding dress?"

"Are there any suitcases or holdalls missing?" she
asked.

"I checked on the cases. Nothing's missing. She could
have put her nightclothes in a big carrier bag, I suppose?

Truth is, Sister, that I can't seem to think straight since the police came. She was such a good, quiet girl. It's true, honestly. I know every parent says that under these circumstances, but Valerie never caused us any problems. She was a bit too shy if you know what I mean. Not many friends."

"No boy-friends?"

"I'd swear to it. No boy-friends at all. She wasn't interested, Sister."

Sister Joan begged leave to doubt that but kept silent. Every father in this situation said the same thing: "She was a good, quiet girl. Never took any notice of boys."

"I won't rest until they get him," Mr. Pendon said, suddenly and savagely. "I won't rest until they've got him. He must be a maniac. You'd have to be a maniac to kill a girl of sixteen. He must be sick in the head."

"And very wicked," Sister Joan said sombrely. "Sometimes I think that wickedness is a kind of madness. I'll pray for Valerie, Mr. Pendon."

The brief burst of feeling had passed and he sounded drained and weary.

"Thank you kindly, Sister. I'm sure the wife and I are very grateful."

He had reached up and taken down one of the stuffed animals, holding it, stroking it while his eyes gazed into a bleak emptiness. Sister Joan left him there, went back on to the landing, drank her too sweet, cooling tea with a slight grimace, and went down the stairs again as Father Malone arrived.

"Thank God, but Mrs. O'Hare is tons better today," he informed her. "You've spoken to the family?"

"Briefly. There isn't much one can say."

"And the poor things will still be in shock, of course. It was good of you to come, Sister."

"You must have known Valerie," she murmured.

"She was a regular communicant." His face was heavy with distress. "Girls these days are not like they used to be, Sister. All late nights and heavy make-up, but Valerie wasn't like that. She was young for her age, Sister. Young and innocent. She was a nice girl."

A nice Catholic girl who went regularly to Holy Communion, who collected stuffed animals and bought religious statuettes during a family visit to Lourdes. A good girl who took no interest in boys. A girl who had risen from her bunk bed in the middle of the night and put on a wedding dress and sneaked out to meet her killer.

"Was she still at school?" she asked.

"She left at the end of the summer term with two good O levels, English and Art. She hadn't made up her mind exactly what she was going to do. I think that she might have been very good with small children. A tragic waste, Sister."

"Good morning, Father Malone." Sister David, blinking up through her spectacles, had joined them. "Are we ready to go, Sister Joan?"

"Yes, we ought to get back. Goodbye, Father. Mrs. Pendon, goodbye." She would have said more but Mrs. Pendon whisked by with a tray, still intent on bandaging her wound with tea and bustle.

There were still people hanging about in the street. The two nuns walked with bent heads and downcast eyes, shielded by their grey habits and white veils. Sister David dived into the car and fastened her seat belt.

"What a sad, sad thing," she said tremulously.

"Yes." Sister Joan started the car and drove thoughtfully down the street.

Sad and squalid and unnecessary, she thought, and wrong.

"There's that nice police detective," Sister David said, perking up slightly. They were just passing the police station and Sister Joan slowed to a crawl as Detective Sergeant Mill signalled to them.

"I'm sorry to bother you, Sisters, but I do have a few questions," he said.

"We ought to get back for lunch," Sister David said worriedly.

"Sister Joan will probably be the one who can be of most assistance. We can give you a ride home in a police car, Sister David."

Sister David, her nose twitching nervously, was crushed by masculine dominance.

"I'll tell Mother Dorothy you were delayed, Sister," she offered, getting out of the car and ducking into the waiting police car. "What is Sister Teresa supposed to make for lunch?"

"It's chilly today so it had better be soup. I'll try not to be long."

Turning to precede Detective Sergeant Mill into the police station, she surprised a twinkle in his eye.

"Is anything amusing you?" she enquired.

"I didn't realize that you were the cook," he said.

"Now that the school has closed down I'm taking over the duties of the lay sister since we don't have one at the moment, but I don't actually do the cooking. Our novice, Sister Teresa, does that."

"And you tell her to make soup." He held open his office door.

"For your information," she said, betrayed into retaliation, "I'm now the one who goes round at five in the morning and wakes everybody up."

"For breakfast?"

"For private devotions in the chapel and then mass. We have breakfast at seven-thirty."

"Not bacon and eggs." He was teasing her now. Realizing it, she forced herself to chill a little.

"You must know by now that in our order we're vegetarian though we do eat fish. Breakfast is cereal, fruit and coffee, eaten standing. What other questions did you want to ask me?"

"What did you find out at the Pendons'?"

"I went there to offer flowers and condolences on behalf of the order. I didn't understand I was there in the capacity of detective."

"You are in a bad mood," he observed mildly.

"I'm sorry." She flushed, biting her lip. "It's only that I've just returned from a spiritual retreat and landed, somehow or other, in the middle of a murder merely because I was stupid enough to want to take a look at the school. I live under obedience in a semi-enclosed order, and having to think about a dreadful crime—most women would find that disconcerting. I didn't mean to be rude, however. No, I didn't find out very much. There were crowds of relatives and friends there, drinking tea and keeping Mrs. Pendon mercifully busy. I did see Valerie's bedroom."

"I hoped you might," he put in.

"Why? You must have seen it too."

"I'm not a Catholic female, Sister," he said. "I've always believed that if you want to find a killer you need to know a lot about the victim. Nothing happens by chance in my opinion. If we build up the picture of the victim then we can draw in the killer who murdered them. Even in apparently random killings there's always the tie that links the two. What impression of Valerie Pendon did you get?"

"From her bedroom?" Sister Joan frowned down at her clasped hands, marshalling her thoughts. "The room was left over from her childhood," she said at last. "She'd shared it with her older sister until—Sandra, yes, Sandra got married last year. Her father told me they'd started doing the room out, redecorating and so on. They hadn't got very far and the room itself, the stuffed animals, the coloured statuettes—they belonged to a younger girl, one about fourteen perhaps. That might have been Valerie's own choice or it might have been the way her parents saw her, as the innocent child they wanted to hold on to."

"She was a virgin," he reminded her.

"Girls can have boy-friends and be interested in the opposite sex without losing their virginity even nowadays," Sister Joan countered. "And we're talking about a Catholic girl from a family of practising Catholics. Emotionally immature possibly. Not an overt rebel. These are simply my personal impressions, Detective Sergeant Mill, and they might be completely wrong. She obviously went out to meet a man, clad in a wedding dress which suggests that she at least meant to go through a form of marriage with him. Perhaps he was someone of whom she knew her parents would disapprove."

"We might find a diary. Girls still keep diaries sometimes."

"Sometimes." Sister Joan hesitated, then went on, "It doesn't seem likely to me that she'd carry on a love affair, plan to run off, buy a wedding dress, all without arousing the slightest suspicion in her parents' minds and then take the risk of keeping a diary about it—

unless she wanted subconsciously to be stopped. Again I might be wrong."

"I think you're probably right," he said. "Anything else?"

"Nothing I can recall. She was a regular churchgoer, had been on holiday to Lourdes with her family last year, had two good O levels; her father said she hadn't made up her mind yet what to do but he thought she would have been good with children."

"In other words a thoroughly blameless, decent girl who, for some reason we've yet to fathom, decided to turn her life upside down and run off with someone. Yes, that's the picture we're building up ourselves."

"There were no suitcases or holdalls missing," she remembered. "I made a point of asking. She could have taken her nightclothes in a carrier bag."

"She was probably killed within an hour or two of her leaving home."

"How do you know?"

"We don't exactly, but she'd been dead long enough for rigor mortis to wear off. She might have been held somewhere for a day or two, of course, but it's not likely. There hadn't been the smallest sign of a struggle."

"And she wasn't killed in the school?"

"Almost certainly not. She was killed somewhere else and then put in the school after that area had been searched. There was a routine search on the moors after she was reported missing so her body was kept somewhere until it was fairly safe to move it."

"The door was unlocked when I went there."

"A couple of our men searched the school and found the front door unlocked too. They left it as it was. I assume it had been unlocked by whoever was there last."

"Not guilty," Sister Joan said promptly. "We usually did lock up during termtime but after the children had taken their things home there wasn't much left for anyone to bother stealing. This isn't an inner city area with lots of petty crime."

"I agree. Crime, when it comes, tends to be big," he said wryly. "You didn't know the girl?"

"Valerie? No, not at all. She never was a pupil of mine and she would have attended the parish church. Father Malone says she was a quiet, good girl."

"Yes. He told us that too. Well, it looks as if you have no further involvement in the case." His tone was faintly regretful. "You found the body and that means you might be called for the inquest though the coroner might be satisfied with a statement. After that it won't directly concern you. You can go back to ringing bells and ordering soup. Surely soup isn't all you get for lunch?"

"We get bread, water and fruit with it. They don't starve us in the order, you know."

"But they don't encourage you to indulge either, do they? Every mouthful subject to discipline."

"Which frees us to concentrate on the important things, like prayer and meditation, but you might not appreciate how vital those things are."

"I reckon I don't." He made a sudden restless movement among the papers on his desk. "Would you believe I tried praying about my marriage once? It didn't make a blind bit of difference."

"Then I'm sorry, but perhaps it's too soon to tell."

"Perhaps. I'll reserve judgement. And I've two fine boys."

"And I have to drive back to the convent. Sister Teresa makes very tasty soup." She had risen, holding out her hand with a frank smile that precluded any intimate revelations.

"Thank you for your help, Sister. I'll see you to the car." He was equally formal.

"There's no need. Surely you have work to do?"

"Plenty, and if I do find five minutes to relax Sergeant Barratt, our new broom in Bodmin, is here with suggestions as to how a conscientious police officer can fill an idle hour."

"You don't like him?"

"He's keen," he said wryly. "Spends two-thirds of his life here since he arrived. You met his wife."

"After you pressured her into giving me a lift. She seems very pleasant, a bit out of things, but then they've only just moved here, haven't they?"

"A couple of weeks ago. Barratt was in Birmingham but he was transferred here to a rural area because the powers that be reckoned his chances of promotion would be enhanced or words to that effect. Ours not to reason why. I wish he wasn't quite so enthusiastic, makes me feel I ought to be getting ready to queue up for a cheap bus pass or something. Give my regards to Mother Prioress—wait."

On the verge of opening the car door for her he stopped, straightening up, as Sergeant Barratt strode down the road. Though he was in plain clothes he looked as smart as if he were ready for an inspection parade. Sister Joan took in the classic profile, the wide shoulders, the light blue eyes that swept over her as if she wasn't a real person at all.

"Detective Sergeant Mill, something's come up." He spoke respectfully but briskly.

"What? You can talk in front of Sister Joan." The other intercepted a discreet glance.

"I went over to the Romany camp to check on the men getting the names of the children whose fingerprints we need . . ."

"Hardly necessary, Barratt. The two I sent are local men who know the Romanies and can persuade them to bring the kids into the station."

"It was on my way, sir," Barratt said stiffly. "It wasn't my intention to exceed my duty."

"Of course not. Go on."

Sergeant Barratt gave Sister Joan another brief glance and went on.

"One of the men was on his way down to the station when I arrived. The Romanies found a body, it seems. They were all for packing up and leaving the district, not wanting to be involved with police business I daresay. Anyway our men arrived and persuaded them otherwise."

"Never mind that. What about a body?"

"There's a hut near the camp where they stack stuff from time to time. Stuff that probably fell off the back of a lorry. The girl was in there, huddled up in the corner on a pile of straw. Wearing a white dress with a wreath of flowers on her head."

"Identified yet?" Only a slight tightening of the mouth betrayed his superior's reaction.

"One of the gypsies—sorry, sir, Romanies, recognized her. Young girl who works in a bread shop over on the new industrial estate. Name's Tina Davies."

"Is she still there?"

"They had the sense not to try and move her, sir. She was in the same position as the other—strangled by what appears to be the same method."

"You've left someone there, of course."

"Yes, sir. I've got them cordoning off the immediate

area. I drove down and parked round the corner. Easier to turn round and drive back."

"Right. I'll come with you. Sister Joan, can you delay your soup for half an hour?"

She had known the request was coming, had steeled herself against it.

"We want you to look at the girl and tell us if she's in the same position as Valerie Pendon was. If she is—we have a harder case on our hands than we even thought we had. Can you follow us in your car?"

"Yes, of course, Detective Sergeant Mill."

Following him, she felt the inevitability of fate close round her. Like it or not she seemed to be involved.

FOUR

✠ ✠ ✠

The Romany camp had existed since time immemorial high on the moor where gorse and bracken created a barrier between the mundane world and the secret enclosed existence of the travelling people. Sister Joan, who had taught several of the Romany children and was accepted by them, if not with friendship at least with tolerance, parked her car at the edge of the clearing and joined the two detectives who were heading for the shed not many yards off. Outside it a police constable stood guard, while another was engaged in marking off a large square with string and pegs, his progress watched by a small knot of men, women and children. A couple of lurcher dogs barked furiously, then slunk away as someone shied a stone at them.

"This is a bloody awful business, ain't it, Sister?"

A loose-limbed, rangy fellow with a cap perched at the back of his curly black head and his sleeves rolled up to reveal brawny, tattooed arms greeted her.

"Padraic Lee, how are you?" Shaking hands, she was aware of Sergeant Barratt's sidelong glance and lifted eyebrow.

"The better for seeing you again, Sister Joan, and that's a fact," he declared. "Time you was back home I was saying to my Madge only the other day. If you'd been around they wouldn't've dared close the school. My Madge was that upset about it. The girls was learning ever so nicely with you and now I'm supposed to get them on that dratted bus every day and me with a business to run."

"We must all do what the education authorities decide," Sister Joan said. "Do you know anything about what happened here?"

"It was me that found her, wasn't it?" Padraic answered with deep gloom. "Went to pick out a couple of things I'd stored there—there's a market for antiques nowadays—astonishing what you can pick up when you've a mind—anyway I came with Luther—you don't know my second cousin, Luther." He nodded towards a thin man who twisted his cap between his hands and scowled darkly at being brought into the limelight. "He's been away a few months—eighteen months to be exact. Anyway, we opened the door and there she was, poor maid, all doubled up on the straw. Gave me quite a turn."

"So you rang the police?"

"No need to ring them. Two of them was just arriving, wanting fingerprints from the kids who went to your school. They said on account of another murder. And that's it."

"Are you certain you didn't touch the body?" Sergeant Barratt asked. "If you did you might as well admit it at once. Saves us and you a lot of trouble in the future."

"Tell the man, Sister." Padraic grimaced, folding his arms and standing a little way off.

"If Mr. Lee says he didn't touch the body then he didn't," Sister Joan said.

"I didn't realize you knew him well enough to serve

as a character witness," Sergeant Barratt said with delicate scorn.

"Sister, will you have a look yourself and tell me if the girl is in the same position as Valerie Pendon?" Detective Sergeant Mill asked.

"I'm quite ready." She folded her hands at her waist and stepped within the roped-off space, unconsciously jerking her chin slightly to meet the emotional challenge.

The police constable pulled open the door and she stepped to the threshold. Inside a variety of objects, ranging from Padraic's precious fireirons to a rusting bicycle, were stacked against the rough plank walls. There was straw piled against the opposite wall with wisps of it lying everywhere. Old sacks and bundles of newspapers created a fire hazard.

No attempt had been made to conceal the body. Tina Davies was huddled on the straw, her white dress neatly smoothed over her bent knees, the wreath of fading leaves crowning the tousled brown hair.

"She's in the same position," she said, crossing herself, keeping her voice low and calm. "I don't see any difference at all."

"Thank you, Sister." Detective Sergeant Mill had drawn in his breath slightly.

She turned away, glad when the constable pushed the door to again.

"Who identified her?" Detective Sergeant Mill looked round the circle of faces.

"I did," Padraic said instantly. "Works in the little bread shop over on the industrial estate. Nice girl."

"You knew her intimately?" Sergeant Barratt spoke sharply.

"I'd seen her a few times. She served me with bread

now and then when I was doing a bit of shopping for the wife. Told me her name was Tina. There's no law against that."

"What were you doing buying bread over on the industrial estate?"

"I was there doing a bit of gardening, wasn't I? There's some ladies that like a bit of help at rock bottom prices."

"And some girls who might find it exciting to be chatted up," Sergeant Barratt said.

"That's a bloody filthy suggestion." Padraic clenched his fists and took a menacing step.

"If I might have a word with you, Sergeant?" Sister Joan spoke firmly as she might have done to a defiant pupil, moving aside several steps, tacitly forcing the other to follow.

"Sister, I'd take it kindly if you didn't . . ." Sergeant Barratt began.

"Didn't provide you with helpful information? Sergeant, Padraic Lee is devoted to his wife. She has—well, she has bad health and he's brought up their children with very little help. He doesn't—play around."

"If you had as much experience of the criminal mentality as I have . . ."

"You think that being a nun insulates one entirely from reality? Padraic Lee may bend the law occasionally but he's very far from being a criminal. And he most certainly isn't a murderer."

For a moment he faced her coldly, his authority threatened, his judgement called into question. Then he said annoyingly, "If you say so, Sister. Thanks for your help."

"Did anyone see or hear anything unusual last night?" Detective Sergeant Mill was asking.

There were sidelong glances, a shaking of heads.

"No barking from the dogs?"

"They bark all the time. Nobody pays heed," one of the men said.

"And by now any clue will have been trodden underfoot," Sergeant Barratt said. "I must say that I cannot fathom how people can live in this mess."

"You ought to stand for the council," Sister Joan advised sweetly. "Then you could figure out how to get running water and adequate sanitation up here on a very limited budget."

"Barratt, get on to the doctor and the photographer again," Detective Sergeant Mill interposed somewhat hastily. "We'll need some extra men here. I'll go and see the parents. Anybody have an address?"

"They'll know at the bread shop," Padraic offered.

"I'll try there first. Sister Joan, you've been a tremendous help. I may need to call upon you later. Meanwhile give my respects and apologies to Mother Dorothy."

From Detective Sergeant Mill she was more willing to take a dismissal. Padraic stepped forward, escorting her to her car with innate courtesy.

"Who's the other one then?" He jerked his head over his shoulder towards Sergeant Barratt. "Bit of a pig, ain't he?"

"Sergeant Barratt is an extremely efficient officer who's been transferred here from Birmingham," Sister Joan said severely.

"Oh, a foreigner." Padraic nodded as if all was now understood. "This is a rotten business and no mistake. There's been another one done in too, I hear. In the school."

"Put there after she was killed and after the area had been searched," Sister Joan said sombrely. "It is, as you say, a rotten affair. I would advise you to co-operate with the police though, even if you don't like Sergeant Barratt. After all nobody suspects for a moment that anyone from here has had anything to do with murder. The girl wouldn't have been left on the premises so to speak."

"And murder's not in our line except in temper," Padraic said self-righteously. "Now a bit of poaching ..."

"Don't tell me anything about any poaching," Sister Joan warned. "How is your wife?"

"Middling fair." His swarthy face had lengthened slightly. "She has a bad do now and then. We've all got our troubles though, and she's a good wife. I wouldn't swap her for the world."

Madge Lee, struggling halfheartedly against alcoholism, had a better husband than she merited. Sister Joan patted his arm and got back into the car, lifting her hand in salute as she drove away.

Soon another family would hear about the death of a loved one, be inundated by the sympathy of neighbours, the curiosity of passers-by.

"You're very late, Sister." Mother Dorothy, meeting her in the hall, frowned ominously.

"I'm very sorry, Mother. I was needed to help with the police enquiries." Swiftly she explained what had happened and saw distaste and distress on her Superior's face.

"This is a terrible business, Sister." Her hand rose to bless herself while her mind coped with the new tragedy. "Of course, if you can assist further it is your duty as a citizen to do so. You may take my permission as read—provided that you don't neglect your duties in the community. Fortunately Sister Teresa is proving most competent. You had better go and have your lunch and get on with your work."

Since her return she hadn't eaten once with her sisters in the refectory. She went through to the kitchen, accepted the bowl of warmed over soup, slice of bread and ripe pear that had comprised lunch.

The rest of the day passed without incident. Floors were swept, brasses polished and dishes washed. At five the sisters retired to their cells for private study and the writing up of their spiritual diaries. The two postulants, escorted by Sister Hilaria, came to the parlour for instruction from Mother Prioress. Only the rustling of pages and the scribbling of pens broke the silence.

What, thought Sister Joan, have I learned from my recent retreat? What have I learned in six years of convent life? Certainly not to be a living rule. If all the written rules were lost no novice would be able to discern them from the way I carry on.

Her own shortcomings seemed to her magnified like a fly under the microscope. In the Order of the Daughters of Compassion an extra rule, that of compassion itself, was added to the usual three of poverty, chastity and obedience—all spelt with capital letters, she remembered, making hasty alterations in her notebook—as if the rules themselves were sanctified, intrinsically holy.

Poverty wasn't so difficult, she thought wryly, when one lived in a large house in the countryside, assured of bed and board for the rest of one's life. The days when she'd dreamed of roast turkey and Eggs Benedict and strawberries thick with cream and soaked in wine! Chastity and celibacy—she reminded herself that the two were not mutually dependent—were disciplines only slightly shaken by a whisper of longing, a half-remembered dream. Obedience seemed to be the rock against which she constantly stubbed her spiritual toes. Not out-and-out rebellion, but the impulsive action that sent her off on some quest of her own, the stretching of an hour's freedom into two. The little foxes that ate up her grapes before they were ripe. And Mother Dorothy, instead of imposing more discipline, had virtually given her *carte blanche* to come and go more or less as she felt necessary. Which meant self-discipline. She made a note and underlined it, heard the chapel bell ringing and rose, going to benediction with a pleasant feeling of resolution.

Father Stephens was officiating though it wasn't his turn. Probably Father Malone was still with the Pendons. She bowed her head, the curate's mellifluous phrases floating above her, and prayed for the bustling woman with the swollen eyes and the bewildered father who had stood, automatically stroking a stuffed toy, and spoken of his good, quiet daughter.

Father Stephens wafted himself away, and the community settled into silent meditation. Outside night waited on the threshold of a magnificent twilight.

Someone was tugging gently at her sleeve. She came back to earth with a start and saw Sister Teresa giving her a look of apologetic questioning.

O dear Lord, the lay sisters leave early to prepare supper, was her first flustered thought. While she had been indulging in prayer her companions were risking a late supper. Rising, avoiding Mother Dorothy's eye, she left the chapel.

"I do apologize for interrupting you, Sister Joan," Sister Teresa said as they traversed the hall together.

"You did right, Sister. I had completely forgotten the duties of a lay sister. I really must get my head together."

"But it must have been most painful to have to go to the scene of a crime," the other said. "The world is a cruel place, Sister."

"Lit by flashes of beauty and kindness. Shall we get on with supper and then my conscience will be eased?"

"Yes, Sister."

Being a novice in the third year of one's training was difficult, Sister Joan reflected with sympathy. One had left the cocoon of the postulancy and was in but not yet entirely of the community, distinguished by the wearing of one's blue habit instead of the grey of the fully professed, knowing that at the end of the year came the two years of silence and virtual solitude as laid down by the founder.

"I am most grateful for your help, Sister," she said warmly. "I was worried as to how I was going to manage alone. My cooking is awful, and as you're finding out my mind flies off too frequently at a tangent. We must try not to dwell on unpleasant events in the secular world."

In her own ears she sounded impossibly pompous but Sister Teresa nodded and smiled. A nice, competent, dedicated girl, she reckoned. In her early twenties and obviously destined to be an asset to the order. By what strange quirk of fate had this young woman landed in a convent and another, of about the same age, ended as a body huddled in a shed?

The reading chosen for that evening as they ate their meal was the life of St. Maria Goretti, read in a softly hesitating voice by little Sister Martha. No doubt the history of that raped and violated child who had forgiven her murderer as she lay dying had been suggested to Mother Dorothy's mind by recent events. Though

Valerie Pendon had not been violated she recalled, and felt thankful that she had been spared the final horror.

Recreation immediately followed supper, a recreation in which the lay sisters generally didn't join. As Sister Joan hesitated, however, Mother Dorothy paused to speak to her.

"When the dishes are done, Sister, you and Sister Teresa will join us for the hour of recreation. Perhaps you will bring the paintings you did while you were on retreat. We will make our choice of one to hang up and sell the rest at the Christmas bazaar."

Recreation wasn't always the most exciting hour in the day. Sisters were required to bring some useful work with them and expected to sit in a semi-circle, choosing subjects of conversation that would be of general interest. She washed the dishes, slipped out to check on Lilith who greeted her with a reproachful look and went on chewing hay, and made her way upstairs again.

The recreation room opened off the refectory on the first floor. Once the two huge rooms had been a ballroom where the Tarquin family had entertained. Even with the mirrors gone and the gilt cornices tarnished the apartments had an air of vanished grandeur. Apart from the semi-circle of chairs there was a long table on which wool and sewing baskets were laid out ready for use, and the huge fireplace which was innocent of fire since heating was permitted only in the kitchen and the infirmary.

"Ah, you have brought your pictures, Sister." Sister Perpetua looked expectant.

"Only four smallish ones," Sister Joan said. "I also painted two views of the monastery chapel for the monks who take care of the retreat. These are of the loch, with one of the retreat itself."

Laying them on the table, her recent stay in Scotland came vividly to mind—the steep climb up to the cave where once monks had kept watch for Viking long-boats, the community of brothers living their retired lives on the spit of land that jutted out into the loch— that had been a time taken out of time, weeks that were unlikely ever to come again.

"We shall hang the one of the retreat," Mother Dorothy said. "It's many years since I was there and I had quite forgotten how steep the ascent to it is. When the council of prioresses is held we must discuss the matter."

"You are very talented, Sister," Sister David said wistfully.

"But I can't translate Greek into Latin and back again."

"We all have talents that can be put to God's use, Sister," Mother Dorothy said, picking up the remaining three pictures. "These should fetch a very good price at the bazaar."

"Shouldn't they be signed?" Sister Gabrielle who was attending recreation piped up unexpectedly.

"Sister Joan has no wish to bring herself to public notice," Mother Dorothy said.

"Hasn't she?" Sister Gabrielle's face expressed inno-cent astonishment. "My, but the retreat has changed her a lot then!"

There was a ripple of laughter as the sisters took up their work and settled down.

"I think it's wonderful the way Sister Joan helps the police and carries out her duties," Sister Katharine said loyally. "I'm sure I would be terrified if I had to answer questions about a murder."

"It really wasn't like that at all," Sister Joan began. "I found the poor girl so naturally I had to give an account of it. And Sister David and I both went to have our fingerprints taken."

"This is hardly a fitting subject for recreation," Mother Dorothy said, drawing in her mouth severely.

There was an immediate outbreak of self-conscious chatter from several of the company. In the midst of it Sister Teresa's voice could be heard, brightly declaring, "Painting must be so satisfying to the soul but I think cooking can be too. My best friend in school, Tina, used to say that she was convinced a good meal was as important as a poem."

"Tina?" For the life of her Sister Joan couldn't have held her tongue.

"Tina Davies. She and I were in the same class—oh, I beg pardon." Sister Teresa had blushed scarlet. "I completely forgot one must not talk about one's previous life."

If she learned now that her school-friend was a second victim she would never say anything worth hearing. Sister Joan cast Mother Dorothy an imploring glance.

"Speaking of friends can never be wrong," Mother Dorothy said in a thoughtful fashion. "Because we have entered the religious life it separates them from us in body but surely not in spirit. We still wish them well, pray for them, remember them. Your friend, Tina, became a cook?"

"Oh no, Mother." Sister Teresa looked relieved. "She took a job in a breadmaker's though, a really old-fashioned type of shop where they bake their own dough and it smells heavenly. Of course she may have left by now. I haven't seen her since I entered."

"She seems like a nice friend," Sister Joan said with some difficulty.

"She's a nice person," Sister Teresa said. "We took our first Holy Communion together."

"She's a Catholic?"

"She'd hardly be a Muslim if they took their first Holy Communion together," Sister Gabrielle said dryly.

"I had a Muslim friend once," Sister Perpetua said surprisingly. "She had very strict fasting laws and her parents married her off to a cousin she'd never seen."

Impossible to keep custody of the eyes one moment longer. Sister Joan raised her own dark blue orbs and sent Mother Dorothy anther imploring look.

"Sister Joan, bring the three paintings for the bazaar down to the parlour, will you?" Mother Dorothy had risen, her tone casual. "The rest of you will excuse us, I'm sure. I hoping that Sister Joan will prepare a little talk for us on the spiritual benefits she derived from the retreat."

Sister Joan followed her superior, hearing her own footsteps on the uncarpeted stairs as the slow tolling of a bell.

"Close the door, Sister, and put the pictures on the table."

As they entered the parlour she seated herself at her desk and motioned the other to a stool.

"Father Malone was called away?" she ventured.

"So Father Stephens told me though he didn't inform me of the reason. He was obviously called out to comfort the family of this second victim. Two good Catholic girls most brutally killed in the same district. You don't think there is some religious fanatic abroad?"

"It could just be a coincidence, Mother. Not that the man isn't a madman, whatever religion the girls had."

"I would not have blurted out the news of Sister Teresa's friend's death," Mother Dorothy said with a hint of reproach.

"No, of course not, Mother. It was only that—well, as soon as anyone learns that someone has died then they are unwilling to speak frankly about them. The dead are always perfect. I wanted Sister Teresa to be frank."

"She spoke of her school-friend as a nice girl who enjoyed cooking."

"And still works in an old-fashioned bread shop," Sister Joan said. "Valerie Pendon was a nice girl too. An innocent girl, young for her age, with no boyfriends, you know? Two nice, shy, quiet, rather dull girls."

"We don't know they were dull," Mother Dorothy said.

"No, of course not, Mother."

"And it isn't for you or me to speculate on their personalities. Sister Joan, I have given you permission to help the police with their enquiries if they deem it necessary. You do understand that does not give you permission to rush in and offer your services."

"No, of course not, Mother."

"But you want to help. Your heart has a habit of overriding your head, I fear."

Sister Joan bit her lip.

"You think I'm being unjust?" The eyes behind the spectacles were piercing. "I give you full credit for your intentions, Sister. The road to hell is said to be paved with them. These two deaths are not directly connected with our order. We will condole with the families; we will send flowers and pray for the souls of the victims and for the souls of their murderers or murderer, but unless we are asked specifically for help we will not rush in and play amateur detective. That isn't why we entered the religious life, is it?"

"No, Mother Prioress."

"On the other hand, if Detective Sergeant Mill seeks your active co-operation then you must give it in full measure. There is one other matter." She hesitated, frowning.

"Yes, Mother?" What, Sister Joan wondered, was coming now?

"In spite of my initial doubts as to the wisdom of permitting you to place yourself in an occasion of sin, I am disposed to trust your good sense."

"Occasion of sin?" Sister Joan stared at her in bewilderment.

"Detective Sergeant Mill is an attractive man whose marriage, I am given to understand, is not ideal. Your being thrown together could present problems."

"Not as far as I'm concerned," Sister Joan said firmly. "I promise you, Mother, that nothing has or could pass between us that you couldn't witness yourself."

"And no thought that I could not read has strayed into your mind?"

"I can't speak for Detective Sergeant Mill," Sister Joan said with a glint of humour, "but for myself—Mother Dorothy, I already have a Bridegroom and I'm not about to settle for second best."

"You've spoken with good sense." Mother Dorothy had risen, looking down at the veiled head. "Naturally I trust your common sense, Sister. As you say, why should any of us be tempted to settle for second best?

Even before I entered the religious life it never occurred to me for one moment that I might marry—but then I was never pretty, God be praised. Now I must see Sister Teresa and inform her of the death of her old friend. She will, I feel sure, take it calmly. Then there will be chapel, a chance to clear our minds of the unpleasant events taking place beyond our enclosure. We must pray for guidance, Sister."

"Yes, Mother Dorothy." Sister Joan genuflected briefly and rose. Both small women, they stood for an instant eye to eye.

"I hope you can be of help in this matter," Mother Dorothy said unexpectedly. "The violent pointless death of a young creature is an affront to God."

"I'll do my best—if I'm asked."

"Don't be afraid of giving Sister Teresa a few extra duties if you have other things to do. She will grieve less if she has plenty of hard manual work. When we find a permanent lay sister I am thinking of making you assistant mistress of novices."

"What?" Sister Joan forgot every precept of conventual courtesy as she spoke.

"You might provide a little common sense to balance Sister Hilaria's extreme spirituality. She is a true mystic, Sister, and a pure soul, but every day I sense her moving a little further away from the mundane world. I learned from one of the postulants that Sister Hilaria is experiencing visions. She has said very little about them and it's not for me to probe into her soul until she tells me of her own volition, but some extra help would be appreciated once the question of lay duties is totally settled. Send Sister Teresa to me now, will you? And don't encourage talk of any kind about recent events."

"Of course not, Mother Dorothy—and thank you."

Going out, Sister Joan paused, to brace herself for the inevitable questions that would accompany Sister Teresa's summons, to wonder how much Mother Dorothy had been trying, in her own, oblique way, to warn her against.

FIVE

✠ ✠ ✠

Morning woke her before her alarm clock went off. It was, she thought, a good start to the day. She washed herself in the tiny washroom next to the lay cells, put on habit and veil rapidly with the ease of long practice, went into the chapel to light candles and check on the flowers there. It was odd how a good night's sleep changed one's perspective. It was unlikely, she decided, that her help would be needed again by the police. She would be able to concentrate on her duties.

"Whatever task is given you," Mother Agnes had said, "you must do to the best of your ability. If you are told to slop out the pails do it as perfectly as if Our Lord Himself were coming round to inspect them."

Going up the stairs, preparing to raise her voice in the morning greeting, she wondered if the words spoken by one's novice mistress remained throughout the rest of one's life. Mother Agnes, with her El Greco face and beautiful hands, had been first her novice mistress and then her prioress. There were still times when Sister Joan missed her counsel. On the other hand Mother Dorothy was revealing unsuspected depths.

Father Malone came to offer the morning mass and to join the Sisters afterwards for a cup of coffee as they ate their breakfast in the refectory. Father Stephens usually had pressing duties elsewhere. Father Malone enjoyed a mild and unmalicious gossip. This morning he stood, talking quietly to Sister Teresa, whose drawn young face bore witness to the shock her friend's death had afforded.

Somehow or other word of the second murder had spread on the convent grapevine. Nobody said anything but there were glances of sympathy, laced with curiosity, sent towards Sister Teresa.

"Good morning, Sister Joan." Father Malone had drifted towards her, his kind, elderly face heavy with concern.

"Good morning, Father."

"This is a tragic affair, Sister." He had lowered his voice slightly. "Detective Sergeant Mill tells me that you saw the poor child yesterday and were able to help them in their work."

"Not very much, I'm afraid."

"I was hoping you might be able to help me this morning if Mother Prioress can spare you. I have to see the Davies family again and I'm required at the hospital. Father Stephens would go in my stead to both places but he has other duties. I feel very strongly that the Davieses need constant spiritual support at this time, but I was forced to cancel my visit to the hospital last week too and the children get disappointed."

"You want me to go down and see the Davieses?"

"Only for an hour if it's possible. I will make my hospital visit short. I would not have asked but Mother Prioress intimated that you might be able to undertake the task."

"As soon as I've seen to the breakfast dishes and fed Lilith I'll be at your service, Father. If you give me the address I can follow you in my car. Mother Prioress has already given me leave."

"Splendid." Father Malone looked marginally more cheerful. "They live over on the industrial estate— Princess Royal Road, number twenty-five. Very nice people."

"They are parishioners of yours, of course?"

"Yes indeed. I knew Tina very well. A good, quiet girl, never caused her parents a moment's trouble. It's very good of you to go, Sister."

"I will be as quick as I can be," she promised.

Even though she hurried it was past nine o'clock before she had finished clearing away and washing up, helped by a silent and sorrowful Sister Teresa. It was a relief to go out to the stable and check on Lilith who looked as if she expected some exercise.

"Later on, old girl, if I can possibly find time." Sister Joan gave her a sugar lump by way of compensation and went back indoors to leave instructions about lunch.

"Soup again, Sister?" Sister Teresa looked faintly disconcerted.

"Soup and a tomato sandwich, please," said Sister Joan, with a feeling of recklessness. "The sun may be shining but it's a cold day. Oh, and skin the tomatoes for Sister Gabrielle's sandwich. She believes that tomato skins wrap themselves around one's appendix or something."

Sister Teresa, despite her sombre mood, giggled. Sister Joan went out briskly and met Sister Martha coming in from the garden.

"There are some more dahlias, Sister. Mother Dorothy said you were going to offer our condolences to another family. It doesn't seem possible, does it?" She was clearly referring to the murders and not to Sister Joan's suitability as a visitor of mercy.

"Thank you, Sister. That was most thoughtful of you."

The dahlias were streaked with bronze and gold, the petals autumn large. They had a faintly exotic quality.

She put them on the passenger seat of the car, together with the attached card in Mother's neat convent hand and drove away. From the front door she thought she caught a glimpse of Sister Perpetua gazing wistfully after her. Until now Sister Perpetua had frequently driven the car when it was necessary to go beyond the confines of the enclosure. She would find it hard to adapt to staying within bounds.

The new industrial estate wasn't a place where she had ever had occasion to go before. It lay at the end of a track that curved away from the convent, past Farrer's Field with its attendant farmhouse, past the path that wound to the Romany encampment, and looked raw and unused.

What unimaginative, underfunded planner had set the half-dozen streets in parallel lines, each semi-detached dwelling roofed identically in virulent scarlet, each gate bearing an identical wrought-iron nameplate. Attempts had been made to give some individuality by the owners themselves, with rockeries instead of lawns, front doors painted in contrasting tones, a white statue of a nymph brooding sadly over a plastic-lined pool. The general effect was depressing. Sister Joan's artist's eye was offended by dead symmetry and colours that hit the senses instead of wooing them into surrender.

At number twenty-five a crowd of people surged round the gate, held back by a stolid policeman. Stolid was the mask he wore, she guessed, parking her car and edging through the eager, shocked, sensation-hungry faces; some of them looked so familiar that she had the indecent impression they had set off in a bunch from the Pendon gate and dashed here for some glimpse of the latest murder.

"Good morning, Sister." The stolid mask remained in place even as he muttered, shifting his eyes towards the crowd, "Wish they issued us with the odd burst of tear gas."

The house had drawn blinds that necessitated the switching on of the lights. She rang the bell, was conscious of being scrutinized through a spy hole and let in, the door being closed behind her before she had fully squeezed through. She made a grab at her veil and found herself being shaken vigorously by the hand.

"You'll be Sister Joan. Father Malone has told us that you might be coming. God bless you for doing so, Sister. Not that we see anything of the Compassion nuns but we're always aware they're up on the moors, watching over us in a manner of speaking. You'll have a cup of tea, Sister? My sister-in-law's seeing to all that."

Valerie Pendon's mother had found relief in serving food like some robotic waitress who doesn't know when to stop; Tina Davies's mother found relief in talking. Small and brown, twittering like the sparrow her physical appearance brought to mind, she talked about the terrible shock, the kindness of her friends, the awful questions the police had asked, the unnerving curiosity of the sightseers.

"One might almost think that they believed themselves at the cinema, Sister, the way they stand gawping and there's nothing to see. They took Tina to the mortuary. Better that way my husband said. Bill usually knows best."

"Have you had any further news?" Sister Joan broke into the deluge of words.

"About Tina? She wasn't—wasn't interfered with, if you know what I mean, Sister. That's a great comfort to us as you can imagine, since Tina was a good girl. We brought her up to respect her body, not to give herself outside marriage."

"But she had boy-friends?"

"Not for the last couple of years. There were one or two before that, nothing serious. She says—used to say she liked staying home and watching the telly, not ramshackling round Bodmin."

"One of my companions in the convent knew your daughter very well. Sister Teresa? I believe that was her original name—sometimes the name is changed if the Sister wishes to adopt a particular saint."

"Of course I remember Teresa," Mrs. Davies said fiercely, pecking at the words. "I haven't seen her since she went into the convent. My Tina was quite cut up about it at the time. The two of them used to go around together and when Teresa's family moved north she lived here for a few months while she was waiting to start as a novice. She'll be upset to hear, I daresay?"

"Most upset. She would have come to see you herself but she is not yet fully professed and so cannot leave the enclosure. Oh, I brought flowers from the convent."

She handed over the dahlias just as a man taller and broader than herself but with the same facial characteristics came in.

"Look, Bill, what the Sisters have sent for Tina. Isn't it kind of them?" Her tones were flurried and anxious.

"Very kind of you indeed, I'm sure." Bill Davies observed Sister Joan with less than enthusiasm.

"Bill doesn't hold with too much religion," his wife

twittered. "Mind you, he never misses midnight mass at Christmas and the Sacraments at Easter. His side of the family was always secular minded—we were cousins before we got wed. But he converted to Rome. You converted to Rome, didn't you, Bill? But a convert isn't the same as a cradle Catholic."

In Sister Joan's experience converts were usually the keenest but she murmured something indeterminate and met Bill Davies's sardonic gaze.

"If you've a minute, Sister," he said surprisingly, "I'd like a word. Nancy, your sister's looking for you. She wants to know what to do about the ham."

Death and ham went together, Sister Joan thought, following him into a back room the door of which he shut firmly. Ham teas after the funeral had assumed the force of tradition.

"Mr. Davies?" She folded her hands, tilting her head to look at him.

"The police told us that a nun found the body of that other girl and went with them to look at Tina," he said.

"That was me. I'm Sister Joan."

"From the convent on the moors?"

It sounded like the title of a schoolgirls' adventure story. Cheating at hockey and jolly japes in the dorm—did kids still read books like that?

"The Order of the Daughters of Compassion, yes."

"Bit of a mouthful." He gave a humourless, down-twisting smile. "Sisters of Mercy, Sisters of Charity, Benedictines—much of a muchness."

"There are subtle differences, Mr. Davies, but what was it you wanted to say to me?"

"That detective—Mill? He told me that one of the Sisters had been helping them. Spoke of you highly."

"That was very kind of him." She felt a small glow

of innocent pleasure. "I'm afraid there's very little I can do save in the most amateur capacity."

"I've not much patience with religion. The wife spoke the truth there," he said. "Very devout Nancy is. Tina was too, and I never interfered, but going to church is more for women, don't you think?"

Sister Joan, who didn't concur, said nothing but sat down on the chair he indicated.

The room was pleasant despite the long curtains shutting out the daylight beyond the French windows. Pink shades diffused the glare of electric lights shed over imitation pine furniture amid which she noticed a large wall cupboard and a divan bed masquerading as a couch.

"Tina's room," he said, noting her glance round. "She got herself a local job and talked about sharing a flat in town somewhere, but Nancy wasn't too keen on that. Tina was twenty-two and wanted a bit of independence so we came to a compromise. We gave her this room for her own and I had French windows put in so that she could come and go as she pleased. Not that she went out often. But she did have a boy-friend."

"Recently?"

"Seems like it." He looked sad and angry. "I don't know why she never said anything. Nancy and me— we'd've loved to see her settled with a nice husband. The police asked me straight off if I knew of anyone she was serious about, and I said no. That was the truth as far as I knew it, but this morning while Father Malone was chuntering on with Nancy I came in here, just to be quiet and at peace for a little while. I was fiddling about, picking up things, dropping them again, not able to settle. Her writing case was by the bed. I picked it up to put it out of the way and then it came to me that there might be something inside, anything to give us a bit of a clue."

"You found something?"

"In her diary." He opened a drawer and took out a plastic-covered pink book, not small but slightly too big to fit easily into an average-sized handbag. "She had it last Christmas from her auntie. She didn't keep it regular—I mean there wasn't very much to write, but she filled in birthdays and such. And this here right at the end where there are spare pages. I wish you'd read it, Sister, and tell me what I ought to do."

She felt a momentary reluctance to read what had not been intended for other eyes before she bent her head over the neat, round handwriting.

Is this love? Like hunger eating you up, clean to the backbone? Like a fire burning? Is it? I wish I could ask someone but I can't break my promise. I have to wait until it's too late to pull me back.

"Is that all?" She looked across to where he had seated himself.

"I figured it was enough," he said heavily. "It's obvious there was someone we didn't know about. The doctor found out she was still—untouched. Detective Sergeant Mill was good enough to come round and tell us last evening as soon as he got the results. She hadn't gone against her teachings, Sister, but she went off with someone."

"You didn't report her missing?"

"We never knew she was. Night before last we all stayed in. Played Scrabble and watched a quiz show on the telly. Tina said she felt a bit tired and went to bed. Here." He nodded towards the sofa divan. "Nancy went up soon after I locked up the front door and the back door and went to bed. There was no light showing under Tina's door so I figured not to disturb her. She's—she was always first up in the morning on account of getting early to the bread shop so she can start and put the fresh loaves and buns in the window. Five-thirty that'd be, when she left the house. She knocks—knocked off at one o'clock."

"You didn't hear her use the bathroom?"

"We've a little cloakroom next to the kitchen. She uses that in the mornings and has her bath upstairs later on. And she lets herself out through the French windows with her own key. So we never check up. She doesn't bother with any breakfast, has a coffee and some toast at the back of the shop. I got up and went to work—I've a building business—self-employed but not doing so well what with the recession and all. Nancy gets up later. I generally take her a cuppa before I leave."

"And nobody from the bread shop rang to ask where Tina was?"

He shook his head. "She'd had a bit of a cold so I reckon they thought she'd taken the morning off. There's another kid there who helps out so they wouldn't have been stuck. Near lunchtime—no, just after, the police came to ask me to go and take a look for identification purposes. Then I came home and told Nancy." His face twisted suddenly with appalling grief. "She hadn't even been into Tina's room. Usually she went in and had a bit of a tidy round but Tina said she liked looking after things herself so Nancy gave up the habit."

"The diary entry? You've not shown it to your wife?"

He shook his head again. "I only just found it this morning. The police came yesterday to look round.

They wanted to search Tina's room but Nancy took on about that, said she wasn't having our daughter's belongings pawed over and they'd have to get a warrant. I told the detective, quiet like, that she'd come round and let them look at whatever they wanted once she was over the first shock, and the detective said not to worry and he'd be by later on sometime. Now I'm thinking he ought to know about the diary but every time I move two yards Nancy's wanting to know what I'm doing."

"I could call in at the station on my way back to the convent and give the diary to the Sergeant," she suggested.

"Seems a bit steep to ask you after what I've been saying about religion." For the first time he looked uncomfortable.

"Write me a brief note of authorization and I'll take it for you."

"Very good of you, Sister. Give me a minute."

He went out, closing the door softly behind him with an ostentatious show of trust.

Sister Joan remained where she was, the plastic cover of the diary smooth and cool between her hands. Around her the room had the air of having been abandoned for a long time. It was difficult to realize that a young woman had slept here until two days before. Anyone coming in for the first time, not knowing the circumstances, might have identified it as a guest room used by the occasional visitor. Everything was neat, impersonal, with the cover laid smoothly over the divan and cushions plumped up. There was a crucifix on the wall, a row of paperbacks—romances, a couple of poetry books that looked left over from school, some pamphlets from the parish church, a couple of mild thrillers. On the shelf above was a picture of Mother Teresa in a frame and some prettily shaped bottles of unopened perfume.

"I've written a note giving you permission to take the diary." Bill Davies was back, handing her a small sheet of paper.

"I'll see it gets into the right hands," she promised. "I know you don't reckon much to the church but I hope you understand that we all are anxious to do anything we can in this very sad situation."

"Can the church catch the swine that lured our daughter away and killed her?" he asked harshly. "In the middle of the night, and her only in her shortie pyjamas and robe and slippers."

"You've checked her clothes?"

"Nancy did, when she could bring herself to go into the wardrobe. She looked in on us—Tina, I mean—just before she went to bed. Funny, but she came over and she kissed us both goodnight; we're not much of a family for hugging and kissing, so it stuck in my mind. She had on her nightclothes. We were clearing away the board for the Scrabble. Kissed us both and then went into her room and closed the door. Until I found that diary I figured she might have had a premonition. Now I reckon she was getting ready to do a bunk with her boy-friend, whoever he is."

"You're possibly right," Sister Joan said cautiously. "The police will find out the truth of it. Now I'd better go and have another word with your wife. I promised Father Malone I'd stay until he got back from the hospital."

As they left the room she was relieved to hear the priest's voice in the hall.

"A cup of tea would be very welcome, Mrs. Davies.

And you look as if you could be using one yourself. Sister Joan, it was good of you to come and stand in for me. The problem these days is that there never seems to be sufficient time to get everything done. If only there were more vocations . . ." He sighed and Sister Joan shot him a sympathetic look. The lack of suitable men and women entering the religious life was fairly acute. It was a matter that greatly exercised Mother Dorothy's thoughts.

"Goodbye, Father." She went past him as he opened the door and stood for a moment, frowning at the crowd which still infested the space beyond the gate.

"Ghouls, aren't they?" the police constable on duty said.

"Insensitive," Sister Joan said. "I suppose that death fascinates us because we're still alive."

She had parked the car a little way down the road. The diary fitted nearly in the compartment under the dashboard. She sat for a moment, her mind moving over the direction she could take. She could take the way she had come past the convent and down into town or the ring road that avoided the moors and dipped into the other end of the town. It wasn't a road she had ever driven but it had the charm of novelty.

The housing estate failed to improve on further acquaintance. Neatly and logically planned with gardens in which the owners clearly took pride it yet lacked character. It was too new, too raw, an intrusion into the ancient landscape.

"Sister Joan, good morning."

She had slowed to a crawl at the corner where a sign pointed her towards the ring road. The woman who had hailed her had a laden shopping basket and a scarf tied over head.

"Mrs. Barratt, do forgive me. I was dreaming." She leaned to wind down the passenger-seat window. "May I return the favour you did me and offer you a lift?"

"That's very good of you, Sister. It really isn't far, but groceries get heavier the longer you carry them," Daisy Barratt said, wrenching the door open and heaving herself and her bags inside. "My Mini went on the blink this morning and I wouldn't have bothered shopping but we did need a few things and there's quite a nice little supermarket in the shopping precinct here— the people are ever so helpful and they don't mind chatting."

Sister Joan felt a shaft of sympathy. The woman was a newcomer and lonely. Going to the local shops probably constituted her main social activity of the day.

"Have you met any nice neighbours yet?" she asked, driving on.

"Oh, I'm sure they're all very nice," Daisy said, flushing slightly. "It is rather difficult to get to know people though and being the wife of a police officer— people shy off a little. Even quite lawabiding people sometimes."

"Nuns have the same problem," Sister Joan said wryly.

"In the world but not of it."

"Sometimes very much in the world," Sister Joan said. "I just called on the Davies family."

"There was an item about it in the newspaper." Daisy nodded. "Awful business. I thought that living in the country would be peaceful, safer."

"It depends on the people," Sister Joan said, slowing as the other indicated her destination. "On the whole we're fairly lawabiding round here, give or take the odd poacher, but murder is different from the usual crime, isn't it?"

"Different?"

"More—personal. There has to be such hatred involved. I mean you could steal from someone without even knowing them, but killing them—it's different, much more personal. Sorry, I'm not explaining myself very well and I'm holding you up."

"I was hoping you would come in for a coffee," Daisy said with awkward shyness.

"I really ought to . . ." Sister Joan glanced at the mute, disappointed face and changed her reply. "Perhaps for a very quick cup of coffee then. Thank you."

I am accepting, she informed herself, because I am sorry for this shy, quiet woman who's finding it hard to settle in.

At the back of her mind her voice ran on, affectionately mocking.

Come on, Sister. You want to have a look at the house where that insufferable sergeant lives. Be honest.

There were lumps of stone and rock in the front garden. Daisy, shooting them a helpless look, said, as she fitted her key into the lock, "Mark intends to make a rockery but he's so very busy and it's not worth planting out until spring. Do excuse the mess. We still have things in packing cases."

The packing cases were not in evidence as they stepped into the square hall with the parquet floor and the open-tread stairs rising to an upper landing.

"Do come into the breakfast-room, Sister. I only have to set out another cup and boil the kettle. I'm afraid it's instant coffee."

"I never drink anything else," Sister Joan said, following her past a closed door into a back room from which an alcove gave on to a small, gleaming kitchen.

"Do sit down, Sister. I'll bring in the tray."

Dragged down by her laden shopping bags Daisy vanished round the corner of the wall. Sister Joan sat down on one of the upright chairs placed around the uncompromisingly square dining-table. There was a flock striped wallpaper on the walls and curtains echoing the faint green spot at the windows. Beyond the glass was a neatly swept yard and a border of bare rose bushes. Against one wall a dresser held some oddly shaped pieces of blue and rose glass and a selection of patterned plates.

There was a smallish television set with a low chair at an angle to it. One chair, she noted, and wondered what that denoted. Did Sergeant Barratt leave his wife alone to watch the world of moving, two-dimensional images while he sat elsewhere, writing up his notes, thinking about the promised promotion? At each side of the windows were tall, narrow bookshelves. She got up and went over to them, running her eye over the titles. Collections of short stories culled from defunct literary magazines, accounts of true-life crimes, the memoirs of a judge whose reputation for severity had rivalled Judge Jeffreys, Agatha Christie, Chandler, Sayers.

"Mark reads a lot," Daisy said, coming in with a tray on which two cups of coffee, a milk jug and sugar bowl, and a plate of ginger snaps were symmetrically arranged.

"You call him by his second name," Sister Joan remarked, recalling the somewhat ironic introduction that had been provided by Detective Sergeant Mill.

"His first name is David, yes. After his father. He prefers Mark. Do you take sugar?"

"No, thank you."

A Mark by any other name would still be irritating? Sister Joan sipped her coffee and shook her head to the proffered ginger snap.

"I ought not to but I do," Daisy said guiltily.

"You're beautifully slim."

"Oh yes, I can eat anything and not put on an ounce," Daisy said. "I meant crumbs."

"Crumbs?" Sister Joan stared at her for a moment. "Oh, I see. Yes, crumbs."

"Not that they bother me too dreadfully but they seem to get everywhere. I swear they hear the vacuum cleaner and roll away into the most inaccessible corner. Mark cannot bear them."

"You have no children yet?"

It was a foolish question since the answer was self-evident. It was a question she had no business to be asking since it impinged upon others' privacy.

"No, we haven't any children." Daisy put the half-eaten ginger snap neatly on the edge of her saucer and flashed a nervous little smile. "You mustn't think we're bad Catholics. We'd both adore to have babies, but Mark is—not able to fully complete the act—if you understand me."

It was entirely her own fault for asking the question, for forgetting that some people unburdened themselves of the most intimate secrets to a nun as if nuns were not ordinary human beings with normal reactions at all but depositories of hurtful secrets, of confidences they would not have entrusted to anyone else.

"That's very—sad for you," she said inadequately. "I believe there is help available these days—psychosexual counselling, that sort of thing."

"We accept it as God's will," Daisy said, looking unhappy. "And Mark is—men have their proper pride."

Which denied the crown of fatherhood might well be sublimated into excessive interest in all the ramifications of one's work or into a mania for tidiness.

"We don't talk about it, especially to other people," Daisy said suddenly. "I know you won't . . . ?"

"No, of course not," Sister Joan said, feeling colour surge up into her neck and face. "This is very good coffee."

"I always use water that isn't quite boiling," Daisy said, turning with some alacrity to a less sensitive subject. "It makes all the difference."

"I only wish I had more leisure in which to enjoy it," Sister Joan said, "but I have another errand before I return to the convent. You know, if you're looking to make friends, then the public library has a very full list of societies. Or if you attend church regularly then there are . . ."

"The Mothers' Union," Daisy said, her smile no more than the lifting of her lips. "I'd feel a bit out of place there. Anyway Mark likes me to be here when he gets home, and the hours of a police officer are dreadfully irregular, especially when there's a murder enquiry."

And you have a husband who's a chauvinistic pig, ran Sister Joan's thoughts.

"I'll try and call in again if I'm over this way," she said, rising.

"That's very kind of you, Sister. Believe me but it's appreciated." She spoke in a slightly distracted manner, her eyes riveted on a few drops of coffee that had escaped the cup and trickled into the saucer.

"I'll see myself out then. Goodbye, Mrs. Barratt."

"Daisy, please. Was that a car?"

"I don't think so."

"Mark did say he might look in for a bite of lunch if he wasn't held up down at the station. I must get on."

She had also risen, picking up the tray, her head bent. She was poised for flight through the archway into the kitchen where she could wash away the coffee stain and dispose of the uneaten half of ginger snap.

"Goodbye then." Sister Joan tore her own fascinated gaze from the tray and went into the hall. She would have relished a peep into the front room but she had already nursed her curiosity long enough and to no positive purpose. Instead she opened the front door, went through and closed it behind her gently.

Outside the autumn sun had reached its height, splashing gold over the new gardens and the treeless road that ran straight to the turning. It would be wrong to say that the housing estate had been transformed but the place shimmered with light and colour. A Van Gogh might have done justice to it in long, sweeping brush-strokes. Jacob would have found the place stimulating to his art.

Odd but it was ages since she had even thought of Jacob. His face, the lithe hardness of his body, his dark stubbornness had once filled her entire world. All emotions were softened by the passing of the years. Today Jacob would probably be comfortably married.

Getting into the car and starting it up, she looked back towards the house. No face or waving hand appeared at door or window. Daisy Barratt would be scrubbing the tray and polishing the coffee cups, probably dusting the chairs and setting them at right angles again. And listening anxiously for the sound of her husband's car. It was better to confine oneself to the convent, Sister Joan decided, driving towards the ring road. The world was less intrusive there, less charged with the sad and secret problems of everybody else.

SIX

✠ ✠ ✠

Detective Sergeant Mill was talking to the desk sergeant when she walked into the station. For an instant, before he straightened up and turned, she had a sensation of *déjà vu*. Somewhere before she had seen that self-same turn of a well-groomed dark head, the set of the shoulders—it had been a dance to which she had dragged an unwilling Jacob. He had submitted to having his unruly hair tamed, to wearing a tie, had teased her gently. for her bourgeois notions. But this wasn't Jacob who was part of her past; this was Detective Sergeant Alan Mill who wasn't part of her life at all.

"Good morning, Sister Joan. Did you want to see me?"

"If you can spare me a few minutes?"

"Any time." He motioned towards the open door of his office.

"I visited the Davies house this morning," she said without preamble, taking a seat. "I took flowers from the convent. Her father gave me a diary he'd found. He didn't want to upset his wife needlessly by telling her about it, so he asked me to bring it to you."

"Mrs. Davies cut up rough when we wanted to search her daughter's room." He closed the door and took the diary from her. "One can understand the way the poor woman felt. Rifling through the belongings of a dead person is like violation. Where did he find this?"

"In her bag, he said. No, her writing case. He said it was on the floor by her bed and he moved it out of the way and then opened it on impulse. He said that he thought it proved she must have had a current boyfriend nobody knew about."

He was turning over the pages, pausing briefly here and there, reaching the end papers, reading the pertinent paragraph aloud.

" 'Is this love? Like hunger eating you up, clean to the backbone? Like a fire burning? Is it? I wish I could ask someone but I can't break my promise. I have to wait until it's too late to pull me back.' " He looked at her questioningly.

"She was a romantic young woman," Sister Joan said.

"And still a virgin. A virgin in a white dress with a wreath of leaves on her head. You know what some of the more sensational papers are saying?"

"We don't read newspapers in the convent. Mother Prioress has *The Times* delivered and reads out those parts she thinks we ought to know."

"You probably don't miss much. They're saying these murders have some link with Satanism."

"Nonsense!"

"You seem very sure of your ground."

"Most so-called Satanists are sad, sick people looking for a cheap and nasty thrill. Genuine Satanists, thank God, are thin on the ground. The essence of their power lies in secrecy. The last thing they'd risk is a police investigation."

"You seem to know a lot about it."

"You can't engage your enemy unless you have some idea of his tactics."

"It seems to be a case of *cherchez l'homme*," the detective said.

"Only one man? I mean, isn't it possible that someone copied the first murder?"

"Details of it weren't published. We can't hold off the media any longer though. What I'm worried about is that this may be a serial killer."

"Not here in Cornwall!"

"You sound like Lady Macbeth—'What? In our house?' Murder can become a habit, you know. Someone commits one and is stimulated by the excitement to commit another one along the same lines. In the end the original reason, no matter how crazy, for killing someone is submerged in the excitement of doing it again and again, outwitting the forces of law and order—like a drug addict who needs stronger and stronger doses."

"That's horrific," she said in a low voice.

"Devilish," he said sombrely. "I want to prevent another murder, Sister. There will be another one. There always is."

"If there's any way I can help—Mother Dorothy has given me permission if it becomes absolutely necessary. Not that I could do very much but sometimes people talk more freely to a nun than to some official figure."

"I've made a table of comparisons between the victims. Both young Catholic women, virgin, respectable, one never having had a boy-friend, the other never having had a serious relationship. Both left their homes during the night, clad apparently in their nightclothes. Both were found with wreaths of leaves on their heads and white dresses trimmed with lace. Both were strangled with a wire of some kind when they were completely unsuspecting. One was left in the school cupboard, the other in a shed on the edge of the Romany camp. My own guess is that they were killed elsewhere very soon after they disappeared and in Valerie Pendon's case kept somewhere until she was taken, almost certainly by car, to the Moor School. The other was taken immediately to the shed. This fine weather hasn't helped much. No telltale mud on a fender, no clear tyre tracks—the world and his wife use the moors as a short cut these days. This diary entry certainly points to a clandestine affair. Someone her parents would have deemed unsuitable? A married man, a non-Catholic?"

"That's hardly an insurmountable barrier these days," she objected. "The non-Catholic partner must receive a short course of instruction in the faith and promise to bring up any children of the marriage as Catholics. They don't have to convert themselves."

"As if it mattered provided they want to make a good marriage," he observed.

She was silent, remembering. There had been a time when she had thought the same way herself, when Jacob had thought the same way. In the end their divided traditions, the feelings they had to admit, had defeated them.

"It matters," she said briefly. "What about shoes?"

"The shoes they were wearing, you mean? White plastic sandals—thousands of pairs of similar shoes were sold during the summer at every shoe shop in the country. All we can say about these particular shoes worn by the victims is that they were brand new, unworn. The dresses were of the same design, cheap silk and lace with no labels. Handstitched, very neatly. Wed-

ding gowns for weddings that never were. Oh, and not
a strange fingerprint anywhere so far."

"What happens now?" she asked.

"We slog round the district, asking people if they noticed anything, if they can account for their whereabouts on the nights in question. You'd be surprised
how many perfectly innocent people can't. And we'll be
talking to the families again."

"Nice, ordinary, respectable, loving parents, deeply
distressed by their loss."

"You would be astonished how many nice, ordinary,
respectable, loving parents do away with their children," he said dryly, "but in these cases we're looking
for only one killer. I assume the girls were known to
each other since they attended the same church?"

"Probably by sight," she agreed, "but they weren't
likely to be close friends since they weren't in the same
age group. Incidentally our novice, Sister Teresa, knew
Tina Davies well, but Sister's been in the convent for
two years and hasn't had any contact with her since she
entered."

"No visits?" He looked surprised.

"No visits at all during the two years one spends in
the postulancy, not even any contact with the professed
members of the community. During the third year the
novice joins us in the main house, but during the final
two years she enters a period of almost total seclusion
and silence save when she's in chapel."

"I'm astonished you come out sane at the other end,"
he said bluntly.

"Oh, getting in touch with one's spiritual self isn't so
bad," she assured him.

"So I could talk to Sister Teresa?"

"If it became absolutely vital, but honestly, I doubt if she'd be able to tell you anything of value."

"So it's back to the man." He frowned, tapping the diary with well-tended fingers. "The kind of man who inspires the emotion shown in these words—a man with a charismatic personality, would you say?"

"For Tina Davies, certainly. Detective Sergeant Mill, one thing puzzles me."

"Only one thing? You're fortunate, Sister."

"One particular thing puzzles me," she amended. "Why now? I mean why does a man suddenly commit two murders within the same week? Something must have triggered him."

"It's a good point, Sister, but I'm not qualified to answer it. For that you'd need a psychiatrist."

"Some traumatic event perhaps?" she hazarded.

"Who knows? First we have to catch him. What happens afterwards isn't my job."

"And I must leave you to get on with it." She rose, holding out her hand.

"I stole an hour back here," he confessed. "There's always the papers to be written up. Sergeant Barratt has energy enough for both of us."

"He'll probably go home for lunch," Sister Joan informed him.

"You've seen him this morning?"

"I gave his wife, Daisy, a lift from the local shops and she asked me in for a coffee. She seems very lonely."

"Being married to a police officer as keen as Barratt must be rather like living alone. Mind you, it's a complaint most police wives have, in common with Members of Parliament, doctors and the like. You wouldn't know about that."

"Indeed I wouldn't." Her eyes were dancing. "My

Bridegroom is always available, always ready to listen. Good morning to you, Detective Sergeant Mill. If you need any more help please let me know."

"Off to make soup, Sister?" He shook hands warmly.

"Soup and a salad sandwich today," she informed him. "I'm quite a little rebel in my way."

She heard him chuckling as she went out.

On the steps a young police constable stopped to greet her. "It's Sister Joan, isn't it? The nun with the pony?"

"How odd to be remembered thus!" It was her turn to chuckle. "You're the officer who kindly rode her back for me. I hope Sister Perpetua gave you a cup of tea."

"Afraid not, Sister. She was in the yard at the back when I walked the pony round and she just took the reins and marched off. Not to worry. It must have been the grand silence or something."

"Not at that hour—and Sister Perpetua dispenses tea like manna during the exile. I'm sure she didn't mean to be discourteous."

"Oh, I wasn't complaining, Sister," he said hastily. "I just wanted to be sure you got her back all right. She's a nice old girl."

"I'm very fond of her," she confessed. "Of course the car is faster but one cannot feel affection for a pile of machinery."

"Oh, I wouldn't say that, Sister. A lot of people fuss over their cars like they were babies. Take Sergeant Barratt now. He drives his own car most of the time and every spare minute he's polishing it and vacuuming it and the Lord knows what else. Proper puffed up about it he seems to be."

"Well, we all have our little ways. Thank you again for bringing Lilith home." Nodding at him, she went on into the parking space where the convent car stood. Perhaps she ought to give it a name, get better acquainted. At the moment she couldn't think of one suitable.

She drove back briskly, taking the more direct route that led past the Moor School. There were still tapes marking off a fairly wide area all around and two constables were pacing slowly back and forth. She drove on and turned in at the convent gates in time to swerve aside as Sister Perpetua came down the drive.

"Missed!" The older nun beamed as she uttered the exclamation.

"Sister, I'm sorry. I'm not late, am I?" Sister Joan stuck her head out of the window and shook her head at her own foolishness. "Were you coming to look for me?"

"Sister, this may astonish you but I do have other duties apart from looking for you which isn't one of my duties at all," Sister Perpetua said with heavy irony. "As a matter of fact I'm looking for Sister Hilaria. You haven't seen her?"

"No, Sister. Surely she's in the postulancy."

"I went there first off," Sister Perpetua said, turning and keeping pace with the slow crawl of the car. "Mother Dorothy wanted to see the novices for a little talk. They've heard garbled rumours about these dreadful murders and she wanted to put the whole thing in perspective. When Sister Hilaria didn't come over at the appointed time she sent me to look for her. The novices were there, writing up their spiritual diaries, dear souls, so I shepherded them across to the parlour and then set off again. Not that I expected her to be outside the grounds. But she has become very much vaguer of late. Never quite with us, if you know what I mean?"

"I do indeed, Sister." Sister Joan spoke feelingly, recalling several occasions when she had been the one deputed to get Sister Hilaria where she was supposed to be.

"Sister Teresa has made soup and a salad sandwich," Sister Perpetua said, changing the subject and panting slightly.

"I decided we needed both," Sister Joan said.

"Well, I don't suppose that Mother Dorothy will object," the other said. "You must be worn out, dashing about all over the place."

"And I must find some time in which to exercise Lilith." Driving into the yard, she pulled up and switched off the engine. "One of the police constables rode her back for me the other evening."

"Did he? I didn't see him," Sister Perpetua said, looking round the yard as if she expected Sister Hilaria to pop up from under a stone.

"But . . ." Sister Joan broke off, frowning. Obviously one of the other members of the community had been in the yard and sent the constable away tealess.

"She might be up in the library," Sister Perpetua said with an air of inspiration. "I'll go and take a look at once. It's almost lunchtime, Sister."

She bustled off, while Sister Joan alighted from the car and went into the kitchen where Sister Teresa was piling sandwiches on to a tray.

"I'll help you carry them up, Sister." Seizing the nearest tray, she hurried out into the passage and up the stairs.

Luncheon, like breakfast, was eaten in the refectory. Up to now it hadn't been a meal that Sister Joan had attended regularly. When teaching at the school she'd usually made do with an apple and a scone or brewed up hot Bovril or soup on the primus stove for herself and her pupils. She set down the trays and started laying out the spoons. Someone had already put out the bowls and a platter of apples. Sister Teresa, she decided, was going to be an asset to the community with her calm efficiency.

Much better than me, Sister Joan decided without envy. She has already achieved custody of the eyes, that stillness of the body that reflects a quiet soul. I do hope Sister Hilaria turns up safe and sound.

There was absolutely no reason why she shouldn't. Sister Hilaria wasn't a young girl still living with her parents, at the mercy of her own youth and inexperience. She was past forty, so attuned to cloistered life that she was incapable of taking a step into the outside world unaccompanied. She had suffered a toothache during the summer and Sister Joan had driven her into town, bought her a hot drink in a café. Despite her pain Sister Hilaria had made quite a little holiday of it.

The clanging of the luncheon bell woke her from a reverie that was oddly disturbing. The trouble was, she thought, hastening to help Sister Teresa with the heavy tureen, was that she was not yet assimilated back into the life of the community. She had travelled back from the retreat in Scotland and was suddenly dealing with an unfamiliar job as lay sister and wrestling with the questions surging into her mind about the deaths of Valerie Pendon and Tina Davies.

The others were filing in, hands clasped, eyes lowered. If nostrils were aquiver with anticipation they concealed it well. Nobody, looking at the two lines of figures, ranged down both sides of the table, would have divined that Sister Martha had probably just come in from a strenuous spell of digging or that old Sister

Mary Concepta, leaning on her sticks, was in the most
intense pain from her knotted and swollen joints.

"Sister Mary Concepta, how nice that you are well
enough to join us." Mother Dorothy, entering, spoke
with pleasure.

"I do feel much better today," Sister Mary Concepta
said brightly.

"As long as you don't overdo it, Sister." The Prioress
let her sharp glance note the fact that two places that
should have been filled were empty and bowed her head
to intone the brief grace.

At lunch, as at breakfast, short remarks were permis-
sible, a welcome respite from a morning generally spent
in solitary work. Today, however, nobody seemed inclined to talk. Even Sister Gabrielle was unusually silent, her old face brooding above her soup. It was as if
what had happened beyond the enclosure sent forth cold
tentacles that chilled the fellowship.

"Soup and salad sandwiches," Mother Dorothy commented. "Sister?"

Did one have to ask leave for every blasted departure
from custom? Sister Joan quelled a spurt of irritation
and answered meekly, "Since it was rather cold today,
Mother, I thought that for once it might be a good idea
to have both?"

"It's liable to become a great deal colder before the
winter sets in. However, for once, both are very welcome. We will forego the dessert."

The apples were as red and plump as the apples of
Eden. Sister Joan's mouth watered with a completely ir-
rational desire to snatch one up and bite into it, to cry
aloud, "Two young girls are dead and Sister Hilaria is
missing, and all you can do is chatter on about the

meal. Why don't we all wake up and start talking about the things that really matter?"

"Mother Prioress, Sisters in Christ, I beg pardon for being late." Sister Perpetua spoke hurriedly, sliding to her knees.

"Have you found Sister Hilaria?" Mother Dorothy asked, waving the other to her place.

"There's no sign of her anywhere, Mother Dorothy. I've looked high and low."

"Eat your lunch, Sister. We will excuse your lateness. Afterwards we will have another look. Sister Joan, you will escort the novices to the postulancy and stay with them until Sister Hilaria is located."

Her eyes, shrewd behind their spectacles, said clearly, It will do your inflated ego a world of good to have to remain tamely indoors while others rush round on quests.

"Yes, Mother Prioress." She swallowed her sandwich, waited for the blessing that would release her and led the two novices out.

Sister Elizabeth and Sister Marie walked ahead of her when they had descended the stairs, bonneted heads bowed, hands hidden in the short black cloaks that hung from their shoulders. Their ankle-length pink smocks made them look like overgrown models for a Mabel Lucie Atwell painting; the Flemish-styled bonnets reduced their features to doll size. She knew nothing about either of them.

They made their way across the tennis court with its rusted posts and through the gate into that small yard where the first and second year novices took their exercise. Memories of her own postulancy rose up. Had she really worn that hideous outfit without a smile? Walked round and round to exercise the "limbs," with her head bent and her eyes fixed on the ground? How, in Detective Sergeant Mill's words, had she contrived to emerge sane?

"As I'm taking Sister Hilaria's place for the moment," she said aloud, "it will be permitted for you to talk to me."

Sister Elizabeth and Sister Marie looked at each other. Then the latter said, "Please, Sister, is it true there's a maniac about?"

"Two young women have been murdered locally, yes. Surely Mother Prioress told you?"

They entered the narrow hallway of what had once been the dowerhouse on the Tarquin estate and turned into the bare room with a table and a few stools beneath a three-dimensional crucifix where the novices had their own recreation.

"She told us that the news was very sad but that we mustn't allow ourselves to dwell upon it," Sister Elizabeth said.

"Mother Prioress was right. These events are sad and tragic, but there is nothing you can do about them except pray for their souls—and for the soul of their killer also. Words like 'maniac' don't help."

"Yes, Sister." Sister Marie answered meekly but Sister Joan caught the flash in the eyes before she lowered her gaze again.

That one had spirit, she thought. She might well prove a good nun. Too soon yet to tell, of course, but something indefinable about her betokened character.

"Ought we not to pray for Sister Hilaria's safe return, Sister?" Sister Elizabeth asked.

"Yes, of course, but the matter is scarcely desperate yet," she answered with a faint smile. "Sister Hilaria is, as you must both know, a most spiritual soul, and occasionally such souls get a trifle lost in the mundane world."

"She is awfully absent-minded," Sister Marie said, the twinkle in her eyes muted but not banished. "She starts praying on one subject and then veers off to another and then stops talking altogether and takes off into a dream."

"A most spiritual soul," Sister Joan said firmly, resisting the temptation to grin. "Apart from 'going off into a dream' does she—she is always here, I take it?"

"With us, or in her cell, Sister," Sister Elizabeth said.

"But she must occasionally take a walk by herself? When you are in bed?"

"No, Sister. I don't think so." Sister Elizabeth looked bewildered.

For no reason the image of a nun flitting across the tennis court had come into Sister Joan's mind. Where had she . . . ? Yes, of course, she had been given leave to take a brief stroll after the last blessing on the night of her return. She had seen someone else, had assumed they also had permission to take a walk. Without consciously thinking it out in words she had assumed that it was Sister Hilaria.

"What are we to do, Sister?" It was Sister Marie speaking, a faint dimple in her cheek hinting at private mirth. She must think that all professed nuns go off into trances, Sister Joan thought.

"I think that you had better get on with your sewing," she said aloud.

"Yes, Sister." They turned as one and went to the cupboard to bring out their workboxes.

There would be no delicate embroidery to engage their interest. Instead there were sheets to be turned and hemmed, stockings to be darned, nightcaps to make—

black, white and grey were the prevailing colours. The
pink smocks struck a note of gaiety amid the prevailing
sombreness of shade.

"You may talk if you wish." She addressed the two
silent girls in a voice full, in her own ears at least, of
patronage.

"What about, Sister?" Sister Marie replied respectfully, but the twinkle was back in her eye.

She knew as well as her professed companion that
denied the opportunity to gossip, to reminisce about
one's past life, there remained little else to discuss if
she were not to appropriate the function of the novice
mistress.

"I will find a book and read something," she said, rising.

There were books on the shelves in the other room.
Lives of the saints, half a dozen Victorian novels, some
essays by Cardinal Newman—no Teilhard de Chardin
to upset the dutiful progression of their religious vocations. She pulled out a copy of *The Wide, Wide World*
and looked at its battered cover with an indulgent smile.
There had been a freshness, an innocence about the
books she had read first in her grandmother's house
where she had spent holidays and met again during her
own novitiate. In the world of Meg, Jo, Beth and Amy,
on the island where Anne Shirley dreamed her teenage
dreams, there was no room for a killer who strangled
young girls with a loop of wire and left them, dressed
like parodies of brides.

She took the book back into the other room and began to read it aloud.

The afternoon passed slowly. The novices sewed, Sister Joan read. Outside a harsh wind rustled the few trees
and whipped up gravel from the paths.

"Sister, we usually have a cup of tea at this time," Sister Marie inserted neatly at the end of a paragraph.

"Sister." Sister Elizabeth gave her fellow novice a chiding look.

"I'm so glad you reminded me," Sister Joan said, closing the book. "We will have our cup of tea and perhaps, before it is drunk, we shall hear good news of Sister Hilaria."

"Sister Hilaria makes the tea on the primus stove," Sister Marie volunteered.

"Fine. You two finish off your seams and I'll make the tea."

It was a relief to be doing something practical. She went into the tiny kitchen where Sister Hilaria and her charges could make themselves a hot drink, their meals being taken in the main house. Lighting the stove, finding mugs, getting the milk out of the tiny refrigerator, she felt the elusive shadow of Sister Hilaria at her side. The novice mistress spent most of her time in this bleak little building, often absent from recreation, bound to her novices as if a cord tied them all together. Perhaps Sister Hilaria's flights of mysticism were her escape from the confines of the postulancy.

"Do you need any help, Sister Joan? I put away my sewing." Sister Marie stood on the threshold.

"I'm just waiting for the kettle. The tea ought to steep for a minute or two."

"Stewed," Sister Marie said. "Up north we brew it for five minutes. Oh, sorry."

"It's hard not to chatter about one's previous life, isn't it?" Sister Joan said with sympathy. "I come from up north myself originally. If you listen closely you can still catch the tailend of a flat vowel."

"I like it here though," Sister Marie confided. "I

can't say that I go along with all the pettifogging rules but they're there to teach us obedience, like recruits drilling in the army, so one puts up with it. And the countryside is beautiful here. I wish . . ." She hesitated.

"Pass me the jug. What do you wish?"

"That this awful thing hadn't happened—I mean those two poor girls getting murdered," Sister Marie burst out. "I always promised myself that when I'm fully professed I'd get the chance to walk out on the moors. They seem so sheltering, so safe—and now it's spoilt. Just like at home when . . ."

"Please, Sister, Sister Perpetua wants a word." Sister Elizabeth had fluttered to the door.

"I'll be there at once. Finish making the tea." Sister Joan hurried out.

Sister Perpetua, every freckle prominent on her square white face, was outside, her large capable hands clasping and unclasping the rosary at her belt with a little clanking sound.

"What has happened?" Sister Joan asked and thought within herself, Don't tell me.

"Sister Hilaria has had an accident," Sister Perpetua said breathlessly. "She must have been hit by a car. Sister Katharine found her in a pile of bracken just off the track. We've sent for an ambulance but Mother Dorothy wants you back at the main house, and I'm to stay with the novices."

"Go along in, Sister. They're just making tea." Sister Joan set off at a run, across the tennis court where the wind played kites with her veil, through the gate into the enclosure, and hence to the stableyard.

In the kitchen Sister Teresa's hands rattled the crockery as she brewed tea.

"Mother Prioress told me that we would all need a

cup." Her voice also shook slightly; in her face was the question, Why?

"Will you make an extra one for me, Sister? I must speak to Mother Dorothy." She went on through to the parlour.

"Please come in and sit down, Sister Joan." Mother Dorothy, betraying her agitation, added the customary, *"Dominus vobiscum."*

"Et cum spiritu sancto," Sister Joan said. "Mother, what happened? Is Sister Hilaria badly hurt?"

"She's unconscious," Mother Dorothy said. "Sister Katharine found her and ran back to tell me. I summoned help over the telephone and went to see for myself. She was only a few yards from the front gates, Sister, but the ground dips down into a shallow ditch and the wind had blown the bracken—I stayed with her until the ambulance came and Sister Katharine and Sister David went with her to the hospital. I came back here and told Sister Perpetua to relieve you at the postulancy. Normally she is the one I would have sent with the ambulance, but she was badly shaken by what had occurred."

"She said that Sister Hilaria must have been hit by a car."

"She could not have sustained such an injury by falling over. There's nothing to fall over near where she lay. It looked as if she had received a heavy knock and been flung through the air into the decline. You didn't . . . ?"

"Reverend Mother, how could you possibly think that I'd run over poor Sister Hilaria and say nothing about it?"

"No, of course you did not, but you might have seen

something? Another car behind you on the track?
Something?"

"I didn't notice anything, but then I wasn't paying
particular attention," Sister Joan said, knitting her
brows. "Drivers have started using the moor road more
frequently, haven't they? It saves going through the
town. No, I didn't see anything."

"A hit-and-run driver." The older woman pronounced
the words with icy distaste. "How could anybody run
somebody over and then drive on? How could they?"

"They couldn't at that particular spot unless they
meant to run them over."

"Sister, we have no . . ."

"No proof? Mother Dorothy, anyone driving along
the moor road has an uninterrupted view all round.
There aren't any blind corners; there aren't any corners
at all. And it's broad daylight. Even a drunkard would
have seen Sister Hilaria clearly."

"But why would anyone wish to hurt her? Ah, the
tea. Sister Teresa, set it down here and make sure that
everybody else gets a cup. You had better have a word
with Sister Gabrielle and Sister Mary Concepta—don't
alarm them more than they must be alarmed already.
And see that you drink the tea yourself."

"Is there any news, Reverend Mother?" Sister Teresa
asked.

"Not yet, but we will remain hopeful." Mother Dorothy dismissed the novice with a nod and sipped her tea
in an abstracted manner.

"Mother Dorothy, what was Sister Hilaria doing outside the enclosure?" Sister Joan asked.

"I have no idea." Mother Dorothy put down her cup
and laced her fingers together. "She had been missing

since midday when she didn't bring the novices over for the little talk I planned to give."

"Then something took her outside the gates. Someone deliberately ran her over and drove on. It must have been a short time before I came back from town. Mother Dorothy, Sister Hilaria would never have gone outside without permission save for the most pressing reason."

Mother Dorothy observed her closely for a long moment, then reached for the telephone. With her left hand she dialled the number of the local police station crisply and calmly.

SEVEN

✠ ✠ ✠

"I rang the hospital on my way here," Detective Sergeant Mill said. "I've also taken the precaution of putting a colleague on duty by her bed in case she regains consciousness and says something."

"Is there any doubt of that?" Mother Dorothy asked sharply.

"They didn't say very much over the telephone," he answered soothingly, "but I was given to understand that she is suffering from severe concussion, shock and extensive bruising."

"That is what Sister David told me when she rang up. She and Sister Katharine are still at the hospital. Sister Joan will be picking them up later. I hope I did right in calling you, Detective Sergeant Mill."

"Absolutely right, Mother Dorothy. Whoever knocked Sister Hilaria down must have seen her clearly and seen that she had been hit and flung a considerable distance. Unless she flung herself in front of the vehicle and that, I suppose, is not a possibility?"

"Not in the smallest degree," she answered firmly. "Sister Hilaria can be very absent-minded at times, but that she should deliberately—no, out of the question."

"Then we are left either with a hit-and-run driver

who panicked and made off or with someone who tried, deliberately and coldly, to kill Sister Hilaria," he said.

"But that's ..." Mother Dorothy checked her first exclamation and spoke with a calm authority. "Sister Hilaria hasn't an enemy in the world. She entered the order more than twenty years ago when she was in her twenties and she has rarely left the confines of the enclosure since. I called her absent-minded. That is not, strictly speaking, accurate. Sister Hilaria has a deep spirituality that often leads her mind into realms where the rest of us strive and fail to follow. She is a wonderful example to our novices. However, not all of mystical inclinations are able to balance this with practicality as Saint Teresa did, and upon occasions, she gave the impression of being somewhat distracted in mind."

"And nobody was ever killed for that reason," Sister Joan put in.

"You'd be amazed what motives for murder have surfaced in my experience," Detective Sergeant Mill said gloomily. "However, I take your point."

"Surely someone is examining the spot?" Mother Dorothy said. "For tyre tracks and so on?"

"Rough, pebbled surface, dry weather. Whoever hit her must have dented the bumper, I imagine, but until someone turns up at the garage with a damaged car—of course I'm putting someone on to check the spot. The trouble is that with two murder enquiries going on we haven't many resources left to stretch. But we'll do our best, I promise you."

"Which is all I can ask. Thank you." Mother Dorothy made a small gesture of dismissal.

"I'll get my report in and get back to work then." Rising from the chair on which he had been sitting, leaning forward slightly to shake hands with grave courtesy, he added, "Thank you also for allowing Sister Joan to give me some help with the other cases. Sometimes it's valuable to get the views of an outsider."

"As Sister Joan is carrying out the duties of a lay sister at present she is less confined than the rest of us," Mother Dorothy allowed. "Sister, you had better drive over to the hospital and bring Sister David and Sister Katharine back."

"Yes, Mother." Sister Joan knelt briefly, aware of the detective's faintly amused glance as the words of blessing were exchanged.

"You find us medieval?" She spoke challengingly as they went through the front door and towards the yard.

"Quaint in some ways," he admitted. "However, since I don't really understand what causes a perfectly healthy, attractive young woman to lock herself up in a convent then I certainly can't pretend to understand what keeps her there."

"Not bolts and bars," she assured him. "The few there are fasten from the inside. You know I might have seen the—accident to Sister Hilaria if I'd been a few minutes earlier getting back. I must have driven right past where she was lying."

"And you saw nothing?"

"Only Sister Perpetua, just inside the gate. She was looking for Sister Hilaria. She was supposed to take our two novices over to the parlour in the main house so that Mother Dorothy could say a word concerning tragedies in the outside world having no bearing upon their spiritual development."

"Do you believe that, Sister?" he asked abruptly.

" 'Every man's death diminisheth me.' No, not really, but one comes to terms with the contradictions when one is professed. Novices are usually looking for certainties. Do you think that someone was deliberately trying to kill Sister Hilaria? The same man who killed the two girls?"

"The only thing they all have in common is their Catholicism, surely?"

"And you think that might be a coincidence? Cornwall, by tradition, is more of a Protestant stronghold, you know. We are fairly thin on the ground. But as for Sister Hilaria being lured away by a man—it's unbelievable. I simply cannot think what could possibly have brought Sister out beyond the gates without permission."

"Something may turn up." He nodded as he got into the police car.

Following him down the track in the convent car, she glanced out towards the lone policeman who was measuring the ground painstakingly. Clues were obviously few. Perhaps non-existent, she amended, frowning as she turned into the main street.

The hospital stood outside the town proper. What had once been a cottage hospital had been enlarged into a series of gleaming white buildings, each one neatly labelled. The nurses in their short veils and low-heeled shoes looked as if they were pretending to be nuns.

In the corridor Detective Sergeant Mill joined her. "Sister Hilaria's been put in a side ward," he said. "Fortunately I know the layout of the complex. My job brings me here all too often."

Sister David and Sister Katharine stood like twin guardian angels at the foot of the bed. At the side of the bed a police officer sat with notebook and pen ready. In the bed, as narrow and austere as her bed in the convent, Sister Hilaria lay, a drip attached to one arm, bandages coifing her head.

"I'm to drive you home," Sister Joan said, lowering her voice instinctively.

"The doctor says that her pulse is strong," Sister David whispered back. "They are going to take some more X-rays soon. Ought not someone to remain with her?"

"The police constable will be staying. There's nothing more you can do here."

"She hasn't said anything yet," the constable interposed. "Anything your end, sir?"

"On the other matter? Not yet, but it's early days though you'd not think so to hear the Press baying. Someone'll relieve you later on, Constable." The detective sounded brisk and normal as if coma and injury were too ordinary to whisper about.

"I'll keep an eye open, sir."

"Keep two," Detective Sergeant Mill advised. "Sisters."

"Will you be trying to find the car?" Sister David ventured as they went back down the corridor.

"Yes, Sister. The problem is there are plenty of garages in the area and even at this end of the year tourists travelling up and down. It may take a long time."

"Not that Sister Hilaria would want revenge," Sister Katharine said. "She would be the first one to find excuses for the person who ran her down. Oh, but how anyone could do such a thing is beyond my comprehension. Surely he must have seen her."

"One would imagine so," he said non-committally.

A poker face, Sister Joan reflected, was probably one of the greatest assets a police officer could have. She wanted to ask him if he'd reached any fresh conclusions but he was turning away, getting into the police car. Perhaps it was a measure of the difference between him and Sergeant Barratt that he took any police car available, frequently driving himself, while his subordinate drove a sleek private car. She curbed her thoughts, realizing that she was allowing herself to dislike a man whose only faults, as far as she knew, were an officious manner and a mania for tidiness that clearly upset his wife.

"He seems a very able officer," Sister Katharine said from her seat in the back of the convent car. "Poor Sister Hilaria—one cannot imagine what she was doing outside in the first place."

"Perhaps she had one of her visions," Sister David said. "Or she might have strolled through without noticing."

"She'll be able to tell us soon."

Her companions murmured, "Please God," and fell silent.

When she entered the convent kitchen she almost skidded on the wet floor. Sister Teresa, on hands and knees, uttered a warning cry.

"Oh, do be careful, Sister! We can't risk another casualty."

"Then don't lay traps for your unwary companions." Sister Joan righted herself. "What possessed you to start washing the floor at this moment?"

"It was something to keep my hands busy, Sister. I'm sorry."

"Not your fault, Sister. I'm as tetchy as a wasp today," Sister Joan said in quick contrition. "Of course you need to keep your mind off it. Sister Hilaria is not yet conscious but the doctors are very hopeful. She has concussion with bruising and shock. Not that it isn't most painful and serious, but it might have been worse.

Can you finish off here? I must go and see Mother Prioress."

"Yes, Sister. I'm ever so glad about Sister Hilaria."

Sister Joan bit her lip as she went down the corridor. She trusted she hadn't been too optimistic in her reassurances. Sister Hilaria might—but please God not—take a turn for the worse, or the person who had run her down might—she stopped dead as the question leapt into her mind. Did every victim of a hit-and-run driver have a couple of policemen taking turns to sit by her bed? Or did Detective Sergeant Mill have some reason for thinking that the driver of the car might return, find his way into the hospital, finish off what had been begun?

She reminded herself firmly to curb her imagination and went on to the parlour. It was nearing the hour when the various members of the community settled for their private studies. She herself was expected to write something about her recent retreat that might be used as the basis for a talk and a general discussion, but at this moment her week in Scotland had taken on the shifting hues of a visit paid many years before to a place only dimly recalled.

"It seems that Sister Hilaria is resting quietly," Mother Dorothy said, looking up as Sister Joan tapped and entered. *"Dominus vobiscum."*

"Et cum spiritu sancto. Yes, Mother, she seems to be. We didn't see any of the medical staff but Detective Sergeant Mill must have had information. There is a police constable by her bed."

"I have telephoned Father Malone and informed him of what has occurred. He will go to the hospital the moment he's had his tea. I made him promise he wouldn't rush off without anything. We will have an extra hour in chapel this evening instead of recreation in order to pray for Sister Hilaria's swift recovery. Thank you for picking up the Sisters. They are relieved to be home again."

She made it sound as if Sister David and Sister Katharine had been away for weeks, instead of merely in the hospital for an hour or so, but to them it would seem like that, Sister Joan thought, kneeling for the blessing. Sister David had helped out at the Moor School, but though she had been fond of the children she had never managed to keep any discipline among them on the occasions when she had deputized as teacher, and going alone across the moor had made her nervous. She was much happier acting as secretary for the Prioress and working at the translations that were published in obscure journals and brought in a meagre but fairly steady stream of royalties. And Sister Katharine whose embroideries brought in more revenue was lost once she stepped beyond the grounds.

And I, Sister Joan reflected wryly, am quite different. I love the cloister but going out into the world, involving myself, is still an exciting challenge.

Firmly she shut the door of her cell, as firmly banishing the thoughts that jostled in her mind, and concentrated on the benefits and trials of her recent retreat. Had she learned in that Scottish fastness to know herself a little better, to cope with her faults? Had she succeeded in transcending her own littleness in the contemplation of a greater glory? Seated crosslegged on the floor she opened her notebook and read over what she had written, the outside world falling away as she pondered.

In chapel Father Stephens was celebrating the Benediction. Sister Joan slid into her place, a sidelong glance

showing her Sister Perpetua in charge of the two novices. When Father Stephens had processed himself out
into the sacristy where he disrobed and left without the
cup of tea that Father Malone always accepted, there
was an expectant stir among the community.

"Sisters in Christ, after we have had our supper, we
will return here to pray for Sister Hilaria's speedy recovery and return to us," Mother Dorothy said, rising.
"The loss of one recreation may be offered up for that
intention. Sister Joan, you have done something about
the preparation for supper, I trust?"

Sister Joan's cheeks went scarlet with mortification.
This was the second time she'd forgotten that the lay
sister left a few minutes early to set the tables and see
to the final stages of cooking.

"I'll see to it at once, Mother." She went out hastily,
catching up with Sister Teresa in the main hall.

"I would have attracted your attention, Sister, but Sister Perpetua was looking in my direction," Sister Teresa
said apologetically. "There's vegetable lasagne to heat
up and I made a syrup pudding earlier on. Is that all
right?"

"Sister, you're worth your weight in gold," Sister
Joan assured her. "I must be the most inefficient lay sister ever thrust into that job."

"Your mind's on other things, Sister," Sister Teresa
said. "Now I am never more content than when there's
a floor to scrub or a dinner to cook."

"And that makes you a real asset, Sister. Especially at
a time like this when outside events impinge upon our
life in the cloister. I'll see to the cutlery."

If Mother Dorothy considered that the portions of lasagne were overgenerous she wisely held her peace, and
with equal wisdom had chosen some incidents from the

life of Saint Joseph Copertino as the mealtime reading. Nothing was better calculated to raise one's spirits than the anecdotes of that delightful flying monk. For a little while the faint air of menace that seemed to be creeping about the convent was dispelled.

The syrup pudding duly demolished and the reading completed, Mother Dorothy rose.

"Sister Joan, when you have seen to the dishes please join us in chapel," she said formally. "If you can manage them alone .... ?"

"Yes, of course, Mother. Sister Teresa has done most of my work today," Sister Joan said.

"I will also require you to sleep over in the postulancy tonight," the Prioress was continuing. "Sister Perpetua is more accustomed to seeing to the needs of dear Sister Mary Concepta and Sister Gabrielle. After the great blessing take your things over there, will you?"

"Yes, Mother."

She would have liked to spend the full hour in the chapel but Sister Teresa had earned her praying time. Sister Joan heaped up the cleared plates, piled them on the trays and began the toilsome business of carting them down to the kitchen. In the Tarquins' day there had been a narrow flight of steps linking the kitchen to the upper storey so that maids could scurry up and down unobserved by the guests, but that had long since been blocked off.

Outside darkness had fallen in the disconcerting suddenness of late autumn. Faintly from the chapel she could hear the sound of singing. Like sweet voices raised against the forces of the night, she thought, and frowned because the notion was disturbing.

There was Lilith to feed. The next morning she

would take the pony for a trot round, she decided. Lilith was used to being ridden to and from school and the accustomed exercise ought not to be entirely abandoned. She slipped on her cloak and went out into the cobbled yard. The wind caught at her veil and swirled it across her face, causing the pony to whicker nervously.

"Steady, old girl. It's only me." She leaned against the half-door, stroking the velvety nose. "I've a lovely lot of feed for you if you'll be patient."

The feedbag against the inner wall of the stable was nearly empty. Aided by the light streaming from the uncurtained kitchen window she opened the stable door and went in to refill it.

Behind her Lilith gave a sudden snort and clattered out happily, obviously more intent on exercise than supper.

"Oh no! Bad girl, come here!" Sister Joan made an unavailing grab at the pony's mane but Lilith merely tossed her head, kicked up her heels in a defiant display of elderly skittishness and headed through the open gate with more energy than she ever showed when Sister Joan was riding her.

"Lilith, here!"

The pony trotted just beyond her grasp over Sister Martha's cherished herb beds. Sister Joan changed direction, running round the walls with their fringes of peach and walnut trees to where the second gate led into the patch of open ground before the sunken tennis court and the postulancy beyond. The further gate was open. Perhaps someone had neglected to close it when Sister Perpetua had escorted the novices across for chapel.

A cowled and veiled figure flitted past the open gate.

The moonlight was not strong enough to define, only to suggest, and the figure was gone in an instant.

"Sister? Sis—"

Sister Joan had reached the open gate. She closed it with a little snap and leaned against it, straining her eyes across the rough ground. The wind rustled the clumps of grass and threw a shower of tiny pebbles up into the air. They glinted like hailstones under the emerging moon and fell to earth again.

Lilith, deciding on contrition, nuzzled the back of her neck.

"Bad girl. Come and eat now." Her fingers twined in the rough mane she led the pony back through the garden. By the time the stable door had been secured only ten minutes remained before the great blessing. She wiped her hands, adjusted her veil and walked swiftly through to the chapel. All the Sisters except Sister Hilaria were in their places, heads raised to the altar, rosary beads gliding through their joined fingers. Nobody looked as if she had moved since the hour of prayer had begun. Sister Joan knelt in her place, her hand moving to the rosary at her belt, the accustomed discipline of prayerful calm smoothing her face.

The figure she had seen on the evening of her return, the figure she had glimpsed tonight, the nun who hadn't offered the police constable the customary cup of tea—surely they were all the same person. Seen twice near the postulancy and once near the stableyard. Who?

". . . and in the hour of our death. Amen." Her voice chimed in with the others just before the final Gloria began.

"I will let you have news of Sister Hilaria the moment that I hear from the hospital," Mother Dorothy said. "Sleep well, Sisters in Christ." She moved to the Lady Altar where Sister David waited for the small lamp which was raised over each member of the community as she knelt for the final blessing before the grand silence.

There was no point in reporting what she had seen now. The figure was long gone, and it would be fruitless to demand a search.

Sister Elizabeth and Sister Marie were waiting in the hall. Sister Joan, going past to collect her nightclothes from the lay cell, wondered if either of them ever felt the frustration that had bubbled up in herself when, as a novice, she had been escorted everywhere as if she had neither wish nor will of her own.

Sister Perpetua, looking more at ease now that she was carrying out her accustomed duties, smiled at her from the doorway of the infirmary where she was helping the two old nuns into their beds.

She rolled her things into a bundle and went back to the main hall. Mother Dorothy had remained in the chapel and Sister David waited to bolt the main door.

It was as dark as midnight; the moon fled. Sister Joan switched on the torch she had snatched up, wishing she had had it earlier on, and led her charges through the garden and down into the tennis court. When she glanced back towards the main house she could see a faint glow from one or two of the upper windows. Then, one by one, they went out.

The postulancy was unlocked as it always was until its occupants were within for the night. Pushing open the door, she wondered if that was such a good idea. In the old days the usually unlocked exits and entrances had signified trust in the general public and in the members of the community. But unlocked doors were not always wise.

Sister Elizabeth and Sister Marie went noiselessly up the narrow stairs to their cells. The former had learnt custody of the eyes well. The latter shot a brief anxious glance towards Sister Joan as if she longed to break the grand silence before trailing after her companion. Well, whatever she wanted to say would have to wait until morning.

Sister Hilaria's cell was at the end of the upper passage. It was marginally larger than the other cells as befitted her position as novice mistress, but it was completely austere. The walls, bare save for a crucifix, the narrow bed with its hard mattress and grey blanket, the basin and jug in the corner, the hooks behind the door on which her change of habit hung, the box in which a change of linen was laid—nothing had been added to this perfect model of a cell. The vase in which professed sisters were allowed to place no more than three flowers was empty. On the bookshelf a Bible and a missal were the only volumes.

Something was missing. Sister Joan stood in the middle of the room and gazed round, knitting her brows. Something that ought to have been in the room wasn't there. She had kindled the paraffin lamp automatically as she entered and its light revealed every corner, every crack in the whitewashed wall.

Sister Hilaria's spiritual diary wasn't on the shelf. Every sister, professed or not, kept a spiritual diary, used as the basis for private devotions, as a check on the progress she believed she was making in the religious life. Only she ever read her entries. Not until after her death did the prioress read the record and use it as the source of the obituary notice that would be sent round the other houses of the order. Sometimes, when she thought of her own entries, Sister Joan permitted herself a wry grin at the thought of the prioress who would, one day, be called upon to decipher them.

But Sister Hilaria's diary wasn't here. And Sister Hilaria who, despite her fits of absent-mindedness, never bent a single rule, would certainly not have kept it elsewhere.

Feeling a complete fool, Sister Joan lowered herself to the floor and looked under the bed.

The thick, black-covered volume lay on the floor, in shadow but unmistakable. She stretched out her arm and drew it out.

Spiritual diaries were sacredly private. The fact they were always kept in full view made them paradoxically more private. To open one, to read the struggles of a fellow soul, was an invasion of privacy almost beyond forgiveness.

She scrambled up, still clutching the notebook, and went over to the shelf to replace the book. It teetered for a moment and then, as if endowed with an energy of its own, toppled to the floor again.

Bending to pick it up, grimacing at her own clumsiness, she saw without meaning to see that nearly half the pages had been ripped out, leaving long margins of torn paper.

It wasn't for her to investigate further, though her fingers itched to explore. She would take the book to Mother Dorothy in the morning and ask for her superior's advice. Laying the book down on its side, she began to undress, turning her eyes resolutely away from temptation.

When she had extinguished the light and knelt to say her last prayers, her lips moving silently in accordance with the rules, she hoped for weariness. A good sleep would set her up for whatever the next day would bring.

It was impossible. She lay beneath her blanket; she lay on top of her blanket; she sat on the edge of the bed while half-formed images danced through her head. The veiled figure glimpsed briefly on two occasions, Sister Perpetua not having received Lilith back from the constable, Sister Perpetua in the driveway not many yards ahead, something Sister Marie had begun to say—outside a stone crunched under an unwary foot.

On her own feet, every nerve quivering, Sister Joan groped for the torch, but by the time she felt its heavy weight in the palm of her hand the sound had ceased.

There was no rule to prevent her from investigating an attempted break-in. Switching on the torch, she opened the door and went softly along the corridor, her bare feet curling up against the cold boards.

"At least have the sense to put on some slippers and your dressing-gown." She could hear Mother Dorothy's voice as clearly as if the prioress stood in the passage with her.

It took only a minute to obey that unspoken command, but it was a delay all the same. She gripped the torch tightly, directing its beam downwards, and made her way to the tiny kitchen out of which a door led into the alley that ran between postulancy and boundary wall. The noise had come from the front of the building. She walked softly to the corner and peered round it, her torch stabbing the dark. The courtyard was apparently deserted. Gaining a little courage, she switched off the torch and moved on into the small courtyard.

The front door was closed, bolted from within as she had left it. She stared at it, one hand flying to her mouth. In luminous capitals across the wood were the words I'M COMING. Just that and nothing more.

EIGHT

✠ ✠ ✠

"Detective Sergeant Mill is on his way here," Mother Dorothy said. "Sister Joan, you will be the one most fitted to answer any questions he has. I'm afraid he will expect to be shown inside the postulancy in order to look for signs of an illegal entry. Sister Elizabeth and Sister Marie, you will remain in chapel until the detective has gone, though he may also wish to question you in which case you will be sent for to the parlour."

Her voice was as calm as if a member of the community came every morning to tell her that a threatening message had been left in luminous paint, but her hands were tense.

Father Stephens had been and gone, bound for a clerical meeting somewhere or other. Saturday, marked out from other days by the general confession in the evening, unfolded rapidly from a cold, grey dawn into a cold, sparkling forenoon.

The two novices knelt and went docilely towards the chapel. The prioress looked at Sister Joan.

"You did well to wait until morning before you informed me of what had occurred," she said with rare approval. "Of course it was impossible to hide it from the novices, but there is no need to alarm the rest of the community. Ah, there is the car now."

She went into the hall and opened the door, Sister Joan at her heels. On the step Detective Sergeant Mill lowered his hand from the bell rope.

"Good morning, Mother Dorothy." He shook hands politely. "Your message was very clear. Sister Joan, good morning. You haven't washed out the paint?"

"Not yet. Sister Joan will show it to you. I have kept it from most of the community but the two novices in the postulancy couldn't avoid seeing it. If it's absolutely necessary to question them they can be summoned from chapel."

"Thank you, but I'll try to avoid it. My driver will be taking fingerprints though I have no hopes in that direction. We will need to enter the building."

"Sister Joan will accompany you. Perhaps you will take a coffee with me when you have completed your business—your—er, driver too, of course."

"Wilcox will be more at ease in the kitchen," Detective Sergeant Mill said with a grin. "He's a rabid Methodist and terrified of being converted."

"Whatever you both wish." If she was amused she didn't show it.

Walking round the side of the main house, the constable trailing at a little distance, he commented, "Your prioress seems marginally less prickly this morning."

"She understands the importance of co-operating with the police. There is something more which I haven't yet mentioned but may well be linked."

"Yes?" He slowed the pace, turning an interested face towards her.

"On my first evening back I received leave from Mother Dorothy to walk for twenty minutes in the enclosure. I had discovered that poor girl's body and I was more shaken than I realized. I saw—caught a fleeting glimpse . . ."

"Of what?"

"Of what I took to be one of the other sisters. I assumed at the time that Mother Dorothy had given one of the others leave to walk too. Then the police officer—Constable Stephens?—anyway the one who rode Lilith back for me, he mentioned that he'd handed over the pony to one of the sisters and that she'd simply led the animal away without even offering him a cup of tea. That was so unlike Sister Perpetua that I mentioned the return of the pony to her in a casual manner, but she said she hadn't seen any constable. And then last night, when the others were in chapel praying for Sister Hilaria I had the dishes to wash and Lilith to feed. She hadn't been properly exercised and she was skittish and got out of the stable and into the enclosure garden. I went after her."

"The gate was open?"

"Yes, which is unusual. Sister Martha has charge of the garden and she is very meticulous about closing the gates. This one was open and the gate at the further end was also ajar. I saw someone flit past over the rough ground—it was again the most fleeting of glimpses but whoever it was wore habit and veil. By the time I reached the gate the figure had gone. I took Lilith back to her stall and then went to join the others in chapel."

"They were all present?"

"And looked as if they'd been there all the time. This is the old tennis court. We keep saying that we're going to do something with it, but there's never quite sufficient money."

"The story of my life," he said with a grin. "How the devil do you all manage?"

"Sister David publishes translations from the Latin and Greek; Sister Martha sells fruit and vegetables; Sister Katharine sells the loveliest lace and embroidery work and when I was teaching at the Moor School there was my salary. And none of it," she added chidingly, "with the help of the devil. That's the postulancy."

Something inside her had denied the reality of that stark threat. When she went back the front door would be innocent oak again.

I'M COMING. It glared out still, only faintly muted by daylight.

"Photographs, fingerprints if any, a close look at the surrounding ground and then you can scrub it off," he instructed the constable.

"Right, sir." The officer gave the impression of rolling up his sleeves.

"We can boil hot water on the primus stove," Sister Joan said. "For the scrubbing, I mean. There's no electricity."

"Very quaint and medieval. No lock either, I see." He watched her open the front door.

"We draw the bolt last thing at night. There's nothing here to steal."

"Was anything taken?" he asked as they stepped into the passage.

"Didn't Mother Dorothy say? Sister Hilaria's spiritual diary had been pushed under her bed and nearly half the pages in it torn out."

"Well, take a look round. There seems a decided lack of home comforts."

"Home comforts are not regarded as particularly desirable in the postulancy," she said demurely. "This is the recreation room—for the first two years the novices join the main community only for chapel and meals.

This is the study. This is the meditation room where they examine their consciences, attempt to come to grips with a Reality greater than the reality we know, and this is the kitchen. The door leads into the alley and, as far as I know, is never locked."

"I'll have a word with the constable. Give me a moment." He opened the back door using only the tips of his fingers and went out.

It seemed odd, unnatural to see a man, to hear a male voice in this virgin sanctuary. For all his friendly tact the detective was out of place. And his being here at all was due to the malicious, faceless person who had intruded. A slow, quiet anger was building in her, quite different from the usual bubbling indignation that could be relieved by a short burst of temper.

"I'll have to take a look round upstairs," he said, returning. "No obvious signs of entry anywhere so far, but your community's idea of security makes me shudder. When this is cleared up I'm sending our security officer here to teach you a bit about crime prevention."

"Mother Dorothy won't let him within a mile of the place," she warned, starting up the narrow stairs.

"Trust is a fine quality," he argued, "but times change, Sister. Even here in this quiet place there are burglaries, break-ins . . ."

"And murders," she finished. "We're not fools, Detective Sergeant Mill, but if we have to start surrounding ourselves with burglar alarms and spyholes and trip-wires and the Lord knows what else then we lose something from our communal life, something precious. Don't you see?"

"You're talking about naïvety."

"I'm talking about innocence. These are the six cells

for the novices, with Sister Hilaria's cell at the end next to the bathroom."

Entering, he stood for a moment in silence, looking round. Then he said, "I take it that the cells are all furnished in the same way?"

"Yes, they are. A few are slightly larger than others."

"And you were deputizing for Sister Hilaria here last night?"

"I've been doing lay sister duties since my return," she explained, "but as Sister Hilaria is in hospital I took her place."

"Lay duties?" One eyebrow jerked upward. "Does that mean you've been demoted?"

"It means that now that the school has been closed I have no regular uses so I get moved about a bit. I suppose that makes for a bit of excitement."

"Scintillating," he said dryly.

"Anyway, I brought the two novices over here last evening after the final blessing and we went straight to our cells. Shortly afterwards I noticed that Sister Hilaria's spiritual diary wasn't on the shelf—we all keep our diaries there. On the shelf in our own cells, I mean. I looked round for it and found it under the bed. After I took it up I realized that nearly half the pages had been ripped out."

"You wouldn't know what they might have contained, I suppose?"

"Of course not. Spiritual diaries are very personal things. Sometimes the diary of a novice might be read, as an example to others perhaps, but of a professed nun, never."

"So you took it to the prioress?"

"This morning," Sister Joan said, "and she won't allow you to read it. Sister Hilaria will be able to help you when she regains consciousness."

"And meanwhile 'someone' is coming," he said without expression.

She shivered, her blue eyes clouding.

"I heard a stone crack beneath someone's foot just below my window. I found the torch and went into the passage and then I turned back to put on my dressing-gown and slippers. Then I went downstairs."

"To the front door?"

She shook her head. "To the kitchenette and then through the back door and along the alley to the front. I switched on my torch and held the beam low and then I saw the luminous paint on the front door."

"And what time would that be?"

"The grand silence begins at 9:30. It would have been a few minutes after ten. I'm afraid I neglected to look at my watch." She indicated the neat fob pinned to her grey scapular.

"And you didn't run to the main house to inform anyone?"

"It was the grand silence," she said. "Nobody was in danger of death or anything like that. I couldn't leave Sister Elizabeth and Sister Marie here by themselves and I couldn't have woken them and frightened them for so little reason. I came back into the postulancy."

"All very commendable and in accordance with the rules," he said. "It never entered your head that someone might have crept back and murdered the three of you in your beds?"

"Oh, no, they wouldn't," she said triumphantly, "because I sat at the top of the stairs all night with the heavy torch."

For the first time since she had known him he put

back his head and roared with laughter. Hearty, unashamed, masculine laughter that made the prim walls dance and shimmer.

"I may be small," she said with dignity, "but I'm really quite tough."

"Exceedingly tough," he agreed, grinning broadly. "Yes, Sister, I can see that."

"Is there anything else you need to know, Detective Sergeant Mill?" she asked, concealing her own mirth.

"Not at the moment, Sister. We'll leave the constable to finish off here and walk back to the main building. I was promised a cup of tea."

"And I have my own duties to perform." She led the way downstairs.

"We'll need prints taken from Sister Hilaria's cell," he said when they were outside again. "Not that I expect any joy. I'll get through on the car radio and have them send an extra man along to get the job done. Excuse me, Sister."

He went over to the constable who was scrubbing vigorously at the paint. Flakes of it clung to his uniform and his face was scarlet with exertion.

Sister Joan folded her hands within the wide cuffs of her sleeves and walked on across the waste ground and into the tennis court. It was cold with the coming of winter on the wind. Somehow it chimed with the chill that had gripped her mood. Someone had strangled two young girls. Someone had knocked down Sister Hilaria and torn up part of her spiritual diary and then sneaked back to paint a warning on the door. What exercised her mind was whether or not the same person was involved in all these actions. On the face of it there was no connection at all, but the alternative—that more than one person lived in the vicinity and was sufficiently unbalanced to perform such acts—was a terrifying one. Suddenly the enclosure seemed not a refuge but a place as vulnerable as anywhere else.

"Have you any word of Sister Hilaria?" Detective Sergeant Mill asked, catching her up. "I haven't rung the hospital this morning. I was about to do so when your prioress rang."

"Mother Dorothy rang up and they said she was still unconscious." Her tone held pain.

"It sometimes happens after concussion. I've no doubt they are monitoring her condition very carefully. Well, Sister, have you any thoughts on this?"

"None that please me," she said soberly. "Is there a connection between the two killings and what is happening here? Your coming out here simply to investigate writing on a wall makes me think that you suspect there is."

"I think it's possible," he agreed, "unless several inhabitants of Cornwall have all run mad at the same time."

"You see madness in all this then?"

"Don't you, Sister? A coldly calculating mind, indifferent to normal moral precepts, acting with its own remorseless, lunatic logic? Doesn't that strike you as madness?"

"Evil certainly. And there has to be madness in that, I suppose. I mean real evil and not mere sinfulness."

They had traversed the tennis court and were crossing the garden. Sister Martha, bent over her marjoram with its grey winter stalks bruised by Lilith's hooves, looked up reproachfully.

"I am sure you didn't mean to allow Lilith to rampage through the garden," she said. "Oh, good morning, Detective Sergeant."

"I'm afraid Lilith gave me the slip when I went to feed her last evening," Sister Joan apologized. "Has she done a great deal of damage?"

"Fortunately it can be remedied," Sister Martha assured her. "At this end of the year most plants lie fallow. Is there any word of Sister Hilaria?"

"Only what Mother Dorothy heard when she rang before breakfast," Sister Joan said.

"This must be very distressing for you," the detective began.

"Oh, it's not too bad. As I said the plants are often fallow in winter—oh, you mean poor Sister Hilaria. At least she is in good hands."

"The doctors are very efficient," he nodded.

"I was talking about God," Sister Martha said, looking at him blankly.

"Yes, of course. That too." He looked faintly embarrassed.

"And of course we are all praying for her," Sister Martha said.

"You were praying in chapel last evening?"

"After supper, instead of having recreation, we returned to the chapel for an hour before night prayers and the blessing."

"Was anyone absent?" He asked the question casually, bending to pluck a grey sprig and twirl it idly in his fingers.

"Yes, I think so. Sister Joan came in late because she is helping out with lay duties now," Sister Martha said. "Sister Perpetua went out for about ten minutes. She had a bad coughing fit and didn't wish to disturb anyone."

"Nobody else?"

"No, I'm sure not. I might not have noticed but I

think not. I'm afraid my attention was not as concentrated as it might have been. I was thinking about Sister Hilaria, trying to work out why she had gone beyond the gate. I must remember to mention my fault in general confession this evening."

"Thank you for your help anyway, Sister." He smiled at her and walked on.

"It isn't possible," Sister Joan said vehemently as soon as they were out of earshot. "Sister Perpetua wouldn't dream of hurting anyone. She's the infirmarian."

"She may have seen something," he said mildly. "In any case she ought to have mentioned her absence."

"Why should she? She doesn't know anything about the luminous writing," Sister Joan protested. "Mother Dorothy considered it wiser not to alarm the rest of the community."

"Then it's time Mother Dorothy thought again," he said with a touch of sourness. "Ignorance is no protection against lunacy."

"You can tell her over your cup of tea," Sister Joan said sweetly, leading him into the anteroom and tapping on the parlour door.

She herself went swiftly into the kitchen where she began collecting tea cups and hunting for the biscuit barrel. Outside Sister Teresa was sweeping the yard and crooning to the pony who occasionally tossed her head and whinnied in lieu of applause.

Elsewhere in the convent came the small sounds of industry that marked each morning. The soft tread of Sister David coming across the hall with a pile of textbooks, the swishing of Sister Katharine's broom as she cleared up the bits of cotton left over from her latest piece of embroidery. In the infirmary there was the click-clack of knitting needles and the sound of an occasional remark dropped by one of the old nuns into the pool of silence.

The kettle added its singing to the day. She brewed the tea, picked up the tray, and carried it through to the parlour.

When she entered, placing the tray on the desk, kneeling to answer the traditional greeting, she felt immediately the tension in the atmosphere. There was nothing overt but it was present in Mother Dorothy's thinned lips and the detective's long fingers drumming softly on his trousered knee.

"You may remain, Sister." Mother Dorothy indicated a stool, but didn't suggest that she bring an extra cup.

Sister Joan sat down, folding her hands, feet neatly side by side.

"Detective Sergeant Mill is of the opinion that we need more security precautions at the convent," Mother Dorothy said stiffly. "What is your view of the matter?"

"Of our having extra security? On a temporary or permanent basis?" She asked both questions as a delaying tactic, aware that two opposite reactions were expected from her by the other two.

"Permanent," Detective Sergeant Mill said firmly. "I'm not talking about armed guards and barbed wire, but of a simple system of electronic ..."

"Far too expensive even if we wanted it which we don't," Mother Dorothy said.

"This is in an isolated situation," Detective Sergeant Mill said. His level voice held barely suppressed impatience.

"Sister?" Mother Dorothy looked at her. They both looked at her.

"I think that it would go against the spirit of our or-

der if we surrounded ourselves with security devices,"
she said slowly. "There would be initial expense and
running costs, but I do understand we live in a changing
world. A more violent world."

"You're sitting on the fence," he accused.

"I was wondering . . ." She hesitated, then went on,
"I was wondering if it might be possible to get a
dog—a good guard dog whom we could train to patrol
the grounds at night and give warning. There isn't anything in the rules against the keeping of animals, is
there, Mother Dorothy?"

"Pets are discouraged," the prioress said.

"But a working dog, trained to accompany any of the
sisters when they were alone anywhere in the area and
to give warning of intruders at night? An Alsatian, perhaps?"

"I shall put the idea to the community after general
confession," Mother Dorothy said. "I must say it strikes
me as an ideal compromise, but we shall see."

"If you decide in favour," Detective Sergeant Mill offered, giving in gracefully, "I'll look out a good one for
you from a healthy litter. And in future it would help if
you made sure the doors were bolted in both the main
house and the postulancy."

"You really take this threat seriously, don't you?"
Mother Dorothy lowered her head bullishly and stared
at him.

"Yes, I do." His tone was uncompromising. "Someone ran Sister Hilaria down and someone painted those
words on the door of the postulancy and tore up the diary. And someone killed two young girls in a particularly nasty way. I strongly advise you to inform the
whole community of the risks and move your novices
into the main house. I take it you have room?"

"Yes. We number only eleven, counting everybody. Except myself." She smiled slightly. "I'm afraid the habit of humility can lead to inaccuracy sometimes. We are twelve. I think twelve of us can deal with any trouble. Is there anything else—excuse me."

At her elbow the telephone shrilled. She lifted the receiver, listened, spoke briefly and replaced it. "That was the hospital," she said. "Sister Hilaria, thank God, has woken up. Sister Joan, you had better go down to the hospital. Take the car."

"She can come in the police car," Detective Sergeant Mill said. "I'll see she gets back safely."

"Very well. That's very kind of you, Detective Sergeant. Sister, you will stay with Sister Hilaria for as long as you deem necessary, and do make sure she is not subjected to a long inquisition of what she may or may not have seen. Our first concern must be Sister Hilaria's speedy return to full health. Is that clear?"

"Yes, Mother. Of course."

Kneeling for the blessing, conscious of the detective's somewhat jaundiced gaze, she went out into the hall. Outside a second police car had drawn up, presumably having brought the extra police.

"Get in, Sister. We'd better get to the hospital as fast as we can," he said.

"Yes, of course." She got in and fastened her seat belt rapidly.

"What an obstinate crowd of females you are," he commented, half amused and half annoyed as he started the car. "Determined to cling to your independence."

"There are twelve of us," she reminded him.

"So there are." He cast her an ironic glance. "Mother Dorothy who is small and wears spectacles and has more power in her tongue than her fists, the two old dears in the infirmary, three young novices conditioned not to think for themselves, the one that looks like a rabbit . . ."

"Sister David," Sister Joan said incautiously and flushed.

"I see you know the one I mean," he said, straight-faced. "Sister—Katharine and the gardener."

"Sister Martha."

"Three more delicately made, smallish women."

"And Sister Perpetua," she added.

"Tough enough, I grant you, but close on sixty. Hardly an army."

"You're forgetting me."

"No indeed, Sister Joan. You are the one I don't for-get," he informed her. "The oddest mixture of medieval superstition and hard common sense I ever knew. I'm sorry for the woman who had you as a novice."

"It isn't the way you think," she said earnestly. "We are encouraged to think for ourselves but within the limits of canonical discipline. Can't you go faster?"

"Not without breaking the speed limit. Hold on to your veil, Sister. We're almost there."

He swung the car round a curve and at a speed per-ilously close to the illegal roared in at the hospital gates.

Here was the scrupulous cleanliness and swift, pad-ding footsteps of women that reminded her of the clois-ter, but the smell was different. It was, she thought, as she accompanied the detective along the corridor, the smell of suffering and death. In the cloister it was life that was celebrated, and that was something she couldn't explain.

"She woke up and had some tea," the constable said,

rising from his seat as they came in. "She said her head was aching, that's all. Then she dozed off again."

Sister Hilaria had been slightly propped up. Her cheeks held a faint and welcome tinge of colour and the blue tint about her lips was fading.

"Sister Hilaria?" Sister Joan bent over, keeping her voice low and calm. "It's Sister Joan. You're looking much better, Sister."

"There may be some degree of amnesia for several days." A white-jacketed orderly had entered. "She's in no state to be questioned yet."

"Of course not. I merely wanted to assure her that she's in good hands and the entire community is praying for her," Sister Joan said.

"Which she probably knows," the orderly said.

"Yes, of course. Everybody sends love and you're to have a good rest, Sister." She spoke gently, her tone conventual. Inside she wanted to raise her voice, to demand . . .

"Sister?" The novice mistress's eyes were open, her expression puzzled.

"You're in the hospital and you're going to be fine, thank God," Sister Joan said.

"You don't understand." Sister Hilaria's voice was gratifyingly strong. "It ought to have been a donkey, you see. That was the whole trouble."

And, lids fluttering down, she slipped into healing sleep.

NINE

✠ ✠ ✠

"Did the remark make any sense to you, Sister?" Detective Sergeant Mill asked.

"Not yet, but I haven't had time to think about it."

They had left the side ward where Sister Hilaria lay and were pacing the forecourt of the hospital. Around them the air was cold and brilliant, the silence punctured by the sounds of cars and ambulances stopping and starting.

"It ought to have been a donkey," he repeated thoughtfully. "That has to mean something surely, unless it was one of those meaningless remarks people make when they're emerging from unconsciousness. Some very respectable people swear like troopers."

"Not Sister Hilaria," Sister Joan said decidedly. "She meant something when she spoke."

It occurred to her with a little shock that the novice mistress, for all her dreaminess, had a habit of bringing forth phrases that, though slightly out of context, illumined the situation.

"Let's hope the amnesia doesn't last long," he said. "I'll make sure there's someone with her at all times."

"No luck yet in finding the car?"

"No luck at all. Of course it's possible it wasn't damaged when it struck her, in which case it won't have

been handed in for repair at any garage. In any case our
main concern still has to be the murders."

"And there's no news there else you'd have mentioned it."

"Only the negative kind. The dresses the girls were
wearing were made of a cheap silk that can be bought
almost anywhere including in the markets, and thousands of those cheap sandals have been sold during the
last year or two. Same goes for those lace insets—cheap
lace you can buy anywhere by the yard though it was
all hand-sewn beautifully. They were wearing their own
underwear and we haven't found their nightclothes yet.
I'm trying to keep the media interest low-key to prevent
public panic and so far it seems to be paying off."

"But not having information must be frustrating," she
sympathized.

"Ninety per cent of police work is frustration, five
per cent is sweat and five per cent is the lucky hunch,"
he told her. "So far I haven't had the lucky hunch. Now
we'd better get you back to the convent or we'll have
Mother Dorothy on our tails."

"I'm going to get the bus back," Sister Joan said
firmly. "There is one that drops me off not far from the
industrial estate and it's only a fifteen-minute walk from
there—no, honestly, it's a fine morning and it'll be in
the nature of a treat for me."

"You're not thinking of indulging in a spot of amateur deduction of your own?"

"No, of course not. I promise."

"If that's what you want, Sister. Thanks for coming
down with me."

"Sister Hilaria will be safe in the hospital, won't
she?" she paused to enquire.

"There'll be a police officer with her at all times until

she's well enough to return to the convent. What I'd like to do is put a couple of men on lookout there as well, but the truth is that I can't really spare anyone. One advantage of a place like this is the generally low crime rate; the big disadvantage is that when there is a serious crime we're hard pressed to find extra men."

"There's always Sergeant Barratt," she said demurely.

"Hardworking, competent, meticulous—all the right qualities but so far he hasn't lowered the barrier to let us find anything behind it."

Because he used these qualities to advance his career and thereby avoid the pain of admitting his sexual impotence? She said nothing, not being at liberty to betray a confidence.

"Take care, Sister." His parting salute held an undercurrent of anxiety.

"I will."

Shaking hands, she turned and went with the swift gliding walk of the professed out of the forecourt and along the road to the bus-stop. One of the rare buses of the day was just arriving and she clambered aboard and seated herself by the window.

People watching was always a fascinating occupation. Settled near the door she was able to run her eye unobtrusively over the other passengers. A couple of women with shopping bags, another who sat by herself with a little secret smile on her face—Sister Joan noted the maternity smock over the faded jeans, and smiled too. A first baby perhaps? Eagerly awaited by a loving young couple. It was a pleasant thought to balance against violence and murder.

A group of teenagers shoved their way on, arguing and gesticulating. Sister Joan noticed that they scrupulously avoided the empty seat next to her and rushed up to the back to sprawl over the seats there. The bus driver glanced at them but said nothing. Nobody ever did say anything these days, she thought, for fear of possible retaliation. It was a sad comment on the way the world was going. Yet their brashness might well serve them as armour against greater dangers. The girls who had died had been young for their years, well reared, polite. Their innocence had been no protection. She frowned at her faint, shadowed glass reflection as the bus stopped again.

"Hello, Sister. I didn't expect to see you here," Padraic Lee said in surprise, plonking himself down beside her. "What happened to the convent car?"

"Nothing at all. Good morning, Padraic. I went into town by police car."

"You want to watch it, Sister," he advised earnestly. "You'll do your reputation no good if you ride round in police cars too often."

"Oh, I hope my reputation would stand it," she said solemnly. "Why are you on the bus?"

"Some fool borrowed my pick-up and dented it," he said gloomily. "Not too badly, but I take a pride in that pick-up so it's being seen to and I'm taking buses."

"At which garage?" she asked sharply.

"Do me a favour, Sister," he implored. "Why would I let myself get ripped off at a garage when I can do a fair repair job myself? I thought I'd paint the old girl too. A nice cheerful blue."

"Padraic, have you any idea who borrowed your pick-up?" she asked urgently.

"If I had you'd recognize him by his black eye," he retorted.

"Would you mind if I paid a visit this morning?" she asked.

"Glad to have you visit any time, Sister," he said welcomingly. "We can walk over together if you like."

"Fine. I'd like to have a cup of tea and a chat." She smiled at him, deciding to say nothing yet about Sister Hilaria.

The bus stopped at the corner where the raw, red roofs of the houses on the industrial estate began. Padraic, alighting from the vehicle with Sister Joan at his heels, gave them a scornful look.

" 'Orrible," he pronounced gloomily.

"I'm inclined to agree with you, but people have to live somewhere," she said.

"Me and the wife will stick to our caravan," he said firmly. "The council can grumble about it until the heavens fall down. If they put some money where their mouth is and laid on a decent water supply and a few drains we'd be a lot better off."

"How is your wife?" Sister Joan asked delicately.

"Not too well if the truth were known," he informed her. "Gone to stay with her cousin for a bit. These murders have shook up her nerves."

Which meant either that Padraic's adored wife had vanished on one of her periodic binges or was drying out in some clinic. Padraic himself would never say and she honoured him for his loyalty and regretted that it was spent on someone unworthy of it.

They strode together along the track that straggled to the Romany camp. The caravans, some brightly painted, others faded and in need of repair, the washing lines strung between them, the small bonfires with the cooking pots hung over them, the odorous midden round which the lurcher dogs snuffled, had no place in a clean, sanitized society, but it was her considered opinion that something of value would be lost when the day of conformity arrived. Padraic, less romantic than herself, nodded towards the camp as they approached.

"Smells to high heaven when the wind's in the wrong direction," he said. "The kids don't think much of the new school, by the way. Too many in the class and no Sister Joan."

"I miss them too," she confessed. "Right now I'm helping out with lay duties."

"And with the novices until Sister Hilaria gets on her feet again?"

"You know about that?"

"Give me credit," he said.

Sister Joan, remembering the mysterious grapevine that ensured the Romanies knew about everything that happened almost before it occurred, gave him credit with a questioning glance added.

"Found with her head stove in, wasn't she? I'd've mentioned it but you didn't say anything so I figured you wanted it kept quiet."

"She was hit by a vehicle, fortunately not as badly as you seem to have heard," Sister Joan began.

Padraic was ahead of her, his black eyes kindling as he spoke.

"You think my pick-up hit her? You should've said, Sister."

"I didn't think you were the one driving," she protested.

"Even so . . ." He gnawed his lip for a moment, then relented. "You'd not want the rest of them on the bus to hear our private business. Well, someone borrowed my pick-up and put a dent in it. You'll be wondering whom."

"Surely not one of your people," she said.

To her surprise, instead of agreeing vehemently, he

gave her an uneasy sideways glance, saying, "You take a stool, Sister, and I'll bring out the tea. Gets a bit lonely with my good lady away."

Surely not one of his people, she reflected, seating herself in a patch of sunlight. Poaching, occasional petty thieving, the odd drunken brawl were the limits of their criminality. No Romany of her acquaintance would deliberately run down a nun and leave her there. No Romany of her acquaintance . . .

"There we are then, Sister. Nothing like a cup of tea on a cold morning." Padraic emerged with two mugs and a flowered china bowl of sugar arranged rather touchingly on a tray.

"Nothing in the world," Sister Joan agreed, noting the over-hearty manner.

"One thing I must say," he continued, "is that the kids are getting a good midday meal at that town school. No reflection on you, Sister, because I know you used to feed 'em hot drinks off that little primus, but the school food is pretty good."

"I'm very pleased," she assured him. "Sooner or later all the children would have grown far beyond my teaching powers. But I shall miss them for a while. Padraic, hasn't your cousin recently joined you?"

His swarthy skin had reddened but he answered coolly enough, "Luther? Yes, he's joined us."

"After eighteen months—away?"

"In gaol," Padraic said reluctantly. "And if you're thinking Luther pinched my pick-up then you're way off course, Sister. Luther ain't a thief."

"But he was in gaol?"

She watched the inward struggle mirrored in his face. At last he said, "Can you keep this to yourself?"

"Not if it has a bearing on Sister Hilaria's accident," she said honestly.

"It don't have—doesn't." In moments of stress his carefully articulated sentences unravelled. "It doesn't have, Sister. Luther wouldn't run anyone over."

"Why was he in gaol?" she persisted.

"When I said gaol," Padraic said uncomfortably, "I didn't actually mean gaol. I mean not gaol exactly— more hospital really, for tests."

"Psychological tests?"

"So they call them," he nodded. "Nothing wrong with Luther but nerves . . ."

"Nerves?"

"He gets notions," Padraic said with extreme reluctance. "He gets notions that young girls fancy him and he follows them to give himself the chance of being courted by them if they've a mind. It's a harmless fancy but some folk complained and he was taken to the hospital. He's cured now. He must be else they'd not have let him out, so it hasn't anything to do with anything."

"Where was he in hospital?" she demanded.

"Up in the Black Country. One side of our family camps out by the Wrekin."

"Near Birmingham."

"In that area, yes. But he was never brought up for anything. He agreed to go for treatment, and he's cured of following now."

"I agree with you that it doesn't seem likely he'd have knocked Sister Hilaria down," she agreed, finishing her tea. "Padraic, where's your pick-up now?"

"Beyond the camp under a tarpaulin," he said, obviously relieved to change the subject. "You'll be wanting to take a look?"

"If you don't mind?" Rising, she waited for him to

lead the way beyond the caravans where the few older people sitting on the steps greeted her as she went by, past the shed with chalkmarks still visible on the grass though the restraining string had gone, to the tarpaulin cover stretched over tent poles under which the pick-up truck stood forlornly.

"I've not knocked out the dent yet," Padraic said. "I'm looking for new tyres—well, as good as new but at this time of year and with the recession—it's all money and the lack of it, isn't it, Sister?"

"I'm sure you're right." She stooped to the dented bumper. Whoever was driving it would have hit Sister Hilaria a glancing blow but surely low down. Unless Sister Hilaria, in turning to flee, had tripped and fallen and the truck had swerved towards her, then swerved away again. Panic or design? She shook her head and straightened up again.

"You have to report this to the police," she said. "Before the dent is knocked out. You must, you know."

"Couldn't you report it for me, Sister?" he asked.

"If you like." She nodded reluctantly. "Meanwhile, don't touch it."

"But I don't want the police bothering Luther," he warned.

"But they have to be told," she protested. "Surely you can see that ..."

"What I told you about Luther was in strict confidence, Sister," Padraic said. "Luther never took my pick-up anyway. Why would he when he only had to ask? And he certain surely wouldn't knock down a nun. You'll say nothing, Sister."

"For the moment," she temporized unwillingly, "but if you mention it to Detective Sergeant Mill he'll be able to eliminate your cousin from his enquiries."

"Pardon my frankness, Sister," Padraic said with dignity, "but you don't know what you're on about. There were complaints made about Luther and though he never meant any harm or got into the dock his name's known. Detective Sergeant Mill is decent enough but that new fellow, Barratt, is an unholy terror. Throws his weight about something shocking. Only let him get a whisper and there'd be no peace for poor Luther."

"At least think about what I've said," she begged.

"I'll think about it and you'll tell Detective Sergeant Mill that my pick-up was borrowed and there's a dent in it. Just that, Sister."

"Very well. Unless it becomes absolutely necessary I'll say nothing," she said. Being backed into a corner wasn't a pleasant sensation but there was nothing she could do about it.

"Shall I walk back with you?" he was asking.

"Stay and keep an eye on the pick-up," she advised. "I'll get permission to phone the station and let Detective Sergeant Mill know about its having been taken and damaged. Thank you for the tea."

It was only natural that he should wish to protect his relative from police questioning, but her manner was somewhat constrained as she parted from him. The burden of keeping silent in obedience to his wishes threatened to be a heavy one. She hoped he would change his mind and give her leave to speak.

Meanwhile she could at least point the detective in the direction of the pick-up. That might alert him into interviewing the newcomer to the Romany camp rather more thoroughly, but one couldn't be sure. One couldn't, she thought, gripped by the sense of unease that seemed to overhang her since her return, be absolutely sure of anything.

She had neglected to take the shorter track that would lead her to the front gates of the convent and, either by chance or subconscious design, found herself still on the path that curved towards the Moor School. If she left it now she would be forced to blunder through low bramble and bracken to reach the wider track. She hesitated a moment and then continued on her way, hastening her pace, thankful for flat heels and ankle-length skirt. In her pre-convent days she had sometimes worn high heels despite Jacob's gibes.

"You can't stand being insignificant."

"Neither would you if you were only five feet two!" she had retorted.

When she had decided—or something had decided for her—that she was going to be a nun she had eschewed the orders that clung still to their medieval costumes and approved the neat grey habit of the Daughters of Compassion with its shoulder-length white veil. Practical but without any risk of being mistaken for a district nurse, she had thought, feeling a slight guilt that such considerations should matter.

"You'll not last six months," Jacob had said sourly.

"I'll last for life," she had answered stubbornly.

Yet at that time he might have induced her to change her mind, might have agreed to lay his Jewishness aside instead of insisting that his wife, the mother of his future children, must convert to his faith. And this from a man who cheerfully broke the laws of kashrut and never went near a synagogue. In the end their separate ancestries had proved stronger than their mutual loving.

The schoolhouse had no attendant constable. She went up to the front door and tried it experimentally but someone had locked it and the blinds were drawn down over the windows.

Wasting time definitely wasn't encouraged even though she had been granted a certain amount of freedom. She sighed briefly, recalling the happiness of young pupils spilling out to play on a sunny afternoon, and turned away.

In the high bracken that grew beyond the short, feet-trampled turf, something moved and was still. Sister Joan felt the short hairs at the back of her neck bristle with a knowledge of their own. Somebody watched her from the fastness of the bracken, someone who had ducked down as she moved.

Not a child, she told herself, willing her mind to calmness. A child cast a different aura, something more mischievous. Children didn't watch with an intensity that burned up the space between.

She began to walk slowly towards the track, wishing she were mounted on Lilith or safely ensconced behind the wheel of a car. Out here, a small grey figure in the vastness of moors and sky, she was vulnerable.

Whatever watched her had moved again, was keeping pace still hidden by the tall bracken. Out of the corner of her eye she followed the undulating movement.

"You had better come out."

She had planned on sounding confident and brisk, but her voice wavered slightly as she flung her challenge into the air.

There was absolute stillness again, the bracken holding its breath, and then the tall figure, lank black hair falling in a cowlick over a sallow face, rose up and stood before her, arms hanging at his sides.

"It's Luther Lee, isn't it?"

Oddly though her heart hammered with fright her voice was suddenly cool and steady.

"I wasn't doing no harm," he said in the curious flat accents of a Brummie.

"I am Sister Joan from the convent. I believe I saw you the other evening?"

She had begun to walk on, sensing rather than seeing his loping gait at her side.

"The coppers came," Luther said. "Asking questions. Always bloody questions."

"Yes, well, that's their job," Sister Joan said.

"Persecution," Luther said, and repeated the word with a certain pride as if he had just learned it off by heart. "Persecution."

"What were you doing at the school?" she enquired, increasing her pace slightly, aware as she did so that his strides had lengthened too.

"They found the other one there, didn't they?" He spoke with a dreadful, brooding excitement. "T'other lass?"

"Yes. Yes, they did."

"Like a bride," Luther said. "I like brides in pretty dresses I do. All clean and shiny like apples you bite."

He suddenly bared excellent white teeth in a wide and wolfish grin.

"But she isn't in the school now," Sister Joan said. "The police took her away. There isn't anything interesting for you to see."

"There's you," he said and gave a high-pitched giggle as unnerving as it was unexpected.

"Oh, I'm not very interesting," she answered lightly. "I used to teach at the school, you know? Your cousin Padraic's children were in my little school. Your cousin is a good friend of mine."

"Padraic's a good 'un," he said. "Speaks up for me when they tell lies. They do tell lies. All the women gang up and tell lies. S'not fair they should take my character from me. S'not fair."

"No indeed, but here in Cornwall it will be different."

"Not likely, is it?" He shot her a brief, bitter glance that held in its depths a flash of sanity. "Not when your name's written down. Written down and the doctors taking notes about it. Not right, not fair. Not fair!"

His long arms, raised suddenly, thudded impotently against his sides.

The moor was empty still, the convent only a tiny shape in the distance, unreachable as a mirage. If a car would only come, a solitary walker . . .

"Well, it must be nice to be back with your people again," she said inadequately.

"Nice?" He tasted the word and giggled again. "Fun," he amended.

"I mean—there's Padraic. And his pick-up."

"It got a dent," he said. "Padraic was mad. He's going to do it up lovely."

"Paint it? Yes, he told me."

"I drew a picture once," he confided suddenly. "All coloured and singing. Big red flowers and green leaves, and brown leaves and red leaves and—dead leaves."

"It must have looked lovely."

"How d'ye know?" His black brows lowered over his eyes. "You ain't seen it."

"No, but you just described it and I paint and draw myself sometimes."

"And pray," Luther said.

"Oh, that most of all," she agreed fervently.

"That other one was praying," Luther said.

"Other one?" Sister Joan stopped short and turned to face him. "What other one?"

"The tall one with the bulging eyes. On her knees, praying. Not pretty like you."

"Where was this?" She forced herself to walk on, to speak casually.

"By the gates. On her knees. Praying."

He had moved a few steps ahead of her, stepping into the track, his long shadow barring her way.

"You saw Sister Hilaria?"

"On her knees. Praying is on your knees, isn't it?"

"Yes, but not always." Not at this moment when inside I'm praying harder than I can remember praying for a long time. Without words. Without thought. Only a silent striving for help from anyone, anywhere.

"Luther, have you told anyone about seeing Sister Hilaria?" she asked aloud, moving to the side, skirting around him cautiously.

"They'll send me back to the hospital for following," he said. "It's not right to follow them, you know. It makes them nervy like. But nuns aren't women, are they? Not proper women in white dresses. Like brides."

"I think you ought to talk to Detective Sergeant Mill," she said carefully.

"To the coppers? No, I'll not, and you can't make me." His tone had become petulant, the accents of a sulky child.

"No, of course not, but Sister Hilaria was hurt. You wouldn't want . . ."

"I never meant to hurt her," he said on a high wail. "I put her under the branches. It was off the track away from the road. Safe in the bracken. Are we going to make a hat out of leaves for her like the others?"

"No, we're going to telephone Detective Sergeant Mill and ask him to come over for a chat," she said steadily. "He's—he's not like other policemen. He'll listen."

"I'm not coming anywhere to no telephone." He had stopped, his hands rising, twitching. "Voices say bad things down telephones."

"You don't have to talk on it. I'll call the detec . . ."

"Not your job," he said sullenly. "You pray instead. You go on praying. You let me be."

He had curved his hands together and was staring at them thoughtfully as if some new thought had presented itself. Then he began to giggle on a high, meaningless note.

They were almost at the gates and beyond the gates lay the grounds, the walled enclosure, the main house.

"Think about it," she said clearly and calmly. "Have a little think about it, Luther."

Turning her back again, walking smoothly and swiftly without a backward glance, feeling no alien breath on the back of her neck, no strangling grip, but with the high giggling sounding in her ears and blotting out all other sounds, she gained sanctuary, not daring to run, not daring to look round until she had reached the front door when a glance showed her open gates and empty moorland beyond and the last giggles echoing into the distance.

TEN

✠ ✠ ✠

She felt as if she had been away for days, had lived through a lifetime of new experience, but the others were just filing up the staircase to the refectory. Sister Teresa, bringing up the rear, smiled to indicate that everything had been done. Sister Joan smiled back, composed her face to tranquillity and climbed the stairs.

Today was soup only. She was surprised to discover that her hand shook when she lifted the spoon. Mother Dorothy had already cast her an enquiring glance that demanded explanations later.

Lunch finished and Grace pronounced she began to collect the used dishes, piling them on to the trays, thinking how pleasant it was not to have to scrape wasted food off the china. The rule that demanded everything on the plate must be eaten was a blessing for the lay sister.

"I'll see to the dishes," she informed Sister Teresa. "You go and get on with your studies, Sister."

With hands plunged into hot water it was easier to think. She would have to tell Detective Sergeant Mill about Luther. Not to do so would be tantamount to withholding information from the police. On the other hand by telling him she was breaking her promise to

167

Padraic and might be exposing an innocent man to police harassment.

"Something is worrying you, Sister?"

Mother Dorothy, pausing just within the kitchen door, gave her a sharp look.

"Yes, Mother." Sister Joan reached for the hand towel. "I ought to telephone the police with some information that came to me after my visit to the hospital, but other people are involved. Sister Hilaria is better, by the by."

"I rang the hospital before lunch," Mother Dorothy said. "Sister, if you have information that may be helpful to the police then it is your duty to reveal it whatever the consequences to others. You may use the telephone."

Sister Joan bit her lip. In Mother Dorothy's world there were no uncertainties, very few shades of grey.

"I want to make sure that Detective Sergeant Mill gets my message," she said.

"He being discreet and tactful? Then telephone and find out if he's there at the station."

"Thank you, Mother."

"If he isn't," Mother Dorothy said, "surely there's somebody else equally competent?"

"Competent, yes, but not perhaps fitted by temperament to deal with a delicate situation."

"You, of course, being qualified to judge?"

"Well, no, I suppose not." Sister Joan flushed.

"Make your call."

"Thank you, Mother." Sister Joan frowned as the prioress went out.

She had been given permission to telephone the station, been implicitly rebuked for setting herself as judge, but she hadn't actually been forbidden to do anything.

"Obedience to the rule," Mother Agnes had said, "does not mean mere lip service to its outer aspects. It means following the spirit of the rule."

She went out into the passage where a second telephone, installed for emergency use only, was on the wall and rang the station.

"Detective Sergeant Mill isn't in his office at the moment, Sister. May I take a message?"

She thought she recognized the tones of the constable who had ridden Lilith home.

"Do you know where he is?" she asked.

"Up at the Romany camp, I think. I can try and get hold of him over the car radio."

"No need. I'll go over there myself."

Lilith, she reminded herself as she hung up, required exercise.

Lilith not only required it but was craving it. Saddling up and mounting, Sister Joan felt a pang of compunction. Lilith had grown accustomed to the regular trip to the school. It would be unkind to deprive her now that the school was closed.

With the afternoon had come the eastern wind, flattening the grass and bending the bushes in one direction. She rode sedately down the drive, giving Mother Dorothy plenty of opportunity to forbid the short excursion, but no bespectacled face loomed at the parlour window.

Once out on the moor she gave Lilith her head, only checking her when the pony showed a tendency to take the path leading to the school.

"Not that way, girl. We're off to find the detective," she told her gaily. Too gaily? Was she perhaps in danger of seeking out Detective Sergeant Mill from motives of personal friendship? She examined the possibility as she rode.

There was no doubt that she both liked and respected him, and no doubt, if she were honest, that he, on his side, felt for her an emotion that would grow stronger were she to afford him the slightest encouragement. On the other hand she thought that he too was alert to the danger and in this particular instance, where it involved the breaking of a confidence and the peace of mind of a mentally disturbed individual, she could think of nobody to whom she would have preferred to confide beyond him.

As she reached the camp she was relieved to see Detective Sergeant Mill already in full view, talking to Padraic.

"No need to come checking up on me, Sister," the latter said reproachfully, coming to help her dismount. "I thought over what you said and went and rang the police myself. They're looking at the pick-up now."

"Though not with much expectation of fingerprints," Detective Sergeant Mill said. "However, it means I can pull a couple of men off the task of inspecting all the garages within a fifty-mile radius. That dent on the bumper certainly seems to correspond with the blow Sister Hilaria received to her head. I am fairly certain that she was trying to get out of the way, stumbled to her knees and was caught a glancing blow by the pick-up. What happened then is still unclear. She may have risen to her feet and stumbled dizzily into the bracken—what is it, Sister?"

"I met your cousin, Luther, this morning," Sister Joan said to Padraic. "He—followed me."

"He'd never do any harm," Padraic said protestingly. "It's just his way."

"To follow people?" Detective Sergeant Mill spoke sharply.

"Women," Padraic said, with a heavy shrug that indicated surrender. "Some of them complained—not that he ever did anything to them. Just followed. Shy like. He never got taken up for it, but he went for treatment—psychological treatment."

"Where?"

"In the Black Country. Near Birmingham."

"I know where the Black Country is," Detective Sergeant Mill said, still sharply. "You should have informed me about this before."

"Put the finger on poor old Luther? Why the 'ell should I?" Padraic's "h" was smothered in righteous indignation. "He don't do any 'arm—harm. Just a bit mixed up mentally, that's all. And he never took my pick-up neither. He wouldn't."

"But he did put Sister Hilaria in the bracken and covered her over," Sister Joan said.

Both men stared at her. Then Detective Sergeant Mill said, "Very kind of you to tell me, Sister. You couldn't have made it a bit sooner, I suppose? Rung the station for example? Or did you hope to combine it with a nice leisurely ride on that . . ."

"I did ring the station. You were out here so I decided to come and tell you personally so that you could deal with it in a tactful manner." She flushed. "In future perhaps you ought to question prospective witnesses more closely, and then I'd be spared the job of doing your detecting for you."

"Hold it, Sister." He put up a restraining hand. "Look, my apologies if I lost my temper for a moment. You're quite right, of course. This is obviously something that calls for tact—of which I seem to be woefully deficient at this moment. But you're wrong about not questioning the people here. Sergeant Barratt made what looked like a pretty thorough job of it—not quite thorough enough, it seems, in the light of this new information. I'd better have a word with your cousin, Padraic, and the address of the sanatorium where he received treatment."

"Luther's shy," Padraic objected.

"Then he'll have to get over his shyness, won't he? Good Lord, man, I'm not arresting him. I daresay even you can see that if he was in a position to lift Sister Hilaria up then he would probably have seen who caused the accident. That makes him valuable."

"And vulnerable," Sister Joan said before she could stop herself.

"Possibly that too," Detective Sergeant Mill said. "Padraic, where's Luther now?"

"How d'ye expect me to know?" Padraic demanded, with a brief return to belligerence.

"You're not your cousin's keeper?" the detective said, gently ironic.

"He needs a bit of peace does Luther," Padraic said. "Time to settle down."

"While he's settling he can talk to me," the other said with a touch of grimness. "Sister, you'll excuse my ill manners but I have to get on. Thanks for bringing me the information personally. You ought to have done so immediately . . ."

"I asked her to keep what I said quiet like, for Luther's sake," Padraic interposed.

"And the horns of a dilemma are not comfortable to have to perch upon, eh, Sister?" He gave her a rueful look.

"Not very."

"Then I'll keep in touch. I hope that sensible plans have been made to keep the novices out of harm's way."

"We shall do whatever Mother Dorothy decides. Good afternoon, Padraic."

So much, she reflected as she remounted, for her illusion that she had a special place in the detective's considerations. At the moment he thought of her as a somewhat uncooperative woman who fed him information in her own time and when she judged it expedient. Her mood as she turned Lilith's head towards home was a sombre one.

She jogged home, keeping Lilith's head firmly away from the direction in which the school lay. It was, of course, possible that Luther Lee was far more dangerous than he appeared to be, but her instincts told her a different story. What she needed was a little space in which to jot down the questions and conclusions jostling in her brain.

At this hour the convent was silent, the swishing of brooms and clatter of dishes replaced by the quiet work done usually in isolation within each cell. She unsaddled Lilith and saw her safely into her stall, went into the kitchen where Sister Teresa had evidently dried the dishes and wrung out the cloths, padded down the corridor into the main hall. The parlour door was closed. Mother Dorothy used this period on Saturday afternoons to catch up on her correspondence. If anything further had been heard from the hospital no doubt she would tell it in her own good time. And I, Sister Joan resolved, had better take my judgemental attitudes and my hurt pride and offer it up on the altar of humility.

In the chapel she found, as she almost always did,

the unquestioning, uncritical peace that was always there to be accepted or rejected as one chose. Kneeling, her hands feeling the coolness of her rosary beads, she sought peace.

How to set one duty against another and choose the right path to take? In the cloistered life it was easy because the rule was always there in its shining perfection, but when life flung one into the world outside then the choices began. The trick of it was to strike a balance between the two. Sister Joan sighed, as her fingers completed the fifth glorious mystery. She sat back on her seat and reached for one of the small missals always piled neatly at the ends of the pews. It fell open as she picked it up and her eye fell on the words printed there: "Render unto Caesar the things that are Caesar's." Was that her answer? It was, at any rate, sound advice. She sent up a grateful thank you and went back to the closed parlour door, hesitating for an instant before tapping at it.

"Sister Joan?" Mother Dorothy finished addressing an envelope and looked up.

"Mother, I apologize for interrupting you, but I need advice," Sister Joan said.

"Which I'll give if I can." The other clasped her hands on her desk and gave her full attention.

"You gave me permission to help the police with their investigations if I could be useful and provided that it didn't interfere with my religious duties."

"Yes, I did."

"I've reached the conclusion that I can't be of much help to them without finding myself forced to break other people's confidences to me and the help I do give—it has fed my own vanity too much."

"So you are opting out?"

The colloquialism sounded strange on Mother Dorothy's lips.

"I'm a religious, not a private detective or a police informer," Sister Joan said.

"Or are you a little disappointed because you expected more appreciation for whatever help you have managed to do?" Behind the spectacles the eyes were shrewd.

"You must be psychic," Sister Joan said.

"Unhappily I can lay no claim to any supernatural talents," Mother Dorothy said, "but I received a telephone call from Detective Sergeant Mill just a few minutes ago, giving me the latest news and asking me to apologize for his short temper. He feared that he had given the impression that he was taking your help for granted. I told him that you wouldn't wish your assistance to be regarded in any other way than your social duty towards the community at large. So what is it you're asking me to do? To confine you to the enclosure and remove from your shoulders any responsibilities your unusual measure of freedom affords you?"

"Freedom," Sister Joan said wryly, "is a two-edged sword."

"Then use it wisely and don't turn it against yourself," Mother Dorothy said briskly. "Two young girls have been murdered and one of your sisters in Christ attacked and injured. If you can be useful then be so and don't muddle yourself up with scrupulosity."

"Yes, Mother. In that case may I take it that I can go into town over the next few days as and when I deem necessary?"

"Provided it doesn't interfere with your religious life. So far," said Mother Dorothy with delicate and malicious humour, "your duties as temporary lay sister have scarcely impeded you."

"Yes, Mother."

And serve me right, she thought, as she went into the hall again, for trying to wriggle out of everything when the going gets tough.

Somewhere a small bell rang, signal for the community to cease what they were doing and recite a silent Gloria. Mother Agnes had rung the bell back in the Mother House at regular intervals to create a pattern of tiny reminders; Mother Dorothy favoured the irregular method that kept one in a constant state of alert. There was something to be said for both methods, she supposed.

In the lay cell, where her belongings still looked out of place, she took pad and paper and sat down on the floor, the Gloria said and her attention turned again to secular matters.

Valerie Pendon	Tina Davies
Aged sixteen	Aged twenty-two
Catholic	Catholic
No known boy-friends	No known boy-friends
No diary found. Is there one?	Message in diary speaks of love affair being kept secret. Who and why?

Both left home in the middle of the night, wearing nightclothes apparently. Both found strangled, apparently by wire loop, wearing white dress (bridal?) and wreath of leaves.

Found in school cupboard.	Found in shed at Romany camp.

Sister Hilaria

What was she doing outside the gates?
What made her stumble?
"It ought to have been a donkey?"
        Who took the pick-up?
        Birmingham?

There were other questions but those would do for
now. She read over the sheet of paper with a vague feeling of dissatisfaction. Nothing fitted exactly, but that
might be because she was trying to fit the pieces into a
picture that wasn't true.

She closed her book with a little snap and reached for
her diary. Caesar had been given his due measure of attention. Now she was free to concentrate on her own
halting progress towards the absolute.

At general confession she avoided everybody else
with her scruples and confessed to general inattention
and failure to help Sister Teresa adequately with her duties. Sister Teresa, who, as novice, was excused as yet
from general confession had been parked in the kitchen
with the two novices younger in the religious life in order to prepare supper. Outside the wind dominated the
creeping dark.

At supper, Mother Dorothy checked the reading of
the life of a saint whom few had heard of with a small
gesture.

"Sisters, I have received some advice from the police
detective," she informed them. "The police are somewhat concerned by the lack of security here in view of
recent events. I made it clear that we have not the
smallest need or desire to live surrounded by electronic
gadgets and the like, but in the world today there are indeed elements that threaten everybody, religious or secular. It has been suggested that we get a guard dog, a

young Alsatian that can be trained to patrol the grounds at night and to accompany the sisters should their work take them alone into some isolated corner. I believe the question is suitable for general discussion."

There was a ripple of barely voiced comment. Sister Martha was the first to speak, her thin face flushing as she realized she held the floor.

"I thought that pets were forbidden by the rule, Mother."

"This would be a working dog."

"Working dog or pet, could it be trained not to dig up all my vegetables?" Sister Martha pursued.

"Has anyone ever trained a dog?" Mother Dorothy looked brightly around.

"When I was a girl I taught our canary to say 'God bless you,' " Sister Mary Concepta volunteered."

"One cannot train a dog to do that, Sister," Sister Gabrielle snubbed. "I can't see what canaries have to do with anything."

"It was a very pretty one," Sister Mary Concepta said wistfully. "But a dog would be very nice too. It would be a lady dog?"

"It would certainly be more fitting," Sister Perpetua said, the corners of her mouth quivering slightly.

"Am I to take it that we're agreed a dog might be a good idea?" Mother Dorothy cast her bright glance round again.

"Who would do the training?" Sister David asked.

"There are classes to which one can take dogs— obedience training," Sister Katharine said.

"That might serve, if the budget will run to it." Mother Dorothy shifted her gaze to Sister Joan. "Since you are assisting with enquiries, Sister, perhaps you will ask Detective Sergeant Mill to look out for a good dog—a lady dog—for us? You must make it clear that we shall be willing to pay for one from a good litter."

Sister Joan nodded docilely, not expressing her opinion that Detective Sergeant Mill had more urgent matters to attend than the finding of a guard dog for the Daughters of Compassion.

"There remains the unfortunate business at the postulancy," Mother Dorothy was continuing.

She had evidently acquainted the rest of the community with the facts during Sister Joan's absence since nobody looked puzzled.

"You've heard nothing further?" Sister Perpetua enquired.

"Nothing at all. In my opinion it may have been a practical joke, but one cannot be at all sure. I suggest that Sister Marie and Sister Elizabeth therefore move their things over to the main house for the time being. Better safe than sorry."

Glancing down the table, Sister Joan saw relief on Sister Elizabeth's face, a flash of disappointment on Sister Marie's more piquant features.

"If it isn't a joke," she ventured, "and somebody is coming wouldn't it be better not to discourage them?"

"Are you suggesting, Sister, that I set up our novices as bait?"

"Only if they were willing and of course certain precautions could be taken."

"Out of the question." Mother Dorothy's tone was flat and firm. "These girls are my personal responsibility and I have no right to expose them even to the threat of danger or unpleasantness. Of course if any of the professed sisters is mad enough to go and sleep over in the postulancy at this time then the results must be on her own head, but I hope none of us is sufficiently featherbrained."

But it was not, Sister Joan reflected, actually forbidden. Not that she had any intention . . .

"Sister Perpetua will go with the novices to help them pack what they need and to ensure that the postulancy is locked," Mother Dorothy was saying. "Shall we continue with the reading, Sister Martha? These Roman martyrs offer such a wonderful example to the rest of us."

The reading continued, Sister Martha speeding up since it was her meal that was getting cold at the end of the table.

"There will be recreation this evening," Mother Dorothy announced as they rose. "The last bulletin I received from the hospital informed me that Sister Hilaria is greatly improved. She has been sleeping most of the day but the doctors are pleased with her progress."

It was Sister Gabrielle who asked the question that hovered on the tip of Sister Joan's tongue.

"Has she said what happened?"

"Apparently she is suffering from a slight degree of amnesia, not uncommon in the circumstances," Mother Dorothy said. "She may remember everything in a few days."

And that, thought Sister Joan, beginning to pile up plates, was something that someone wouldn't be able to risk.

"You look tired, Sister," Sister Teresa had paused to say.

"Old age is creeping on," Sister Joan said vaguely.

Her disturbed night's sleep was catching her up. It would be sheer folly to try and achieve anything useful before she had enjoyed her customary slumber. What

was gratifying to recall was that Mother Dorothy had
not forbidden any of the professed to go over and sleep
in the postulancy. Neither had she actually forbidden
any of them to turn somersaults all the way round the
enclosure, she reminded herself, and felt a chuckle rising in her throat.

"Shall I see to this, Sister?" Sister Teresa was asking.
"It isn't any bother, and I like to keep busy. It stops me
thinking about all the dreadful things that are happening."

"Thank you, Sister. I'll go and check on Lilith." Sister Joan slipped from the room and went downstairs
towards the kitchen quarters.

Above her she could hear the subdued murmur of
voices as the sisters took up their sewing and knitting
and settled themselves in the recreation room off the refectory. Sister Perpetua had already led the two novices
out to collect what they would need for a night in the
main house.

Lilith was docile tonight, not troubling to make a run
for it. Sister Joan fed her, checked there was fresh water, promised herself that come Monday morning she'd
muck out the stable properly, and walked on through the
yard past the shelter under which the convent car was
lodged.

Ahead of her a foot struck against stone and she
froze, aware of darkness and the piercing wind that
blew the bushes in the garden.

Not any of the nuns now settled at recreation, nor
Sister Teresa whose shape blocked the uncurtained,
lighted kitchen window when she glanced back to see.
And not Sister Perpetua and her charges.

Her mind having rapidly discounted all these possi-
bilities she took a cautious step sideways which took

her into the deepest shadow of the enclosure wall, and began to tread softly along its length to the gate. Her fingers found the latch and lifted it quietly.

Another step and she was in the garden with its maze of paths and winter-bare beds and gaunt shapes of fruit trees stripped of their autumn bounty.

Whoever walked there had also stopped. For an instant she fancied that she heard breathing but it was only the wind soughing through the branches that spread like black lace against the paler grey of the walls.

"Who is it?" She kept one hand on the gate, raising her voice in what she hoped might sound like a commanding tone.

A bulk of darkness detached itself from the trees and moved towards her.

"Good evening, Sister." The voice was undeniably masculine.

Relief, sweeping over her, made her tetchy.

"Sergeant Barratt, what on earth do you think you're doing, trespassing in the enclosure?" she demanded crossly. "I thought you were an intruder—which, of course, you are. Unless you have permission?"

"Not from your prioress, I'm afraid." Sergeant Barratt didn't sound particularly regretful. "However, in view of the circumstances surrounding the attack on Sister . . ."

"Hilaria."

"Sister Hilaria, yes. In view of that it is as well to check the grounds now and then."

"Not without letting someone know!"

"The police are under no obligation to reveal their methods, Sister." His voice was irritatingly chiding.

"Even so, there is a certain code of etiquette," she

persisted. "Please ask Mother Prioress in future if you wish to—to stake out the enclosure. This is a most private part of the convent."

"I'll make a note of it, Sister." He actually had the gall to sound amused as if he were humouring her.

"Thank you," she said stiffly.

"Perhaps it would be more sensible if you didn't wander about in your own time in the dark," he went on to say.

"I heard you walking here and came to investigate," she returned. "I am not very far from the house."

"And Sister Hilaria was not very far from the gate," he countered. "She is improving, I understand?"

"Yes. Yes, thank God."

"And remembers nothing of the accident. Perhaps she will recall details in a day or two."

"I hope so," Sister Joan said, frowning slightly, trying to bring his face into clearer focus in the dark. The moon had hidden herself and she was trying to talk to a uniformed pillar with a faint shine of fair hair barely discernible in the gloom. But it was certainly Sergeant Barratt; she knew the cold, clipped, unattractive tone of his voice.

"My apologies then, Sister, for startling you," he said.

"I suppose you're only doing your job," she relented. "The truth is that we're all feeling jumpy. Have you— has there been any further developments?"

"Nothing for public consumption, Sister. Shall I walk back with you to the house?"

"No thank you."

So she was now a member of the public. So much for vanity. She felt an unexpected surge of amusement.

"You're quite right, Sergeant. The police have every

right to keep their methods to themselves," she said briskly. "But Mother Dorothy would appreciate it if she were told when our grounds were being patrolled."

"I'd just completed my inspection," he said woodenly. "You'll not be troubled again tonight."

"Thank you, Sergeant." Some impulse caused her to linger, to add, "I had the pleasure of drinking a cup of coffee with your wife, Daisy. Did she mention it?"

"Yes, I believe she did. That was kind of you, Sister."

"Moving to a strange part of the country where one hasn't any friends can't be very easy," she sympathized.

"My career makes it difficult to have close friends," he said. "It was kind of you to take an interest in Daisy, but I've no doubt she will settle down eventually. She has the house and garden to attend."

"That must be very fulfilling to her," Sister Joan said with delicate malice.

"Fulfilment lies in doing one's duty," he said sententiously. "At least I've always found it so, haven't you?"

Sister Perpetua was coming into the garden, followed by the two novices. Her cheerful voice boomed across the dark. "Come along, Sisters. We must get your things into the cells before we go into chapel. Keep close behind now."

"Good evening, Sister." Sergeant Barratt spoke briefly to Sister Joan and was gone before she could reply.

She frowned after him, then went through the gate into the yard again just as Sister Teresa opened the back door and peered out nervously.

"Is that you, Sister?"

"Right here, Sister. You go into recreation and I'll finish up here." She spoke calmly, pleasantly, stepping into the arc of light thrown from within. "I was just checking on the gates. Sister Perpetua's on her way with Sister Elizabeth and Sister Marie."

"Everything's done, Sister. Thank you." Sister Teresa untied her apron and hung it neatly on its hook, hesitating as she reached the passage door to say, "Are we going to lock the back door early tonight?"

"That's a good idea. I'll see to it," Sister Joan said.

She waited while Sister Perpetua bustled through with her charges, then looked out again across the yard. No footstep sounded; nothing moved.

Locking the back door and taking off her own apron, she stood for a moment, irresolute.

Then before she could give herself time to think she went into the passage and lifted the telephone receiver.

Her call was answered at once.

"Police station. May I help you?"

"Would that be Constable Stephens?"

"Yes, ma'am. Is that . . . ?"

"Sister Joan from the Daughters of Compassion. I was wondering if Sergeant Barratt was available."

"Let me have a look at the duty roster, Sister. No, no, tonight he has time off. He doesn't come on duty again until Monday morning. Did you want to leave a message?"

"No message," said Sister Joan and replaced the receiver gently.

ELEVEN

✠ ✠ ✠

On Sundays manual work was kept to a minimum so that in the morning before High Mass there was time for longer private devotions. In the afternoons there was leisure to read, to write letters, to catch up on work left unfinished during the week. Sister Joan enjoyed the Sabbath seeing it as a blank page on which she could write her plans for a week ahead which she hoped to make perfect. That she hadn't yet succeeded in her aim didn't spoil the possibility that one day she might do so.

On this Sunday it was Father Malone who came to offer the mass, and joined the community for coffee afterwards in the refectory. There was something infinitely reassuring about the small, elderly priest in his shabby cassock, Sister Joan thought, sipping her own coffee and watching the two oldest nuns giggling like teenagers as he joked with them.

Catching her eye, he excused himself and came over to her.

"Good morning, Sister. You will have heard that Sister Hilaria is making good progress?"

"Yes, Father. It's good news."

"Apparently she recalls nothing of the accident. Shock, I daresay. The mind puts up a protective shield. I am giving Mother Dorothy a lift to the hospital and then she will have lunch with Father Stephens and myself at the presbytery."

"It will do her good to have a break for an hour or two," Sister Joan said.

"Indeed it will. Being the prioress carries heavy responsibilities. The two girls are to be buried tomorrow. One funeral following another. I understand that a representative will attend from this convent."

"Mother Dorothy hasn't said."

"Mother Dorothy hasn't said what?" The prioress had joined them.

"Who is to represent the Daughters of Compassion at the funerals tomorrow," Sister Joan said.

"I will be sending you and Sister David," Mother Dorothy informed her. "As you already know both sets of parents slightly you seem to be the obvious choice."

"Yes, Mother."

"And Sister Perpetua will be in charge while I am lunching at the presbytery. If you have time this afternoon, Sister, you could take Lilith out for some exercise."

"Yes, Mother."

She had planned to spend an hour sorting out her thoughts on the two murders and on Sister Hilaria's accident, but she could think as well on horseback as in a chair.

Even so it was past three before she had finished washing up and clearing away. Saddling up the pony, she glanced skywards, noting the scudding grey clouds lit by an occasional ray of sunlight. Winter was drawing in steadily. In the spring she would be thirty-seven. Thirty-seven in years and about six years old in common sense, she reflected with wry humour, mounting up and waving her hand to Sister Teresa who had settled herself at the kitchen table with a couple of vegetarian recipe books, presumably in the hope of creating some new and tasty dish for the community to relish.

Hope, she thought, springs eternal and set Lilith at a trot for the main gates. At this end of the year the moors lost their colours, blending into grey and brown with only the occasional red-berried holly bush to remind the world that Christmas was on the way. It would be a sad time for the Pendon and Davies families. Could any parent ever come to terms with the murder of a child?

She took the narrower track that led to the school, partly because Lilith had swerved automatically in that direction, partly because she wanted to talk to Luther Lee again and thought he was more likely to follow her in that direction. To seek for him in the Romany camp probably would be useless, since he would avoid her and Padraic Lee would erect a protective screen for his cousin to hide behind.

The school door yielded to her tentative push and her blood chilled. The police had locked up when they had completed their investigations. Bending to the lock, she saw the telltale scratches where force had been applied.

With an overwhelming sense of *déjà vu* she pushed the door wider and stepped into the passage. On her left, empty hooks and the washbasins and lavatory met her gaze; on the right, the door into the classroom stood ajar. The empty desks and the bare blackboard reminded her of the pupils she had taught there, now scattered into the "big" school, and probably forgetting her rapidly in the way of children.

Someone had entered the room behind her. She heard hurried breathing and slowly turned, pinning a casual smile to her face though her heart had begun to race.

"Good afternoon, Luther. How are you today?"

"Not doing no harm," Luther said whiningly.

"Of course not. Why should you be?" She sat down in the seat from which she had, so recently, surveyed her young pupils and studied him thoughtfully.

"It were hard to get in," Luther said, "but I broke the lock. I can break any lock into any place."

"If you had asked me I could have lent you the key," she told him.

"Then they'd know I was here," Luther said. "I don't plan on anyone knowing. If I stay here they won't find me."

"They? Who are they?"

"Police," he muttered. "Bobbies asking questions—always bloody asking questions."

"If you know anything that can help them," she began, but it was evidently the wrong thing to say.

He shook his shaggy head vehemently, saying in a tone blended from fear and obstinacy, "I don't know nothing and I don't see nothing. You tell them that, Sister. You tell them that."

"But you did see who knocked Sister Hilaria over, didn't you? You were—behind the wall? And Sister Hilaria went through the gate and Padraic's pick-up van came and knocked her over, and drove off as you ran out to help. Was that how it was?"

"I never saw," Luther repeated. "You tell them now when they ask you. I never saw. And you never saw me, Sister. You never did."

"If you're hiding from someone this isn't a good place to be," she argued. "In camp you'd be with your people. Padraic wouldn't let anyone bother you."

She was wasting her breath. He merely fixed glittering black eyes on her, said in a threatening tone, "Don't you tell on me, Sister. Don't you dare!"

"Luther, wait . . ." She half rose, but he had turned and loped out, shutting the door with a little slam.

Sister Joan subsided into the seat again with a muffled exclamation of impatience. Luther knew something important, she was convinced, and with his muddled view of the law preferred to hide rather than speak out. If she went after him now she would only make matters worse. If only Sister Hilaria would remember what had happened. Meanwhile there was no point in hanging round here. She took a last look about the memory filled room and went out again, remounting with the distinct impression that Luther watched from one of the nearby thickets of bracken and bramble.

She completed the ride back without incident and had just led Lilith into the stable when Mother Dorothy came into the yard.

"You will be happy to hear that Sister Hilaria is making good progress," she said briskly.

"Does she remember what happened to her?"

"She recalls going to the gate but nothing after that until she woke briefly in the hospital. The doctor assures me that she will recall the entire sequence of events in time, but this cannot be hurried."

"And there is still a police officer with her?"

"A Constable Stephens, Sister. Apparently what she will have to say when she does remember may have a bearing on these other crimes. At least so the police think. For my own part I shall be glad when this whole unpleasant business is over and we can get back to normal."

"After the funerals tomorrow may I go to the public library?" Sister Joan asked abruptly.

"Yes, of course. I'll inform Sister David so that she can get out any books she requires. Our own library will have to be brought up to date when finances permit."

She gave her briskly dismissive little nod, without questioning further. And if she had asked questions, Sister Joan thought, I'm not sure how I would have answered her, save to say that I'm acting on a hunch.

The rest of the day passed in Sabbath calm. That a killer had struck twice, had probably attempted a third time, that the two novices were now in the main house, were items not mentioned. For Sister Marie and Sister Elizabeth, forbidden to join in the recreation of the professed members of the community, the day must have seemed long as they sat reading in their allotted cells, and helped Sister Teresa to prepare supper—a meal which was as bland as usual despite her reading of the recipe books. It was as if, by unspoken consent, they drew the sanctuary of the cloister around them, shutting out what was unpleasant and frightening.

For perhaps the first time in her religious life Sister Joan was glad when Sunday came to an end and the grand silence heralded the quiet night.

Funerals were not her favourite way of spending a morning, but at funerals one sometimes glimpsed people with their masks torn away for a single, searing moment. Fastening her seat belt the next morning and glancing at Sister David, she said politely, "Did Mother Dorothy tell you we have leave to go to the public library?"

"Yes indeed, Sister, and I'm very glad of it," Sister David returned promptly. "I want to look up some references about Saint Augustine which don't seem to be in our own library. I am writing a series of booklets about the lives of the Saints for children. In alphabetical order, you understand, and one must get the facts right."

"For children?" Sister Joan cast her an interested glance. "That's a change from your usual translations, isn't it?"

"Mother Dorothy feels they might sell well," Sister David said, ducking her head modestly. "Actually it will be quite a little adventure for me to try a new line for a change."

So little Sister David, all timidity and spectacles, occasionally dreamed of change too. Sister Joan, driving towards town, scolded herself for not giving sufficient credit to her sisters for being more original than they appeared on the surface.

Outside the parish church there were two lines of dark cars, two hearses. The two victims were evidently to share a requiem mass. Slipping unobtrusively into a back pew, she prayed briefly, then allowed her eyes to range swiftly over the congregation.

The immediate relatives were at the front; she could see their backs, the dark clothes and armbands of the two fathers, the mothers in veiled hats.

There was a large contingent of schoolchildren in their uniforms, probably from Valerie's old school, neighbours who greeted one another in carefully hushed voices and, conspicuous despite their plain clothes, several police officers. She caught Detective Sergeant Mill's eye and inclined her head slightly. He was escorting Daisy Barratt into one of the pews, his dark head slightly bent. Sergeant Barratt must be on duty elsewhere then.

In front of the altar the two flower-decked coffins lay on trestles. For the two girls, at least, all questions were answered, all fears fled. Bowing their head, she resolved silently that if, through her help, their killer could be found and any further deaths prevented then she would not hold back.

Though the mass had been a shared one the mourners formed two separate groups, the respective sets of parents scarcely glancing at one another. It was as if by acknowledging a parallel grief they feared to diminish the terrible reality of their own loss.

"Sister Joan, are you coming to the cemetery?" Daisy Barratt approached shyly as the processions formed.

"Sister David and I, yes. It's only a short walk. Good afternoon, Detective Sergeant Mill."

"Sisters." He acknowledged them both gravely.

"Detective Sergeant Mill was kind enough to escort me," Daisy said with a little flirtatious upward look. "Mark is on duty at the hospital."

"The hospital?" Sister Joan's voice was sharp.

"With Sister Hilaria," Daisy said. "He volunteered."

"He is certainly conscientious," Sister Joan said. Her mouth felt dry.

"Oh, we get used to being grass widows," Daisy said. "Of course I don't know any of the people here—those poor girls—but Mark felt I ought to come. Oh, we're moving off now. Nice to have seen you again."

They moved off *en masse* in an ungainly procession. The few shops between the church and the cemetery had their blinds drawn down in the old-fashioned way of showing respect. Sister David and Sister Joan brought up the rear, the former with her rosary beads sliding through her prayerful fingers, the latter trying not to think of Sister Hilaria with bandaged head and quiet breathing alone in the side ward with the impeccably correct and efficient Sergeant Barratt.

Each funeral drew in turn to its close. The parents stood, still private in their separate grieving, as the mourners moved from one grave to the next. Nobody from the Romany camp was present which wasn't surprising since instinctively they shied away from death.

"Shall we visit Sister Hilaria before we go to the public library?" she asked, as finally they left the few scattered knots of mourners standing in the bleak wind.

"Mother Dorothy went yesterday with Father Malone," Sister David reminded her.

"It won't hurt to pay a quick call. Mother Dorothy dislikes telephoning the hospital too often so she will be glad of news."

"I'll be glad to see Sister Hilaria," Sister David said. "It leaves a big gap, her being absent from the community."

"Yes. Yes, you're right." There was faint surprise in Sister Joan's voice. Her companion's remark had been a perceptive one. Sister Hilaria drifted through the days, seldom it seemed speaking to any purpose, yet without her there was something valuable lacking from the community.

"May I offer you a lift?" Daisy Barratt, slowing her Mini to a crawl, put her head out of the window.

"Thank you but we're going to the hospital," Sister Joan began.

"I can run you there," Daisy said eagerly. "It will give me the opportunity to ask Mark what he fancies for supper tonight."

"It must be difficult when one's husband is on night duty," Sister Joan remarked as both nuns squeezed themselves in. "I mean, especially on Saturday nights, when most couples like to go out together."

"Oh, Mark and I are terrible stay-at-homes," Daisy said brightly, gripping the wheel tightly as they turned the corner. "We like to watch television and then I have my sewing and Mark has his stamps. He's building up a very nice collection."

"So he wasn't on duty this weekend?" She had spoken too quickly.

Daisy threw her an agonized glance and said on a high, brittle note, "Mark and I spent the weekend together, Sister. He went on duty again this morning."

"Oh." Sister Joan lapsed into silence as they drove into the hospital car-park where Daisy drew to a halt, exclaiming with a note of triumph, "Done it! Since I had it fixed it's been behaving like a lamb."

She would have liked to go with only Sister David to the ward but Daisy Barratt was trotting along behind them and there was no way of shaking her off save through the grossest rudeness.

For a moment she fancied that Sister Hilaria lay alone but then the white-coated doctor who had been bending over her straightened up as they looked in and frowned officiously.

"Visiting hours begin at two," he said sternly.

"We just wondered how Sister was," Sister Joan said placatingly.

"Coming along very nicely as I told your prioress yesterday. Sleeping most of the time but getting nourishment at the right times. We're very pleased."

"Daisy, what are you doing here?" Sergeant Barratt, coming down the corridor, stopped short, barking the question at his wife.

"I was just—I wondered what you fancied for supper," Daisy said. Her face had paled and her hands clutched at her bag.

"Anything that can be heated up quickly. I may have to work late. Good morning, Sister. I didn't expect to see you here."

"Oh, we like to keep an eye on things," Sister Joan said, meeting his cold stare with a sunny smile of her own. "Has Sister Hilaria said anything to you yet?"

"Only that she had a slight headache. Constable Benson is waiting to relieve me. Daisy, surely you have better things to do than run round trying to find out what I want for supper?"

"Yes, of course." Poor Daisy, clearly flustered and embarrassed, was beetroot red. "Yes, I've simply heaps to do. Can I drop you anywhere, Sisters?"

"It's not far to walk to the library," Sister Joan said. "Thank you for the lift here. Is this Constable Benson?" There was relief in her voice as she saw the approaching figure.

"Three minutes late." Sergeant Barratt consulted his watch with another slight frown. "Since he's here I'll follow you back, Daisy. If I don't you'll spend the entire day worrying over what to cook for supper tonight. Sisters."

He had taken his wife as firmly by the arm as if he were arresting her, his only greeting to Constable Benson a curt nod.

"Sometimes," Sister David confided as they left the hospital, "I am more thankful than I can express that I haven't got an earthly husband to please."

"I know exactly what you mean." Sister Joan favoured the arriving constable's stolid back with an almost maternal smile. "Sergeant Barratt bullies his wife dreadfully I wouldn't be surprised. I don't expect to be too long in the library. We can walk back to the car and hope that Sister Teresa has saved a little lunch for us afterwards."

There was always something about the façade of a library that made her heart beat faster. Books—the smell of them, the richness of old bindings, the shininess of new, the delicate illustrations in Victorian children's books, these things excited her in the way a great painting sometimes took her breath away.

Today however her aesthetic sense was not engaged. She was following a hunch born out of random facts and remarks that might lead nowhere.

Leaving Sister David happily poring over an immense *Life of St. Augustine* she went off to the newspaper reference section.

"Birmingham?" The library assistant gave her a helpful, enquiring look. "Are you interested in any particular year, Sister?"

Sister Marie had joined the community about eighteen months before. Sister Joan did a quick mental calculation and hazarded, "The year before last. I need to look through a popular newspaper that reports murders."

It was to the assistant's credit that she never raised an eyebrow but accepted the statement as if nuns came in every day to enquire about murder.

"A tabloid'd be your best source then, Sister," she said. "I'll get one set up for you for the year. All you have to do is turn the dial and the pages flick past."

It turned out to be a little more complicated than that since it took time to set up the apparatus. Eventually she found herself seated before a screen on which the newspaper columns were neatly reproduced.

She was looking for a headline, something connected with the murder of a young girl, something that made sense of the complaints that had been made about Luther Lee, the unfinished comment of Sister Marie about the situation being the same as she had known up north. Up north could mean Birmingham or somewhere in that area. It was, she admitted, flicking the dial swiftly as her eye ran along and rejected the columns of newsprint, the longest of long shots.

In Birmingham and the surrounding districts people fell under buses, were mugged, shot their wives, eloped with their best friends' husbands, gave birth to babies in taxis, had visions of the Holy Virgin, threw toilet rolls on to soccer pitches and presented bouquets to minor royalties opening supermarkets.

Had visions of the Holy Virgin? She flicked the dial back and found the item.

Two schoolchildren whose names have not been released have reported having seen a vision of "a lady" whom both have identified as the Virgin Mary. The apparition appeared to them in the grounds of a local school through which they were taking a short cut on their way home at teatime.

"She was dressed like a nun," one of the children has testified, "but her hair was long and golden and we knew she wasn't real. She came out of some trees and made a big sign of the cross before us. She said God was calling us. We were scared and ran away but when we looked back she'd gone." The school which stands on the site of an Augustinian priory has no record of haunting. The headmistress has made it clear to our reporter that she regards the incident as a silly prank invented by the two girls, aged twelve and fourteen. Both, we understand, are Catholics, but the parish priest whom we consulted informed us that he had absolutely no comment to make.

The item had no follow-up as far as she could see. Whatever their reasons for telling the story the schoolgirls had had no publicity to flatter their egos.

She flipped the dial more slowly, grateful for the ability she had acquired during her years in art college for speedreading so that the kernels of information could be extracted from the surrounding verbiage.

Child Visionary found dead.

She had almost turned past the item before it registered on her mind. She adjusted the dial and read the item with painful concentration.

Fourteen-year-old schoolgirl, Carol Preston from Perry Barr, was judged to have died accidentally at the inquest held on her on Thursday. Carol Preston was found by her father, hanging by a wire noose from a tree in the grounds of her school by two teachers. One of these, Miss Frances James, testified that Carol was a well-behaved and cheerful pupil who was doing well in her studies and had never shown any signs of strain or unhappiness. It was revealed during the course of the inquest that Carol was one of the two girls who, last year, reported having seen an apparition of the Virgin Mary in the grounds of her school, a story which was speedily quashed by the school authorities and not, as far as is known, persisted in by the alleged visionaries. Miss James, however, testified that Carol had remained deeply religious and convinced of the truth of her experience.

John Preston, father of Carol, testified that Carol, a keen science student, had talked recently of ways in which it was possible to "get high" without resorting to glue sniffing or drugs. She had cited the case she had read of an American schoolboy who had accidentally died while experimenting with the "half-

*hanging" believed to induce psychedelic experiences.
Mr. Preston, giving his evidence, stated that he had
warned his daughter of the dangers of such experiments.*

*A rider was added to the verdict, warning against
such practices, and sympathy expressed with the family of the dead girl.*

She read the item over again, her flesh cringing from
the stark image the newspaper account conjured up.
Carol Preston, accidentally dead. Accidentally? No
other person seemed to have been involved. The name
of her companion who, with her, had taken that first
fateful short cut hadn't been revealed. She had expected
something but not this. There were many questions still
to be asked but her instincts told her she was on the
right track though, as yet, she couldn't see the end of
the road.

"Was there anything else you were wanting, Sister?"
The library assistant had returned and was standing respectfully by her side.

"Would you have a list of mental hospitals in the Birmingham area?" If the request was a strange one the
other gave no sign of noticing.

"They'll be in the Yellow Pages of that particular directory. Shall I fetch it for you?"

"And a paper and pencil if you'd be so kind?"

Luther had been a voluntary patient around the time
the girl had died. Were voluntary patients allowed to
come and go as they pleased? That, and another idea
that had leapt into her mind, needed checking.

The relevant directory brought, she hastily copied
down the names and the numbers of mental hospitals in
the area. Then, on impulse, she turned to the schools

section and made swift notes on the Catholic secondary schools in the area. By the time she had finished her watch warned her it was past lunchtime.

Sister David, still happily wrestling with Saint Augustine, had clearly not missed her or noticed the passage of time.

"Did you find what you wanted, Sister?" She dragged her gaze reluctantly from the hefty volume. "This is a splendid work. I could read it all day."

"We can borrow it for a fortnight and take it back to the convent," Sister Joan said. "I think one fills in a form or something. Wait here and I'll see to it for you."

Ten minutes later, with Saint Augustine tucked lovingly beneath her arm, they left the library, Sister David looking as pleased as if she had just managed to decipher the Dead Sea Scrolls.

"This will be a real treat for me," she said confidingly as they made for the car. "Finding out what one never knew before is always an occasion for satisfaction, isn't it?"

"Is it? I hope so, Sister. I certainly hope so," Sister Joan said. Her tone was sombre and, for an instant, her face had lost its brightness.

TWELVE

✠ ✠ ✠

Mother Dorothy took off her spectacles, wiped them carefully with a tissue, and fitted them neatly on her nose again. When she looked at Sister Joan her eyes, magnified by the shining glass, were shrewd and searching.

"You want permission to speak with Sister Marie?" she said. "You know that during the first two years of their training the novices speak only to the prioress and the novice mistress among the professed nuns save in cases of the gravest emergency."

"Two young girls have been murdered and Sister Hilaria run down and left for dead," Sister Joan said levelly. "Someone broke into the postulancy and destroyed part of Sister Hilaria's spiritual diary and left a warning on the front door. I regard that as a case of grave emergency."

"You believe all these things are connected?"

"Yes, Reverend Mother, I do."

"And Sister Marie can throw light on all this?"

"It's possible, Mother, but I can't be sure until I speak to her."

"Very well, Sister. If you consider it absolutely necessary then you have my permission. You may speak to her alone."

Mother Dorothy, Sister Joan reflected, really had admirable traits of character. In her superior's place her own curiosity would have prevailed.

"I hoped to go over to the postulancy and do some cleaning there this morning," she said aloud. "Sister Katharine will want the pillowslips for the laundry."

"And Sister Marie can help you out. I'll tell Sister Elizabeth to help Sister Teresa. Thank you, Sister."

For what? Sister Joan asked herself the question as she withdrew. For finding a killer before the police did? Or would she? Wouldn't it be more sensible to go and see Detective Sergeant Mill and tell him of her discoveries? Was it mere pride that made her want to wrap up the solution in a neat little package and give it to him? She decided that her motives were basically good even if she didn't care to examine them too closely and sought out Sister Marie who, on this Monday morning, she found washing the front step with a somewhat woebegone look on her grave young face.

"Sister Marie, will you come with me over to the postulancy?" she asked. "It ought to be cleaned even though it's not occupied at the moment, and we have leave to converse."

The woebegone look vanished as the novice scrambled up, her eyes lighting.

"I'll get my cloak, Sister," she said promptly and was off at a speed that would have earned her a rebuke had Mother Dorothy come out of the parlour at that moment. Nobody came and she was back from the kitchen in double quick time, fastening her cloak and straightening the large straw bonnet which first and second year novices wore until they were promoted to the dignity of a white veil.

"Did Mother Prioress really say we could talk?" she enquired as they set off through the grounds.

"Provided we say something to the purpose." Sister Joan cast her younger companion a sideways glance. "Mother wasn't suggesting that we gossip."

"No, Sister." Sister Marie's voice was appropriately respectful but her glance was mischievous. "What subjects are considered safe?"

"Anything I choose to talk about," Sister Joan said, veiling the amusement in her own eyes.

Something about Sister Marie reminded her of herself early in her own religious life. There was the same questioning of tradition, the same barely suppressed humour.

"You're not nervous about coming to the postulancy?" she asked as they reached the farther side of the tennis court.

"Because of the threat painted on the door? No, Sister. It's only because I have your company though that I feel like that. Alone I'd be useless."

"Because you've been in the same situation yourself?" Sister Joan turned as she stepped ahead and gave the other a steady look, noting the sudden paling of Sister Marie's face.

"How did . . . ? Yes, in a way, Sister, though I wasn't concerned directly."

"You come from Birmingham?" Sister Joan asked directly, adding as the other hesitated, "I know that one must not talk about one's previous life but when the situation is grave one may do so and Mother Dorothy has given her permission."

"Yes, Sister. Just north of Birmingham, actually. My family still lives there."

"I'm from the north myself," Sister Joan said. "Manchester originally."

"We never lose those flat vowels," Sister Marie said.

"And nearly two years ago a girl died—she was found hanging by a wire loop from the bough of a tree in the school grounds of Saint Roc's Catholic Secondary School."

"Yes, Sister." Sister Marie gave a strangled little gasp.

"Your old school?"

"Yes, Sister. I'd left when the—the accident happened, of course, but I knew the girl who died. She was in the junior school when I was a senior but I did know her."

"You knew Carol Preston?"

They had stopped at the front door of the postulancy whose door still bore traces of the scrubbing the constable had given it. Sister Joan took out the key and fitted it into the lock, letting them both into the narrow hallway.

"Yes, Sister." Sister Marie's young face was very pale now as she followed into the bleak little recreation room. "She was a nice kid. I knew her because she had a small part in a play we put on in the sixth form."

"What play?" Sister Joan asked, sitting down and motioning to the other to do likewise.

"It was a play about Saint Bernadette of Lourdes," Sister Marie said. "Two of the teachers wrote it and I helped to produce it. Carol had a tiny part in the first scene as Bernadette when she was little. Of course she wasn't very old when she had her visions of Our Blessed Lady but someone from the middle school played her then. It was a big success; we raised a lot of money for the Little Way Association. Carol was very good—it was only a little part, showing Bernadette before the visions started, but she did it beautifully. She was a bit disappointed that she didn't get to play the part right through the play. She told me about it. She thought she could act the whole part."

"And then later on when she was in her teens she started having visions herself."

"Not many people knew that she was one of the two girls," Sister Marie said, "but I met her while the fuss was going on and she told me about it. She said that she hadn't been allowed to see visions during the school play but that Our Blessed Lady had come anyway. I ought to have told her she was talking nonsense, but she was so convinced and it seemed a shame to disappoint her, so I told her—I told her that she ought to keep anything else that happened to herself."

Sister Marie broke off abruptly, looking down at her hands.

"And then she was found dead," Sister Joan said gently, "and you blamed yourself for not discouraging her more."

"She always looked up to me," Sister Marie said unhappily. "To tell the truth she had a bit of a crush on me, the way kids sometimes do. I think I could have influenced her. I didn't and obviously something else must have happened and she—died. They said it was an accident but I never believed that. I never believed it because she'd never been the kind of girl to make silly experiments with wire nooses and trying to get a high."

"What about the girl who was with her?"

"Julie someone or other—I only knew her by sight. Carol told me her name and insisted that Julie'd tell me the same story but I never actually asked her about it. When Carol was found dead I felt—anyway soon after that I entered the Order of the Daughters of Compassion."

"Wasn't that a rather severe penance to impose upon yourself?" Sister Joan enquired.

"It wasn't that," Sister Marie said hurriedly. "I didn't rush into a convent because I felt guilty; I don't think anyone ever really does. I'd been considering it for some time but what happened—it was so—sad, so sad and ugly, that it made the world seem a terribly dangerous place—a place where innocence was mocked. I didn't want any more of it, Sister."

"And now?"

Sister Marie hesitated again. "When Reverend Mother told us what had happened to the two girls," she said at last, "it was as if something was starting here that I'd run away from already. I know that they weren't hanging from trees but the wire loops round their necks—it brought back what had happened before—and then Sister Hilaria—she's a mystic and she sees things the rest of us don't see. She really does, Sister."

"And she was seeing Our Blessed Lady?"

Sister Marie nodded. "She mentioned it to us—to encourage us in our vocations, but she told us not to chatter about it. She said that such experiences lost their flavour when they were exposed to public scrutiny."

Sister Joan bit her lip, considering. What Sister Marie had told her might have been mentioned before had the novice not been under obedience to remain silent.

"Sister Hilaria is going to be all right, isn't she?" Sister Marie asked. "We are very fond of her, you know."

"I'm sure she is," Sister Joan said reassuringly. "Right then, Sister, let's collect the linen and then we can give the place a quick clean-up. Between us we can get it done by lunchtime."

Now wasn't the moment to question further. Sister Marie probably couldn't tell her more than she had told her already and the novice was already fretting over her own small part in the Birmingham affair.

Not until mid-morning when they stopped for a five-minute break and the permitted glass of water did she resume the conversation.

"Do you miss your family in Birmingham?"

It was a foolish question because everyone missed her family, but Sister Marie answered readily and politely, "Terribly, Sister. It does get easier as time goes on, but in the beginning I did wonder if I had any vocation at all."

"We all feel the same way," Sister Joan said, smiling at her memory of the acute homesickness that had gripped her during her own novitiate. "I soaked dozens of handkerchiefs, I can tell you."

"But it is getting better," Sister Marie repeated. "I was beginning to—well, to find my feet—and then these things started happening. I didn't know what to do, whether or not to say anything or not. And then Sister Hilaria was so troubled that I didn't want to burden her further."

"Troubled about what?"

Sister Marie considered for a moment, then shook her head.

"I don't know, Sister," she said at last. "It was after she told us about her vision—a few days later. She never does talk very much but she hardly said anything at all. Sister Elizabeth asked if she was well."

"And?" Sister Joan sipped her water.

"She said she had something to work out, that was all. And then she was run over when she was beyond the gates. Sister Hilaria never went beyond the gates even for one yard. Something very important must have attracted her attention."

"It ought to have been a donkey."

"I beg your pardon, Sister?"

"It was something that Sister Hilaria said when she was coming round in the hospital. Did she ever go into details about her vision? Mother Dorothy would want you to tell what you know."

"She didn't say very much about it at all," Sister Marie said, screwing up her face in an effort to remember. "She said that Our Blessed Lady had appeared in the black habit and veil of a nun with a crown of leaves on her head. She saw her for no more than a few seconds, and then the vision was gone. She only told us because she wanted to impress upon us that the most ordinary day can suddenly be touched by glory. That was all, Sister."

"Well, I don't know how it fits," Sister Joan said, "but it obviously does. We'd better get the linen made up for Sister Katharine."

They went up the narrow stairs and began stripping pillows and mattresses. The wind, which had risen, banged against the window panes. There was a greyness over the day.

From the adjoining cell came a cry of alarm, quickly suppressed.

"Sister Marie, what is it?" Sister Joan whipped into the next cell.

Sister Marie was standing by the window, the pillowcase she had been changing dangling limply from her hand.

"I thought I saw . . ." She broke off, her eyes turning to the window again.

"Thought you saw what?" Sister Joan demanded.

"It must have been my imagination. It couldn't possibly be—a man I used to know very slightly."

"Not an old boy-friend, I hope?" Sister Joan tried to lighten the mood. "Mother Dorothy doesn't encourage that sort of thing at all."

"No, of course not." Sister Marie was too agitated to be amused. "About two years ago, no, less—a man, a gypsy, was scaring people in our district—not actually harming them but following the girls around, watching them and then running away. There were some complaints but I don't know if anything was done."

"Luther," Sister Joan said.

"I don't think I ever heard his name. But I'm sure it was the same man, looking up as I glanced out of the window and then he leapt over the wall and ran."

"Luther went into a mental home as a voluntary patient," Sister Joan said. "He came here recently to stay with his cousin."

"Then it was him?" Sister Marie shivered. "He's weird."

"A bit simple and terribly unsure of himself around women," Sister Joan said briskly. "There's no harm in him at all. He's supposed to be cured of his habit of following people. I hope he is."

"Then why was he here?" Sister Marie asked.

"It was probably coincidence," Sister Joan said, mentally crossing her fingers. "People do occasionally stray into the grounds without realizing they're trespassing. Don't worry about it. And don't waste time gazing out of windows when you're supposed to be changing the linen. Now, have you everything ready for the laundry bag? And did you take over everything you need to the main house? I imagine that you and Sister Elizabeth will be sleeping over there again tonight."

"I think so." Sister Marie cast a troubled look out of the window and bent to open the small locker by her bed. "No, I've remembered everything. Oh, I have some photos of my family in this big envelope—may I take them?"

"I don't see why not."

The modest reminders of home that the novices were permitted to keep were precious.

Sister Marie took out the envelope, then said impulsively as if the idea had just struck her, "I forgot all about it, but I have the programme for the Saint Bernadette play we put on. I kept it as a souvenir because I helped to produce it. Would you like to see it?"

"Yes, I would."

Taking the neatly typed programme with its black and white sketch of the grotto at Lourdes, Sister Joan read it with interest. Here and there a name she had heard jumped out at her—Carol Preston as Bernadette Soubirous as a child ... Marie Brown as co-producer ... Flowers by courtesy of St. Roc's Convent ...

"Sister, may I borrow this for a while?" She spoke abruptly, her eyes still on the typed page. "I promise to take good care of it."

"Yes, of course, Sister. It was a bit vain of me to keep it, I suppose, but I did enjoy working on the play. Is it important—the programme, I mean?"

"I'm not sure," Sister Joan said honestly. "It's given me an idea, that's all."

"Are you really helping the police with their investigations?" Sister Marie asked curiously as they went down the stairs again.

"In a strictly amateur capacity," Sister Joan assured her. "I happened to be the one who found Valerie Pendon and then Tina Davies was found while I was talking to the detective and I was needed to confirm whether or not she had been left in the same position as the other one. And now, well, with no school to teach I am not the most useful member of the community at the moment, so if I can help out with Mother Dorothy's permission then I do so, of course."

"Under obedience," Sister Marie said. Her eyes were amused.

"Under obedience," Sister Joan said, for once not returning the other's smile.

They went down the stairs together, and Sister Joan locked the front door. If anyone watched as they crossed the tennis court, carrying the laundry bag between them, she wasn't conscious of it.

"Am I to tell Reverend Mother what I told you?" Sister Marie enquired.

"If she asks you."

"And you really think that you know who's doing these things?"

"No, of course not, and it would be very wrong of me to start guessing out loud," Sister Joan said impatiently, and glancing at her companion's face gave a reluctant chuckle. "Sister, you don't think that I'm the one with the proof who gets murdered just as she's about to pass it on to someone else, do you?" she exclaimed. "Things don't happen like that in real life."

"I suppose not." Sister Marie looked marginally more cheerful. "Sister, I do feel easier in my mind since we talked. I have been wondering for ages if what I said to poor Carol encouraged her to go on believing that she had a vision—and all the time it must have been someone pretending to be one, mustn't it?"

"I doubt if anything you said or didn't say would make any difference," Sister Joan said robustly. "Take the laundry to Sister Katharine and then come to lunch."

"Can we go on talking?"

"No, Sister." She firmly quashed the hopeful gleam in the other's eyes. "I had permission to speak to you on a particular topic. General chatter wasn't included."

"And that's the hardest thing about being a novice," Sister Marie said plaintively. "You know I never did talk a lot before I came here and now I keep thinking of all kinds of things I want to talk about."

"Then I'll remove the temptation," Sister Joan said severely, concealing a smile as she turned in the direction of the chapel.

There was time for an Our Father before she started laying the table. She knelt in her accustomed place, her hand as it reached for her rosary touching a corner of the folded programme she had tucked into her deep pocket.

The events of the past few days had had their own subtle, insidious effect. What little conversation there was centred upon Sister Hilaria's progress and how soon she might be expected back into the community. Now and then glances were shot towards the two novices who would be sleeping in the main house again. Only old Sister Gabrielle struck an inadvertently lighter note when she enquired, "How soon do you think it will be before someone else is murdered?"

"Really, Sister." Mother Dorothy glared down the length of the table.

"Well, these things go in threes," Sister Gabrielle said serenely.

But there have already been three, Sister Joan thought, as Sister Martha began to talk about the bless-

ing of having root vegetables in winter. Sister doesn't
know that. I wonder if the police do.

"Sister, will you take the car and get the shopping
this afternoon?"

She jumped slightly as Mother Dorothy addressed
her. The request saved her having to ask for permission.

"Yes, Mother. Of course." She was about to continue
when the prioress broke in smoothly.

"Then if you have any other business in town you
can kill two birds with one stone, so to speak."

"Thank you, Mother." Making her way downstairs
with a tray of empty soup bowls, she ran her plan of action swiftly through the sieve of her thoughts.

She could, of course, go immediately to see Detective
Sergeant Mill and tell him her theory, but trying to play
Holmes to his Watson struck her as absurd. The police
were too busy to be able to spare time for women with
ideas that were not even half proved. Everything she
had heard was merely circumstantial.

"We need spaghetti, Sister," Sister Teresa reminded
her.

"And cheese." Sister Joan made the necessary addi-
tions to her list. For fruit and vegetables the community
relied on its own resources. Fish they occasionally
bought but Padraic frequently supplied that need, and
bread was baked on the premises.

"Spaghetti," she said aloud, her tone unconsciously
wistful, "should be served *al dente* with a cheese sauce
flavoured with basil and thinly sliced tomatoes and a
bottle of good red wine."

"I'll try," Sister Teresa said nervously.

Sister Joan, her mind filled with a sudden, sensuous
image of meals enjoyed years before with Jacob,
laughed as she went out. These past memories were not

lessening but the pain they had once brought was diminishing. Nowadays she remembered only the joyous times.

She drove sedately through the front gates, fixing her mind deliberately on the few groceries to be purchased. Sister Perpetua had always relished her monthly excursions into town. She would be glad to resume them when Sister Hilaria was well again.

There were still a few shops where it was possible to buy things without having to drag round a wire basket. The Sisters were loyal to these small businesses though she suspected they might have saved money by going elsewhere, but it was still nice to be treated with courtesy as if one were a person and not a face in a queue.

She bought the spaghetti, sampled and bought some cheese, and added a small jar of olives in a gesture of unashamed luxury.

When she got into the car again the windows were misted by fine rain. Autumn had slipped away without fanfare and winter peered over the horizon.

"So whither now?" she enquired aloud of herself. She could drive to the police station and insist on speaking to Detective Sergeant Mill who, lacking further proof, might snub her as he had every right to do; she could call at the hospital and find out if Sister Hilaria was awake. This latter course struck her as the most potentially fruitful and she drove there briskly.

To her relief it was Constable Stephens and not Sergeant Barratt who rose from the chair by the bed, and greeted her.

"How are you, Sister Joan? Bent on errands of mercy?"

"Just looking in at Sister Hilaria." Instinctively she had lowered her voice.

"She's awake, Sister," he answered cheerfully. "She dozes off and on, but she hasn't had much to say."

"Sister, how do you feel?" Going to the bed, taking the policeman's vacated chair, she bent forward slightly.

"Much better," Sister Hilaria said, weakly but firmly. "Everybody has been very kind. Most kind."

"You've made good progress, thank God." Sister Joan laid her hand briefly over the other's. "Of course we've all been praying for you."

"The novices?" Sister Hilaria hitched herself higher on the pillows. "Sister Elizabeth and Sister Marie? Are they . . . ?"

"Oh, they're both anxious for you to return," Sister Joan assured her, "but Sister Perpetua is deputizing for you at the moment."

"I told them about the vision," Sister Hilaria said, her pale face troubled. "I never do speak of such experiences, as you know, but sometimes it is good to remind the young ones of the joy of a vocation, of how near heaven is to earth."

"The vision of Our Blessed Lady?" Sister Joan said cautiously.

"Yes, but—it wasn't. It wasn't what I thought it was."

"I don't understand, Sister. You mean you were mistaken?"

"Mistaken? Yes, very much mistaken," Sister Hilaria said. "Our Blessed Lady rode a donkey. She did ride a donkey."

"Yes. Yes, so we are told."

"Or walked. There were no motor vehicles in those days. Even if She were seen today one cannot imagine Her on a bus or in a pick-up."

"A pick-up?" Perhaps she had spoken too sharply.

The older woman's lips were suddenly pressed tightly together.

"You went outside the gates." Sister Joan resumed on another track.

"Oh, that was a bad example to set," Sister Hilaria said sighingly. "I was supposed to take the novices across to the main house for a talk from Mother Dorothy, as I usually do. They were writing their spiritual diaries and I went out for a breath of air."

"Surely there's no harm in that?"

"No harm and it was only to the gates. I stood there and then I saw ..." Sister Hilaria stopped abruptly, tightening her lips again.

"Yes?"

"I cannot tell you more Sister Joan. I gave my word," Sister Hilaria said.

"But why shouldn't you tell me what happened?" Sister Joan asked in conclusion.

"Mother Dorothy wishes me to keep my own counsel," Sister Hilaria said. She was drifting into sleep again but her voice remained firm. "It's a question of obedience."

THIRTEEN

✠ ✠ ✠

When it came to a question of obedience Sister Hilaria couldn't be moved and she would be wasting her breath. She stayed a few moments longer, giving the novice mistress encouraging titbits of news about the splendid way the novices were coping, and was surprised to startle a chuckle out of the older woman.

"Sister Marie is quite an original, isn't she? Always ready to drop everything and comment upon the human condition. Sometimes I am hard put to it to answer her queries. Now Sister Elizabeth accepts everything she is told without question. Both of them have strong vocations but I visualize Sister Marie as a future prioress."

"I didn't realize . . ." Sister Joan flushed and stammered herself to a stop.

"That I evaluated the novices?" The pale, prominent eyes were amused. "Dear Sister Joan, but I would be a very bad novice mistress if I spent all my life in the enjoyment of private revelations and neglected the needs of such ardent young souls."

"Yes, of course, Sister Hilaria."

Rising to leave, Sister Joan felt an unwonted humility. It was so easy to put others into neat little categories and leave them there, without troubling to discover other facets of their personalities.

But for the moment she had work to do. She went back to the car and sat there, studying the programme in her pocket and the list of mental homes that she had culled from the library. Later on there would be a telephone call to make but she would be better able to control the expression on her face if she didn't have all the relevant information.

She drove slowly out of the town, taking the road that led to the industrial estate, resisting the temptation to call in at the police station and seek out Detective Sergeant Mill. While she was talking to him other evidence might be destroyed.

The houses with their raw red roofs and half-finished gardens were like a rash over the hillside. She reminded herself that to the families who lived there the characterless houses probably represented security and happiness. In thirty years' time the estate would have mellowed, blended into the landscape. Perhaps a sense of real neighbourliness would have grown up.

Daisy Barratt must have been polishing the windowsill or something since she had opened the front door before Sister Joan had set foot on the path.

"Good afternoon, Sister. Nothing wrong, I hope?" Her hands twisted nervously.

"Nothing at all," Sister Joan reassured her. "I happened to be passing and thought I would call. Is it inconvenient?"

"No indeed, Sister. I'm very pleased to see you. How is Sister—Hilaria?"

"Much better and due to be discharged very soon if I read the signs aright." She stepped into the shining little hall and stood as Daisy closed the door.

"So soon? Then she wasn't seriously hurt?"

"Only her memory." Sister Joan followed the other

into the spotless dining-room. "She has no memory of the accident yet. Well, not any memory she has confided to me anyway. That was a very nasty blow on the head though. It does look as if she was hit by the pick-up truck from the Romany camp. It isn't a large truck but still one wouldn't like to be run over by it."

"I told my husband that it was a disgrace to have those gypsies allowed to wander all over the place," Daisy said, running the edge of her hand across the highly polished surface of the table. "Unhygienic and immoral."

"They really aren't as bad as many people imagine," Sister Joan said. "Once you get to know them they seem almost like everybody else—except for poor Luther of course. He is certainly a trifle peculiar—a little lacking in his wits, I fear."

"I don't know any of them," Daisy said. She sounded prim.

"Well, they provide a certain amount of colour, I suppose," Sister Joan said.

"Will you have a cup of tea, Sister?" Daisy glanced towards the kitchen door.

A cup of tea would have been nice but she doubted if she could stand the fuss and bother that went with it.

"I really haven't time. I merely called in on an impulse, just to find out how you were. Have you made any friends yet?"

"Oh no, Sister." Daisy looked even more prim. "No, indeed I haven't. I came to the conclusion that it really is much better to keep myself to myself—on account of my husband's position, you know. He has always been very strict about that and I may be out of date but I do feel one ought to obey one's husband."

"Then you must have a lot of time on your hands."

"Oh no, Sister." Daisy shook her head. "There's the cooking and cleaning and the shopping and the planning of the garden and—no, I have very little leisure."

"It seems to be a sad feature of modern life," Sister Joan said. "I mean today we have all kinds of electrical gadgets they never dreamed of a hundred years ago, and yet our ancestors seemed to have time for so many things—watercolours and lace-making and tapestrywork and that white-on-white embroidery that looks so delicate."

"I'm afraid I don't sew at all," Daisy said.

"Such a nice way of passing the time. One of our novices looks to me as if she might be talented in that direction—long fingers, you know. I've had a little more to do with the novices since Sister Hilaria was hurt. Sister Marie—but you may know her. She comes from Birmingham."

"Birmingham is a very large place."

"Perry Barr, I believe," Sister Joan said.

"Perry Barr?" Daisy wrinkled her forehead slightly. "No, I can't say that I know . . ."

"A nice child anyway," Sister Joan said. "A trifle too apt to chatter but that's a habit she will learn to control. Which reminds me that a pot ought not to call the kettle black. I've the shopping to take back and you must have lots to do."

Exactly what those would be since the entire house appeared to be in pristine condition she couldn't imagine, but Daisy was nodding and opening the door and then she herself was in the short driveway again. She turned to lift her hand in farewell but the front door was already closed again.

There remained only the telephone call. A kiosk, fortunately not vandalized, stood on the corner where the road joined the track to the moors and the Romany camp. She stopped the car and went in, pulling the door shut, checking the number, sacrificing some of her monthly pocket money in what she thought wryly was rather like a peace offering to her conscience. Not that she had any intention of telling lies and Mother Dorothy had given her permission to act as she saw fit, but she was certainly going to prevaricate a little.

When she came out of the kiosk she was paler than before but quite composed. What she had begun to suspect from the flotsam and jetsam of information she had garnered was proving to be true. The jigsaw was falling into place. The thought of it gave her no pleasure.

"Are you all right, Sister?" Sister Teresa gave her a worried glance as she carried her purchases into the kitchen. "You look tired."

"Don't remind me of my advancing age, Sister." Her joke was half-hearted and she was forced to smile a little too widely. "Put these away for me, will you? I want to go into chapel for a while."

Want? Need? When did one become the other? Kneeling, her hands tightly clasped, she sent her problem into the silence and received silence back again.

When she finally rose her chin was tilted in the way her two brothers would have called "our Joan's mulish look." All the tiny pieces fitted but separately each one might be explained away especially by someone with a vested interest in the result. There was no point in telephoning the police station.

"Sister Teresa?" Returning to the kitchen, she addressed the other.

"Yes, Sister?"

"Will you make certain that the two novices don't leave the house during the recreation period after supper?" Sister Joan asked. "Keep them both indoors and don't leave them."

"Yes, Sister." The other gave her a faintly puzzled look but asked nothing further.

Sister Teresa was a treasure, she reflected. A sound, honest young woman who would make an excellent nun. While the professed sisters were at recreation she would guard them unquestioningly as faithfully as any watchdog.

There remained Sister Katharine to see. Leaving Sister Teresa to get on with cooking the supper, she went in search of her and found her where she usually was, seated on the floor of her cell, engaged in the embroidery of a cope ordered by a provincial bishop.

"Sister, forgive me for disturbing you but may I borrow the keys of the linen cupboard?" she asked.

"Yes, of course, Sister." Sister Katharine detached them from their place on her belt. "Is there anything I can get for you?"

"No thank you, Sister."

Sister Katharine who was blessedly uncurious nodded amicably and drew a silver thread through green silk with an air of absorption.

The linen cupboard so called was actually a small room on the upper floor, its walls lined with deep shelves on which the sorted and numbered linen was laid. It smelt of soapflakes and sunshine and there was a tactile delight in the handling of cotton and starched linen. She stepped to the section where the clean habits lay and took out one of the pink smocks that the novices wore while they spent the first two years in the postulancy. There was a spare bonnet, deep brimmed and of straw, on a higher shelf. She took it down, wrapped both bonnet and smock in a sheet and left the room. She would return the keys later. The word "later" had a pleasantly optimistic ring. She repeated it mentally as she went downstairs again and left both garments and keys in the lay cell where she now slept.

Nothing now remained but to wait. Waiting, she decided, was one of the hardest things in the world to do. She started piling up dishes and getting out knives and forks. At such a time it was better to force one's concentration on to mundane matters.

Supper passed with Sister Perpetua reading some of *The Interior Castle* by Saint Teresa of Avila. Much as Sister Joan relished the brilliance and humanity of that great work she would have preferred something less daunting as she ate her supper. When it came to the exploration of her own interior castle she had the uneasy notion that she was still sweeping the rubbish out of the courtyard.

She sent Sister Teresa a reminding glance as the other collected the two novices and bore them down to the kitchen. She was confident that Sister Marie and Sister Elizabeth would be safe while she herself took her place in the semi-circle and tried to take an intelligent interest in the various unexceptionable subjects that Mother Dorothy raised as suitable subjects for conversation. By common consent nobody spoke of the murders though Sister Gabrielle remarked obliquely, "Isn't it odd how at recreation we always end up chattering about things we have not the slightest interest in?"

Sister Perpetua cast the old lady an apprehensive look and launched into a somewhat muddled account of a holiday one of her nephews was thinking of taking.

"A very lovely country if I could only recall its name. But they alter so."

"Time for chapel." Mother Dorothy brought recreation to an end.

Sister Joan, who had worked only a few rows of the scarf she was knitting, put wool and needles back on the table with relief and filed down the stairs with her companions. She felt a rush of relief for a different reason when, entering the chapel, she saw Sister Teresa kneeling with her fellow novices.

The service proceeded calmly along the usual lines. No shocks or surprises to mar the cadences of prayer and worship. Part of her stood aside and marvelled that nobody turned to give her a puzzled glance. Surely someone could sense the turmoil inside her.

It seemed not. Mother Dorothy rose and went to the door to give the great blessing; the grand silence fell like a curtain over any possibility of conversation.

In the lay cell she swiftly changed her grey habit and white veil for the smock and straw bonnet worn by the novices during the first two years of their training. Her fingers fumbled with the strings and she was aware of her heart beating rapidly.

Perhaps she was being a fool? Perhaps nothing would happen, no one come, or perhaps even now as she scribbled a hasty note and pinned it to the back of her door the last moments of her life were ticking inexorably past.

And that, she told herself scoldingly, was ridiculous. She had always been capable of talking her way out of anything, according to Jacob. Strange that she should think of Jacob now, his clever, dark face, his obstinacy, his gift for making other people look at the world in a different way.

She opened the door and looked out into the kitchen. There was still a faint warmth lingering from the old-fashioned cooker and through the uncurtained window the faint greyness of emerging moonlight. She unbolted the door, tensing as it grated a little, and stepped into the yard. For a moment she stood, feeling the cold as it swept through her smock, wishing she had had the forethought to bring a cloak. Then she dipped her head and set off across the yard into the enclosure. The heavy torch was hidden against her side. As a last resort it might serve as a defensive weapon, but she prayed silently it wouldn't be necessary. Meanwhile she didn't reveal its existence by switching it on, but found her way by moonlight and memory through the gates, past Sister Martha's vegetable plot and neatly pruned roses and the tiny cemetery where other sisters slept even more soundly than those in the main house and went down the steps into the sunken tennis court.

So far—nothing. Not a footfall save her own ruffled the silent ground. Apart from her own somewhat ragged breathing there was only the wind as it swooped down to rusting posts and a tangle of broken net.

She had reached the postulancy. It stared blank eyed from behind the low wall. Her own novitiate had been spent in the London house where the postulancy was a separate wing and not a separate building altogether. She had taken the spare key from its hook and used it now to open the front door. It was a pity that she didn't have a dog with her, she thought suddenly. There was something very reassuring about a large, padding dog with a rough warm coat.

She closed the door behind her with a slight and deliberate bang. It was time to advertise her presence, to tell whoever might be lurking within earshot that the postulancy was occupied again. There was a lamp just within the door. She lit it and carried it up the narrow staircase to the cells above. Whoever had stolen the pages from Sister Hilaria's spiritual diary had almost certainly been forced to look into all the rooms in order to find the right one. Sister Joan hoped they had noticed some evidence of Sister Marie's occupancy of her own particular cell.

She entered it now, setting down the lamp, moving the blind an inch so that its gleam was visible beyond the window, going to the bed to turn it down before she slipped quietly out of the cell again and went noiselessly down the stairs into the tiny kitchen where she drew back the bolt on the door.

Now there remained only the waiting. She backed out of the kitchen and went up the stairs again. She would wait for two hours. After that Daisy Barratt would surely be missed from her bed.

Daisy Barratt with her bullying, impotent husband, her lack of friends, was also the only person connected with the events in Birmingham two years before and the murders of Valerie Pendon and Tina Davies. And she had lied. Sister Joan drew the programme of the school play from her pocket. At the bottom below the cast list, neatly typed, were the names of the backstage crew— Lighting, Prompt, Scenery, Wardrobe Mistress and— Costumes designed and made by Daisy Smithson. Daisy had said she couldn't sew. One small, apparently unimportant lie in the course of a casual conversation might mean nothing but was more likely to mean a very great deal. Taken in conjunction with the telephone call she had made to the mental home it added to the weight of evidence. That brief telephone call echoed in her memory.

"This is Sister Joan of the Order of the Daughters of Compassion. I am making enquiries about an acquaintance of mine, a Mrs. Daisy Barratt? Would it be all right to visit her?"

A moment's silence, the rustling of papers and then at the other end of the line a polite voice.

"Daisy Barratt? I'm afraid you're a little late, Sister. She left us a couple of months ago. Oh yes, she seemed very much better. Fortunately, depression is often quite easy to treat these days."

And Luther Lee had been in the same hospital during the same period. It was no wonder that Luther had gone to ground. Luther too had seen what Sister Hilaria had seen just before she had been knocked down.

It was colder inside the postulancy than outside.

She folded the programme and slipped it back into her pocket, then took a firmer grip on the comforting torch. Whether she would be able to bring herself to use it if it became necessary was something she hadn't yet dared to think about too closely. She prayed silently that she would never be called upon to make the decision. Quietly talking to an unbalanced person usually achieved positive results; at least that was what she had always read. With a little shock Sister Joan realized that in her whole life she had only once been in the situation of talking to an unbalanced person in order to diffuse potential violence. Now she was relying on one brief experience—staking her life on . . .

Her head which had begun to droop jerked upright. The religious life made one used to early nights, she thought ruefully, and shook her head to clear away the mists of sleep. It was essential that she remain awake and alert.

Her ears, straining to catch some sound beyond the coasting wind, caught the soft scrape of shoe against stone. Instantly she was on her feet, her eyes now accustomed to the gloom, fixed on the kitchen door. The handle was turning slowly, tentatively. Then it was released again with a sharp little click. She didn't know if she imagined the soft padding of retreating feet or not.

Someone had tried the door handle and gone away again. Daisy Barratt was a clever woman, one accustomed to avoiding discovery. Only one person must have known of her connection with the Birmingham schoolgirl who had died, must have hastily arranged for her to enter a mental hospital for treatment, had moved from the stresses of his job in a large city to a rural post, had spent his evening off searching the convent grounds for any clue that might lead his superior officer to the truth.

And how, she asked herself silently, could I go to Detective Sergeant Mill with what amounts to nothing more than a few pieces of circumstantial evidence? Whatever solid evidence may exist would have been suppressed by Sergeant Barratt anyway.

There was no point in sitting here any longer. Daisy had been suspicious of the unlocked door and gone away again. She could wait here all night and nothing would happen. Rising from the stool where she had been crouched, she went to the door and gently slid the bolt into its socket. She would go out of the postulancy by way of the front door and return to the main house, drawing her pursuer after her.

Time for one winged prayer that rose through the gentle moonlight as an urgent reminder that she herself, of her own power could achieve nothing, and then she had closed the front door behind her and passed through the gate into the sunken tennis court.

Her shadow ran ahead of her along the ground. A distorted shadow, made more grotesque by the outlines of the poke bonnet she had donned. She wondered if she had been recognized or if Daisy Barratt believed that it was Sister Marie who wandered through the grounds. She had no idea. She knew only that at the extreme rim of her vision another shadow had joined her own and kept silent pace as she walked briskly across the tennis court and up the steps into the enclosed garden.

In the moonlight the simple white headstones in the little cemetery gleamed like ivory. She glanced at them as she went by the low hedge and saw the swift flicker of movement as someone ducked down behind it.

She was safely through the garden and walking rapidly towards the main house. She would have more chance here of being heard if it did come to a struggle. It had perhaps been a mistake to go across to the postulancy but it did seem to have lured her pursuer closer to where others might hear and help.

Lilith whinnied softly from within her stable as Sister Joan went past. The moonlight didn't pierce so far and there was a cavern of deep shadow in which a darker shadow stood. She longed to turn her head and look directly at this other but it was too risky. The final confrontation had to settle the matter once and for all.

She opened the back door, allowed herself to draw one long, quivering breath of relief and then was in the warm kitchen again. Outside the soft footfall rang gently against the cobbles and she half turned just as from behind the door a figure reared up.

Something was round her neck, something that had caught on the brim of her poke bonnet but was inexorably tightening all the same. She hit out wildly with the torch but it spun from her hand and then her hands were at her own throat, last desperate barrier between her flesh and the loop of strong wire that had been thrust over her head.

The torch struck against the cooker and sent a pan clattering down. She kicked out wildly again, aware of the wire cutting into her fingers, of the wind swinging wide the door, of footsteps running. Running from both directions, she thought, as they converged and someone called out:

"You mustn't hurt people. That's a bad thing to do."

The light snapped on with brutal clarity and the intolerable cutting pressure on her fingers ceased. Daisy Barratt, the veil of her nun's habit half torn from her head, was struggling in Luther's grip and Sister Gabrielle stood by the light switch. For an instant they were tableau'd like a Hogarth print and then Daisy tore herself free and ran.

She ran, not through the back door but the other way, blundering into the short corridor beyond, her voice rising into a screech as she called, "Come out and see me. Come and see me. I am going to find you, Sister Marie."

Sister Joan tore the loop from her neck, dislodging her bonnet in the process and stumbled to the inner door. Daisy Barratt had reached the main hall, had her hand on the newel post of the balustrade, one foot lifted to the lowest step.

From the antechamber leading to the parlour a voice spoke sharply, with the habit of old authority.

"Do exactly as I tell you and stay where you are," Sergeant Barratt said.

"But they have to be punished," Daisy said, half turning, her face a white and terrible mask within the disordered frame of her veil. "They can all have babies but they won't. They deny life and lock themselves away.

And that's not right. If no babies are born the human race will die out. We cannot allow unnatural behaviour. We cannot allow that, you know."

"You are to come with us," said another voice. Detective Sergeant Mill had emerged and stood, poised and calm.

There were other policemen in the hall and somewhere among them the small, indomitable figure of Mother Dorothy. Daisy looked at them all blankly and then moved her head slightly to look at the newel post she was gripping so tightly.

"This must be cleaned first," she said. "We cannot allow smears, you know. I'll come as soon as I finish polishing."

And with the edge of her veil began slowly to rub away the faint imprint of her sweating palm.

FOURTEEN

✠ ✠ ✠

Mother Dorothy looked round at the semi-circle of attentive faces and folded her hands neatly together. She looked slightly drawn but otherwise showed no sign that she had passed what must have been an almost sleepless night. Neither, thought Sister Joan, did Sister Gabrielle. The old lady looked, if anything, rather brighter than usual as if recent events had stimulated her.

"I have decided," Mother Dorothy said, "that, in view of the circumstances, Detective Sergeant Mill should be invited to give his account of the events that culminated in last night's arrest. Usually, thank God, such events don't concern us, but since last night's emergency forced us to break the grand silence then we may all benefit from an account. Detective Sergeant?"

She inclined her head politely to the man seated by her. Sister Joan looked down at her own clasped hands, her mouth twitching despite the solemnity of the occasion. He looked as if he would have preferred to be almost anywhere else.

"Reverend Mother. Sisters." He cleared his throat slightly. "As you all know already two young women, Valerie Pendon and Tina Davies, were both murdered recently. There were similarities between the two kill-

233

ings that pointed to their both having been killed by the same person and there were similarities between the two victims as well. Both were quiet, respectable girls, practising Catholics without any known lovers. Yet both of them left their homes in the middle of the night and were found wearing white bridal gowns with wreaths of leaves on their heads; both had been strangled by a loop of wire dropped over their heads and pulled tight. Two particularly nasty murders."

There was a general nodding of heads.

"Murder," said Sister Mary Concepta, "is never very nice anyway. I have always disapproved of it most strongly."

"What I didn't know," Detective Sergeant Mill was continuing, "was that two years ago a schoolgirl in Birmingham was found dead, also with a wire loop around her neck. There was no reason why I should have known. At the time there was no suggestion of foul play. The coroner returned a verdict of accidental death and the affair was never widely reported. The level of crime has risen so sharply in recent years that it simply isn't possible for every incident to be made known to every police force in every county. Sometimes I wonder if a central register of crimes might not be a good idea save it reminds me too much of a police state. However I'm digressing. All that we really had that might be a clue was a note in the diary kept by Tina Davies. The note seemed to suggest that she was having a secret affair."

He paused to glance down at the paper in his hand.

" 'Is this love? Like hunger eating you up, clean to the backbone? Like a fire burning? Is it? I wish I could ask someone but I can't break my promise. I have to wait until it's too late to pull me back.' "

Sister Marie had blushed a fiery red while Sister Elizabeth looked slightly affronted.

"Sister Joan had seen this diary extract," he was continuing, "when she visited the Davies household as your representative and Mr. Davies had just found the diary. She had the good sense to obtain his permission to bring it to me and I naturally began to look for the man in the case. Then Sister Hilaria was run over just outside the convent gates and pages were found to have been torn out of her private diary. Whatever had been written there could not possibly have referred to a love affair, and I assumed that she had recognized someone and connected it with the murders. Sister Joan, I understand you drew a different conclusion."

He was smiling at her encouragingly, inviting her to speak.

"I was in a more favourable position than the detective sergeant," she said. "I knew that Sister Hilaria would never dream of confiding any suspicions she had to a diary meant solely for spiritual matters, and in any case she takes little interest in mundane affairs. But when she first recovered consciousness she said, 'It ought to have been a donkey.' And I also had the advantage of knowing that Sister Hilaria had recently mentioned having had certain private revelations. It was a matter of reading the extract from Tina Davies's diary in a slightly different way. I mean—the words might refer to an imagined religious experience. And then Sister Marie said something about it all starting again just as it had up north. Mother Dorothy kindly allowed me to talk to her further and I learned that a schoolgirl from the district in Birmingham where Sister Marie formerly lived had been found hanging from a tree with a wire loop round her neck. It was too big a coincidence."

"Sister Joan ought to have gone to the police immediately with what she had learnt," Mother Dorothy said severely. "However, she had my permission to act as she thought fit in her assistance to the police and she decided, rightly or wrongly, to wait a while before informing anybody."

"Why was that, Sister?" Detective Sergeant Mill enquired.

"Because Sergeant Barratt had recently transferred from the Birmingham Police," Sister Joan said, "and it struck me as odd that he wouldn't have mentioned the supposed accidental death when these two deaths took place. The three were so very similar."

"I reached the same conclusion by a different route," Detective Sergeant Mill said. "According to Sergeant Barratt he had requested a transfer in order to obtain a better chance of promotion. During the last couple of days I checked up on his transfer. He had certainly requested one to a rural district but the superintendent whom I telephoned informed me that Barratt was in line for promotion anyway. So he had some other reason for requesting a transfer. I wondered about that."

"He suspected his wife had had something to do with the first girl's death?" It was Sister Gabrielle who enquired, her head held slightly sideways like an intelligent bird.

"It seems as far as we will ever tell that the first death was an accident. If you would like to continue, Sister Joan?"

"Sister Marie told me that before she entered the religious life she helped to produce a school play about Saint Bernadette of Lourdes. The girl who died—Carol Preston, she had the small role of Bernadette as a child. It wasn't until Sister Marie showed me the souvenir programme that I saw the costumes had been made by Daisy, Sergeant Barratt's wife. That placed her in the right place at the relevant time. When I mentioned sewing to her yesterday, however, she made it very plain that she couldn't sew at all. It was a totally unnecessary lie. And even though I'd met her several times she never once mentioned to me that she'd helped out in a school play shortly before one of the cast had died in almost exactly the same way as Valerie Pendon and Tina Davies."

"It seems that Daisy Barratt originally decided to test out some theory of her own," Detective Sergeant Mill said, taking up the narrative. "She believed that any vision could be faked if one were dealing with an impressionable child, and she tested out her theory on Carol Preston and her friend. The friend, Julie Jones, took fright and ran off, but Carol insisted she'd had a vision. I couldn't understand how she'd failed to recognize Daisy Barratt who was, after all, making all the costumes, including white dresses and nuns' habits, but as far as we can tell she wore a blonde wig and veiled herself. In one thing she was proved right. Poor Carol Preston was already disappointed that she hadn't been given the main part throughout the play and she accepted the vision hook, line and sinker. Daisy Barratt had been telling us that she meant the joke—she calls it a joke—to end there but she was tempted to go on. She appeared again to Carol but the second time Carol got too close and realized she'd been fooled. Only Daisy knows exactly what happened then. She insists that she picked up a wire loop that was lying around in the undergrowth and tried to frighten the kid into keeping quiet. It's possible but it's more likely that she brought the wire with her just in case she was recognized. Perhaps to frighten? Who knows?"

"And after the poor child died she had a breakdown?" Sister Martha asked.

"Sergeant Barratt insists that he had no idea his wife had any connection with the death of Carol Preston. However, he persuaded her to enter hospital as a voluntary patient and she remained there for nearly two years."

"And Luther Lee was a patient at the same hospital," Sister Joan said.

"Correct." He nodded at her. "Not that they were friendly. Poor Luther follows women around but seldom dares to speak to any of them. However, he saw Sergeant Barratt on visiting days and recognized him again when he was making enquiries up at the Romany camp. Luther is deeply suspicious of the police and terrified of being blamed for something he hasn't done. So he's been keeping out of the way."

"And Daisy Barratt started dressing up and pretending to be a vision again as soon as she arrived here?" Sister Katharine asked.

"Which doesn't say much for the opinion of her doctor who had diagnosed her as suffering from clinical depression when it's clear the problem was far more serious. However, he evidently was never told the full facts. Sergeant Barratt, very understandably, thought a quiet rural posting might suit his wife better. He was very fond of her. It's a pity that he shows his affection by constant hectoring and nagging about cleanliness."

Sister Joan, her mouth open to interpose "He behaves like that because he's impotent," closed it again. That confidence wasn't hers to betray.

"Dressing up as a vision is surely different from setting out to murder people," Sister Perpetua objected.

"Exactly so, Sister," he said briskly. "Not that I'm approving of the mockery of sacred things, though I'm not personally religious, but the deliberate taking of a human life is the ultimate crime because there is no adequate compensation ever to be made. However, Daisy Barratt started at once to choose someone she could manipulate. Being a Catholic helped. Nobody would ever connect the mousy woman with a scarf over her head who slipped into early mass on Sundays with a veiled figure in nun's habit who drifted about near the convent and near the Pendon and Davies homes after dark. She was a shrewd psychologist, unerringly picking out two unsophisticated, impressionable girls, both devout, both living rather restricted lives. Both of them thrilled and flattered at the notion that they might be receiving visions."

"I suppose she ordered them to follow her somewhere or other with the promise of some great revelation," Mother Dorothy said. "Poor, silly creatures."

"Sister Hilaria also believed she had seen Our Blessed Lady," Sister Gabrielle reminded her.

"Through the window of her cell in the postulancy," Mother Dorothy said with a shade of reproof. "Had she spoken to the figure she would indeed have realized at once that it was a mere human being. She did realize it, of course, when she was near the main gates and saw Daisy Barratt driving up the track in Padraic Lee's pick-up. Her own Mini car was being repaired and she simply helped herself to the truck. Sister Hilaria had caught a glimpse of Daisy's unveiled face and now, suddenly, she saw that same woman at the wheel of a pick-up."

"It ought to have been a donkey," Sister Joan said. "Our Blessed Lady would hardly arrive at the wheel of a pick-up truck. She must have run forward and then stumbled and Daisy ran her down."

"I don't think that was deliberate," Detective Sergeant Mill said. "After all it's unlikely that she recognized Sister Hilaria."

"She didn't stop," Sister Teresa said.

"No, she swerved aside and carried on. Since the pick-up was kept under a tarpaulin top at the far end of the Romany camp she found it easy enough to take and return it without being noticed."

"When Sister Hilaria recovered her memory fully she told Sergeant Barratt who was on duty at her bedside that she had recognized the woman—not as Daisy Barratt whom she had never met, but as the woman she had fleetingly mistaken for a vision. Sergeant Barratt tells me that he left the ward, ostensibly to telephone, and then returned, giving Sister Hilaria a message which purported to come from the prioress," Detective Sergeant Mill said. "Under obedience she was to say nothing about the experience to anybody. Sister Hilaria, accustomed to the habit of obedience and quite incapable of realizing that a police officer might be lying, accepted the injunction. Sister Joan, you telephoned the mental home, didn't you?"

"And found out Daisy Barratt had been a patient there at the same time as Luther."

"And instead of bringing the information to me," he said, "you decided to set a trap for her."

"Because all the bits of evidence were circumstantial," she protested. "Anyway Sister Marie was never in any danger."

"But you were in considerable danger yourself," Mother Dorothy said, primming her mouth.

"I did leave a note, Mother."

"Which Sister Gabrielle found. She was wakeful as she so often is and when she heard the back door close she got up to investigate. She didn't see the note at first and assumed you'd gone out to see to Lilith."

"Later on as I hadn't heard you return I got up again," Sister Gabrielle said, "and on that occasion I found that very inadequate note you'd pinned up on the door. 'Gone to complete investigations. Please don't worry.' What kind of note is that?"

"Sister Gabrielle very properly brought the note to me and I judged the situation sufficiently serious to telephone the police," Mother Dorothy said.

"By then my own investigations were sufficiently well advanced for me to have Sergeant Barratt in for questioning."

"I did think at one stage that he was the killer," Sister Joan admitted. "He was wandering round in the grounds one evening when he wasn't officially on duty."

"Checking up on his wife's whereabouts," Detective Sergeant Mill said. "He knew by then that it had to be Daisy and he was doing his best to prevent a further tragedy. It was Sergeant Barratt who painted I'M COMING on the front door of the postulancy to ensure that the novices were brought over to the security of the main house, by the way."

"But he had already covered up for her," Sister Joan said.

"And is being charged as an accomplice after the fact." The detective frowned.

"One corrupt or criminal policeman must cast a

shadow over the reputation of the whole force," Mother Dorothy said.

"Unfortunately that's the case." He shook his head slightly as if to banish unpleasant thoughts and went on. "The two girls were killed almost immediately incidentally. Daisy has been telling us quite frankly that she lured them out of their houses and dropped the loop of wire over their heads as they knelt before the supposed vision. In both cases just round the corner from their homes. Of course she had extraordinary good luck in that nobody came by or looked out of the window at that precise moment. Then she simply put the body in the back of her Mini and covered it with a rug until the area round the school had been searched in the case of Valerie Pendon when she drove up there, dressed the poor girl in the white dress and wreath she'd made and stuffed her into the cupboard. When she killed Tina Davies she dumped the body immediately in the shed on the edge of the Romany camp, first dressing her in a similar fashion. She'd bought a quantity of shoes of the same pattern in different stores and calculated the respective sizes of the victims very accurately before making the white dresses. She was punishing them for not having boy-friends and therefore the chance of babies, you see. Completely mad but in her view logical. Of course eventually she would have killed one of the Sisters here and found great satisfaction in the doing of it."

"And she went into the postulancy?" Sister Teresa's face had whitened.

"Which was unlocked, of course." He cast a reproving glance over the semi-circle. "It gave her pleasure to wander round when its occupants were elsewhere. Then she read Sister Hilaria's spiritual diary in which a full account of the supposed vision had been written. She tore out the pages and shredded them into the dustbin."

"What about the nightclothes in which the girls left their homes?" Sister Joan asked.

"She made two neat parcels and put them in the boot of her husband's car," he said. "We searched high and low for those garments but nobody thought of looking in a car belonging to one of the officers concerned in the case. Barratt swears he didn't know they were there; he may be telling the truth."

"She will plead insanity?" Mother Dorothy looked at him.

"Undoubtedly. Sergeant Barratt doesn't have that excuse."

"You call it insanity?" Sister Gabrielle tapped her stick impatiently on the floor. "I call it wickedness. Wickedness is an unfashionable word these days, but what that woman did was nothing short of wicked. Insanity indeed."

"Perhaps insanity is sometimes obedience to the evil within oneself," Mother Dorothy said.

"Whatever." Detective Sergeant Mill rose, clearly disinclined for any kind of philosophical discussion.

"Was it Daisy Barratt whom Constable Stephens saw when he brought Lilith back?" Sister Joan asked.

"She used to relish the thrill of wandering about near the convent, I suppose," he nodded. "She enjoyed the risk of being found out. Since she had never mixed socially with anyone Constable Stephens took her to be one of the Sisters and gave Lilith's rein to her."

"Didn't he realize that her habit was black whereas we wear grey?" Sister Perpetua asked, her reddish eyebrows shooting up.

"It never entered his head. People don't usually look very closely at nuns, you know."

"I knew it had to be her," Sister Joan said. "Sister Perpetua or whoever was in the kitchen would never have let him leave without a cup of tea."

"We would have got her in the end," Detective Sergeant Mill said, "but Sister Joan precipitated events and may well have foiled another death. I hope not too many rules were broken in the process?"

"Sister Joan had my authority to assist the police in any manner she deemed suitable," Mother Dorothy said. "The manner she did choose was, I admit, somewhat unconventional but occasionally desperate circumstances call for desperate means. We are all particularly grateful to you, Detective Sergeant Mill, for coming so promptly when I telephoned you. I hope that no charges are to be brought against Luther Lee. I know that I speak for the community when I say we are not proposing to accuse him of trespass."

"He's harmless," the detective admitted.

"And was of the greatest help in rescuing Sister Joan when she was attacked. Daisy Barratt is much stronger than her physical appearance would suggest. I believe that too is an attribute of madness."

"There remains the question of security."

"Detective Sergeant Mill, I appreciate your concern, but I refuse to surround ourselves with bolts and bars," Mother Dorothy said impatiently. "I will guarantee that we will bolt or lock all outside doors at night but that's as far as I am prepared to go. Later on we will see about a dog."

"As to that . . ." He broke off, glancing towards the window as a police car drew up outside.

"As to that?" The prioress fixed him with an enquiring look.

"I've taken the liberty of picking out a nice little Alsatian bitch from a local litter. Compliments of the Department—if I can prevail on you to accept the gift."

"We can, at least, take a look at the animal, I suppose," she allowed.

"Excuse me a moment, Sisters." He went out, taking with him the indefinable odour of masculinity.

"A little kitten would have been nice," Sister Mary Concepta said wistfully.

"A cat is not an adequate guard," Sister Perpetua objected.

"The Romans used to employ geese to guard their property," Sister David volunteered.

"Geese," said Sister Gabrielle, "bite."

"This is the puppy."

Detective Sergeant Mill had returned, bearing a wriggling bundle which he deposited on the polished floor.

"Oh, the little love." Sister Katharine was on her knees at once.

"It's far too small to be an adequate guard dog," Mother Dorothy said.

"Better for her to grow up knowing this is her home," Sister Perpetua said. "I daresay that there are obedience classes and so on to which she could be taken."

"When she's six months old. I can arrange it for you, Sisters. Also all the necessary injections etcetera."

"You're being very kind," Mother Dorothy said in a softened tone. "But puppies make messes."

"They can be trained to—er—make them in the right place, Mother," Sister Martha coaxed, "and I am always in search of rich compost for my vegetables."

"Shall we say a period of probation then?" Mother

Dorothy rose with an air of having reached a satisfactory compromise. "We had better think of a name."

"Juno?" Sister Joan hazarded.

"Positively not, Sister. A convent is no place for a heathen goddess."

"Lilith isn't exactly a Christian name," Sister Joan murmured.

"Lilith was named before we obtained her," Sister Gabrielle reminded her.

"Well, not Juno anyway. It ought to be a more respectable name in my opinion."

"Blackie?" said Sister David.

"Alice," Mother Dorothy said, a note of finality in her voice. "Alice is a most respectable name. Alice, come here."

The puppy, engrossed in chasing its own tail, fell over sideways and shot a distinctly horrified look in the direction of the prioress before scrambling up and trotting up to her where it sat, ears pricked and one paw raised.

"It recognizes the voice of authority," Detective Sergeant Mill said with a faint grin. "I'll leave her with you, Mother Prioress."

"Sister Martha," said Mother Dorothy firmly, "will take her into the garden. Now, if you please, Sister."

Sister Martha grabbed the puppy and bore it away hastily.

"Alice," said Sister Joan, fighting down a great desire to laugh. "Alice indeed."

"If you have a moment, Sister?" Mother Dorothy fixed her with a look.

"I must go. Thank you for your time, Sisters." Detective Sergeant Mill shook hands. "Oh, I telephoned the hospital. Sister Hilaria is being discharged in the morning."

"She will convalesce in the main house and Sister Perpetua can take charge of the novices in the postulancy," Mother Dorothy said. "I'll walk with you to your car, Detective Sergeant Mill. Sister Joan, isn't it time you were preparing lunch?"

"Yes, Reverend Mother."

Today it was soup and a thick slice of buttered toast. This evening there would be kippers with vegetables and a rice pudding. The ordered tenor of the days had taken up their interrupted course. The danger and the excitement were over, and she had her regular duties to perform without recognition for any help, however unconventional, she had been able to give.

Going along the passage into the kitchen, she fixed her mind firmly upon soup.

"Mother told me to hang it there," Sister Teresa said, clambering down from a chair as Sister Joan entered.

A small painting of the loch where she had spent her recent spiritual retreat hung on the whitewashed wall. It had been one of her best efforts. She approached it, stood looking up at its rich autumnal colours, at the neat card tucked into the frame.

Painted by Sister Joan of the Order of the Daughters of Compassion

It was, she thought with a lifting of the heart, Mother Dorothy's oblique way of telling her that in the end she had done well.

"Let's get on with the lunch, Sister," she said. "Tomato would be nice, don't you think?"

The Sister Joan mysteries by

Veronica Black

Available in bookstores everywhere.
Published by Ivy Books.